RACHEL & NIKKI JONAS

#PRETTY BOY D

He wants to break
all her rules...
She might just let him.

RACHEL JONAS & NIKKI THORNE

KINGS OF CYPRESS *Pointe*

CONTENTS

COPYRIGHTS

Published July 9th, 2021

KINGS OF CYPRESS Pointe

& NIKKI THORNE

KINGS OF CYPRESS PREP
The Golden Boys
Never his Girl
Forever Golden

KINGS OF CYPRESS POINTE
Pretty Boy D
Mr. Silver

DESCRIPTION

Dane Golden—Best friend. Temptation in football cleats. Roommate?

I'm screwed.

His followers don't call him Pretty Boy D for nothing. The guy is, literally, God's gift to women. I should know. I've watched chicks throw themselves at him since puberty.

Sharing his loft should be simple. Easy. But shortly after I settle in, we realize being "just friends" was so much easier when we weren't sleeping under the same roof.

Seven years of thinking we had this down to a science goes out the window the night Dane sees my "Never Have I Ever" list. Now, he's on a mission to help me cross off the top four items. Some of which aren't quite as innocent as he'd expect.

What he's proposing will break the rules we agreed to when I first came to stay here. He wants me to give in, to let my guard down and face my feelings for once. At least, that's what that wicked look in his eyes and the mounting heat between us suggests.

This isn't how I imagined being roommates would go. But a girl can only stare temptation in its green eyes for so long and not weaken.

My best friend wants to have his way with me and, right or wrong… I think I might let him.

Pretty Boy D is a full-length standalone novel. This book can absolutely be read on its own, but when you're done, it's recommended that you check out more from the Golden triplets and Joss in the complete enemies-to-lovers trilogy, KINGS OF CYPRESS PREP.

Do you enjoy the frustratingly hot push and pull of a good friends-to-lovers or roommates-to-lovers romance? Then you'll love getting to know Dane and Joss. Due to adult themes and sexual situations, this one's only for the 18+ crowd. Expect an HEA and no trigger warnings needed.
One-click and get lost in this story today!

Smooches,
RJ & NT

Thank you for your purchase! I would love to get your feedback once you've finished the book!
Please leave a review and let others know what you thought of
"Pretty Boy D."
You can stay up to date on new releases and sales by joining my newsletter

https://us14.list-manage.com/subscribe?u=
73f44054c9dda516cc713aea7&id=ad3ee37cf1
or by joining my Facebook Group
https://www.facebook.com/groups/141633853243521

**For all inquiries, please contact me using my primary email
address:**
author.racheljonas@gmail.com

Prologue

Age twelve (Nearly 7 years ago)

Joss

You would've thought a tornado had just torn through the room, but this was all him. The tall boy with hair dark as ink and a storm gathering in his eyes—Dane Golden.

I'd only learned his name when Ms. Kent took attendance, right before all hell broke loose.

Shock held me and twenty-plus classmates hostage, huddled in a corner beneath the periodic table. This was where we felt safe and out of harm's way.

Out of his way.

It happened so quickly. One minute, things were quiet. The next, Dane was flying out of his seat, tackling Alex to the floor. While most thought the scuffle was completely unprovoked, I knew better. The outburst happened when a hate-filled slur left Alex's mouth, but it wasn't aimed at Dane.

It was meant for me.

This being my first day of school in a new city, I distinctly remember having prayed for it to be as boring as humanly possible. Clearly, that turned out to be a bust.

He stood at the epicenter of the disaster he created; overturned desks, scattered chairs, and drops of blood dotting the tile.

His knuckles paled when gathering Alex's lapel into both fists, so tightly there was an audible rip when the stitching gave. Still, it was as if Dane was numb to the pleas for mercy, the begging that made the rest of us cringe. Even me, the girl Alex's words were meant to wound.

"I swear, I'll never say it again!" he begged.

Ms. Kent, realizing she'd *completely* lost control, fled for help. Dane, on the other hand, was unmoved by the fountain of blood pouring from Alex's nose, dripping down onto the embroidered crest of his uniform blazer.

"I was only kidding! Chill!" he pleaded again.

That storm in Dane's gaze darkened, threatening to make landfall. At that moment, Alex seemed to notice his excuse hadn't gone over so well.

"Okay, I'm sorry! It was a stupid thing to say!"

"You think *I* need your apology? Say it to *her!*" Dane snapped, flashing a look toward me. It was that same bold green stare that caused a breath to hitch in my throat every time I'd gotten lost in it that morning.

"I'm sorry! I take it back!"

Alex's head bobbed when he was yanked forward by the lapel a second time.

"Tell her again!" Dane growled. "And this time, say it like you *fucking* mean it."

A collective gasp filled the air when he swore. At twelve, I guess we weren't used to hearing that kind of language roll off another kid's tongue, but I'd later realize Dane was nothing like other boys.

Visibly shaken by the threat, Alex stuttered through another apology, hoping to earn Dane's approval.

"I—I'm really, *really* sorry. I swear I'll never say it again," he sobbed.

Dane stared down at him, scowling with disgust as the kid melted into a whimpering mess. Then, in a fit of rage none of us saw coming, his fist slammed Alex's already battered face one last time. A horrified shriek left Ms. Kent's mouth because, of course, she came back just in time to catch Dane in that final, merciless act.

Three suits rushed past her, flooding the room to wrestle Dane into submission. I'd never seen rage like his before—raw, so easily triggered—but there it was, as vivid and wild as his green eyes.

As he was dragged from the room, I managed to mouth the words "Thank you" before he disappeared down the hallway. It wasn't lost on me that whatever punishment he'd face would be because he stood up for me. A shy, wiry girl with braces he didn't know from a stranger on the street.

That day was a monumental one. Not because of the hatred that could've left me emotionally wounded and insecure. It's etched into memory because it's the day I met the guy who taught me the definition of loyalty. As it turned out, the savage I'd seen off his leash became the best friend a girl could ever have.

That chaotic episode was the beginning of something epic.

It was the beginning of us.

Chapter 1

Present Day

Joss

The loud thud that likely just startled Dane's new neighbors was all me—the result of stumbling into the wall, making a less-than-graceful entrance.

A jolt of pain shoots through my shoulder, but it's a small price to pay for not hitting the floor. Had I fallen, I would've landed right on the box in my hands. One that happens to hold thousands of dollars' worth of camera equipment.

Oh, the shit he would've talked if I'd done that.

These cameras are his life.

Speaking of lives, *mine* just flashed before my eyes. Meanwhile, Dane manages to hold back a smile for all of three seconds.

I shoot him a look when his lips start curving upward. "Not even gonna ask if I'm okay first?"

My question is apparently the straw that breaks the camel's back because it's followed by his deep laugh echoing off the vaulted ceiling.

"Dick."

He ignores the insult and finally relieves my hands of the box. "Next time, leave the heavy stuff to us guys," he teases.

"Or maybe, you know, stop leaving your ginormous shoes right in the doorway," I shoot back, shoving his shoulder.

I put all my strength into that push, but you'd never know it. He's freakishly solid, so I moved *myself* more than I moved him.

Trailing behind, I stare at the definition in his back through the ribbed tee he stripped down to about an hour ago. I'm reminded of how much more time he's spent at the gym since graduation. He says it fills the empty hours, but I think it's a distraction.

Namely, from the media circus that's taken a sudden interest in his family.

Having a father who's been named the city's most heinous criminal to ever walk the streets of Cypress Pointe could have that effect, I suppose. It's not every day a father attempts to murder one of his own sons, but it's all true. Including the part where Vin's only motivation was to conceal the many, many horrific acts he'd committed. Needless to say, while my homelife's sucked lately, it's nothing compared to what Dane and his brothers have lived through these past months. For instance, my dad isn't facing years in prison. The only punishment for *his* transgression is having to endure the wrath of the two women scorned by his affair.

Me and Mom.

Despite mine and Dane's fathers' indiscretions being vastly different, Pandora—our city's anonymous gossip reporter—has had a field day flaying both in the public eye. Granted, whoever hacked her several months ago is the one responsible for outing my father's behavior, but Pandora has certainly contributed to the fallout. If Dane and I weren't already close, this might've been the thing that brought us together.

We turn into a room stacked high with boxes and he sets down the one I brought up from the rental truck. While he shuffles things around a bit, my fingertips trace the mortar between the exposed bricks in the wall. My vision's drawn out through the tall window, watching the sun set. From this high up, Dane's view of the city is a work of art—silhouetted buildings against the backdrop of a peach and lavender-colored sky.

A loft apartment in the heart of downtown Cypress Pointe isn't so bad for this being the first place he's had on his own. As a triplet, I used to think the three of them would live together until one married, but I was wrong about that.

West—the oldest by mere minutes—recently settled into the family's second property in nearby Bellvue. It's halfway between the campuses where he and his girlfriend, Blue, are starting college this fall. Sterling—younger than Dane by thirty seconds—wants the full campus experience, so he'll be moving into the dorm by summer's end.

Which brings me to Dane and this bad-ass loft I fell in love with the first time he brought me to see it. It's so huge our voices echo into the rafters, making it perfect for him—a guy who enjoys throwing the occasional party. Plus, it has this extra bedroom he plans to make his studio.

"Decide how you're gonna set up in here yet?" I ask, zoning out while I stare at traffic on the grid of streets below.

"Nah, I'm not in a rush," he answers. "Call me crazy, but I'm still holding out hope my best friend will change her mind and room here for a bit. In which case, I'll set up shop in the great room."

He smirks at me from over his shoulder, knowing I haven't changed my mind. We're friends, yes, but I'm exceptionally cautious when it comes to getting 'too close'. Most days, our friendship is the most solid thing I have, which is why I protect it with my life. So, if that means turning down his offer for a place to lay my head at night, rent-free, then that's what I'll do.

He only stops glaring at me to check the notification on his phone. Saved by the bell. With any luck, it's not more of Pandora's B.S.

"Anything good?" I ask.

He shakes his head and leans against the wall. "Just a message from Rose."

I suppress an eyeroll, which has one of my lids twitching. Rose—brand manager extraordinaire—doesn't let up. She popped into Dane's life at the height of his family drama, hoping to capitalize on his father's infamy, no doubt. She's the ultimate opportunist, and I get pissed every time I think about her only seeing dollar signs when she looks at him.

Dane's done well on his own, managing to garner a few million followers without help. Rose's goal, though, is to turn him into an icon with endorsements and several streams of income linked to his growing platform and football prowess. The sports-related endorsements will have to wait until *after* college, per the NCAA's guidelines, but that hasn't stopped Rose from getting a head start. She's got a whole plan laid out for how he can make the most of this summer before classes start in fall. Hopefully, none of which require the selling of his soul.

"She's been on me about hiring a social media manager," he elaborates with a sigh.

"To do what, exactly?"

He peers up and the last ray of sunlight peeks between buildings, hitting him in just the right way, brightening his eyes like emeralds.

"She thinks I need a gatekeeper, someone to weed through the comments and messages that hit my accounts."

"And… she doesn't trust you to do this yourself?" A laugh slips out when I ask.

He shrugs. "She asked for access to see what goes on behind the scenes and I guess she saw a few things she thinks could mar my image."

Translation: there were chicks laying thirst traps in his DMs, and he likely fell victim to them.

Men.

I'll admit, the tribe of women who follow him are ravenous. One or two have literally sent their panties to his P.O. Box, so this comes as no surprise.

"You should take the job," he blurts out.

I do a doubletake. "Me? Dane, I—"

"Come on, Joss," he cuts in, rasping my name. "It'd look good in your portfolio. Plus, Rose said to find someone I trust, and you know all my login info already."

Listen to him, appealing to my sensible side. That's the problem when debating with someone who knows me so well. He isn't wrong, though. Being able to stack my portfolio with experience now will only help. Marketing is a tough industry to break into. Even with upcoming plans to intern at my uncle's firm—an internship Dane and I were supposed to undertake together until my father put a stop to that—I'm not guaranteed I'll get my foot in the door after graduation.

Still, this feels like a bad idea.

"You do know I've never actually logged into your accounts," I say, trying to deflect.

"Doesn't matter," he reasons, pushing off from the wall to come closer.

He works a hand through his dark hair and, for a second, I forget who he is, forget who *we* are. I'm not allowed to see him the way other women do, so I've become a pro at this now—refocusing my attention quickly, being sure to stare only at his eyes.

Not... everything else.

"I know you don't need the money, but the job does pay," he adds, taking both my hands when his gaze slips over me. I think he meant for the look to come across as innocent, but coming from him, it's anything but.

He's so persistent.

"I'll think about it," I concede, but in my heart, I'm firm on the answer I've already given.

"I'll take that. For now," he adds with a smirk.

He blinks into the fading sunlight and that's when I realize we're still holding hands. It isn't until a sound from the other room brings us back to our senses that we let go, mere seconds before two whose features mirror Dane's to a T bound into the room. Both have boxes in hand. Both seemingly unaware of whatever weirdness just took place before they stormed in.

Thank goodness for that. We'd never live it down if they'd seen.

"I'm expecting pizza for moving all this shit," West grumbles.

"And wings," Sterling adds.

We've been at this all day and we're all exhausted, but years of football conditioning have the guys still going at full steam. My gaze slips to Dane again when I think I feel him watching and, sure enough, I have his attention.

"One with pineapple for me, please," Blue announces when she bounces in, setting down the lamp she likely grabbed just to give the *appearance* of helping.

I smile when her stare persists, but when her brow twitches, I'm certain she's read the room just that quickly, noticing the energy is off balance.

She's an intuitive girl by nature, which comes from growing up much faster than anyone should have to. We've also gotten to know each other pretty well these past few months, so I'm not at all surprised she senses that something's up.

"I, um, think I saw some junk mail on the kitchen counter. Maybe I'll find coupons with it," I say distractedly, having no clue if that's true. Honestly, I just need to make a clean exit before my expression gives too much away.

Without looking, I know Dane's gaze follows me out of the room. Which is why I don't breathe until I clear the hallway, making it to the wide-open area where the great room, kitchen, and dining room all bleed into one grand space. There, my phone sounds off and I take a detour to the couch—which will also dub as Dane's bed until the real one comes.

My eyes settle on my phone screen and there's a name displayed across it. One I've seen more in this past month than I have in the entire year since we met in Cuba, visiting Mom's side of the family. I don't know why I always feel super uncomfortable when he messages or calls when I'm near Dane, but like usual, my stomach twists.

Carlos: You free to facetime? I'd love to actually see you for a change.

I sit up a bit straighter, trying to determine how to word my response. On one hand, I've got no reason to turn him down. After all, I'm completely single, completely unattached. But on the other, the idea of Dane walking in on a conversation between Carlos and me has my anxiety spiking.

I stare at my phone a moment, then decide I'm not feeling quite brave enough.

Joss: Maybe later tonight. Helping a friend move.

I hit send, resenting the hell out of this knot in my gut. It's one of the reasons me living here would never work. I go through these bouts of not quite knowing how to define my feelings while in Dane's company. I know it's probably just because we've cared about each other so long that the lines get blurred, but still. I don't need any more confusion in my life than I already have.

Standing, I've decided to call it a night. The four of them can eat without me and I'll catch them later, but before I make it back to the hall to say my goodbyes, my phone's going off again.

I expect it to be Carlos replying to the text, but I'm wrong. Instead, what I see has me feeling sick to my stomach because nothing good ever follows these four words.

Dad: We need to talk.

Shit. That sounds serious.

My gut sinks and I'm certain my night's about to take a turn, but I can't even begin to guess what this could be about. As if things aren't bad enough already, judging by the tone of my father's text, it's about to get worse.

That's great.

More drama.

Just what I fucking need.

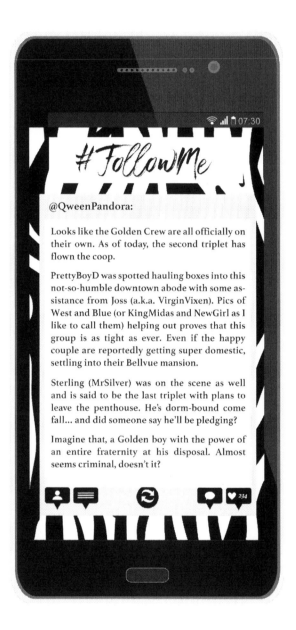

#FollowMe

@QweenPandora:

Looks like the Golden Crew are all officially on their own. As of today, the second triplet has flown the coop.

PrettyBoyD was spotted hauling boxes into this not-so-humble downtown abode with some assistance from Joss (a.k.a. VirginVixen). Pics of West and Blue (or KingMidas and NewGirl as I like to call them) helping out proves that this group is as tight as ever. Even if the happy couple are reportedly getting super domestic, settling into their Bellvue mansion.

Sterling (MrSilver) was on the scene as well and is said to be the last triplet with plans to leave the penthouse. He's dorm-bound come fall... and did someone say he'll be pledging?

Imagine that, a Golden boy with the power of an entire fraternity at his disposal. Almost seems criminal, doesn't it?

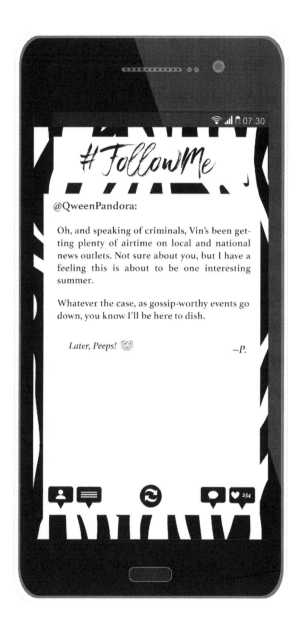

#FollowMe

@QweenPandora:

Oh, and speaking of criminals, Vin's been getting plenty of airtime on local and national news outlets. Not sure about you, but I have a feeling this is about to be one interesting summer.

Whatever the case, as gossip-worthy events go down, you know I'll be here to dish.

Later, Peeps! 😎

~P.

Chapter 2

Joss

Just an hour ago, the sun was setting in a clear sky, but as if acting as an omen of what's to come, a storm has blown in out of nowhere.

The house is quiet when I enter, aside from rain pelting the windows and an occasional rumble of thunder. The only light I see while passing through comes from Dad's office, so I head in that direction.

My steps echo through the hallway as I cross the tile. Now, there are voices—Mom's and Dad's—and it sounds like they're arguing. It's only the tone of the conversation that gives them away, not their volume. They're far too dignified for screaming and yelling, or anything *else* that might suggest there's any level of passion between them. Actually, the only time I've ever witnessed either show some measure of raw emotion directed at the other was when news of my father's affair first came to light. But now, since my mother seems resolved to just move forward like nothing's happened, it's been eerily quiet here.

Too quiet.

I step into the doorway and they both fall silent, which either means I was the topic of discussion, or they're hiding something. Whatever the case, I can't help but wish I was back at Dane's loft with him and the others, laughing and eating pizza while we hang out.

Instead, I'm heading into my father's study, staring as his dark skin creases right in the center of his forehead when he scowls.

What the hell did I do this time?

Mom's gaze slips to the floor where she's seated on the opposite side of his desk. Meanwhile, my father's expression grows even more disapproving as he looks me over.

"Where have you been all day?"

The question feels loaded, because I'm almost positive he knows I was with the triplets and Blue. If not because those are the four I'm *always* with, Pandora's posts don't leave much to the imagination.

Which *he* should know all about.

"I was helping a friend move."

"A friend," he scoffs. "You were with *him* again, weren't you?"

The inflection in his words is always sharper when he's angry, due in part to his thick accent. But it's also sharper when he mentions Dane, having decided he's nothing more than a wolf in sheep's clothing.

I don't answer and his expression darkens even more, likely because he believes I've spent at least *some* portion of my day in Dane's bed. According to him, there's no way a girl and guy can maintain a platonic friendship as long as Dane and I have, therefore we *must* be sleeping together.

It's narrowminded and it's utter bullshit. Not everyone lacks self-control. Not everyone is like him.

Trying to reign in this sudden spike of anger, I glance down at my finger, at the silver ring I was given by him on my thirteenth birthday. It implies a vow that I'll remain a virgin until marriage, pure. I once believed it meant he saw something valuable in me, something worth protecting. My innocence maybe, or perhaps my heart.

But as I've grown, this gift has evolved into much, much more than that.

At times, it's felt more like a ball and chain than a ring. I've come to see it as a means of maintaining control over me from a distance, a means of triggering immense guilt simply at the idea of letting someone get close. In short, it's been my father's way of tormenting me even when he's not present to do it himself.

While I made the promise he asked me to, it's become clear that giving him my word meant nothing.

Which begs the question; why the hell do I even bother wearing the damn thing?

If he knew me at all, he'd know I've never been in Dane's bed or anyone else's for that matter.

"I've told you time and time again, he's only after one thing and you're too stupid to see it," he rants. "And look at yourself! You're a mess!"

His eyes narrow, staring only at my hair. He despises the look of it in its natural state—dark ringlets that just sort of do their own thing if I don't fuss with them. Like this morning, when I just gathered them on top of my head, leaving out my bangs and a few curls in the back. Seemed fitting since I only threw on a pair of stretch pants, a long tee, and sneakers to help Dane transport boxes and furniture. That didn't feel like the occasion to get dolled up, but according to my father, I've left the house looking disheveled if my hair isn't either straightened or professionally braided.

More bullshit.

Mom eyes me as if she's just heard my thoughts and agrees with me one hundred percent. Too bad neither one of us has it in us to speak our minds to the tyrant she married.

"Just say what you need to say, Martin," she interjects, fuming from her seat. The outburst has my father casting a dark glare her way, but she doesn't back down for once.

First drawing in a deep breath, he aims his attention toward me again.

"In light of recent events, your mother and I have made a decision," he declares. "We'll both be taking a leave of absence from our positions, and we think a change of scenery would be the best thing for our family right now."

My brow tenses and I can barely respond. "What are you talking about?"

He breathes deeply again, and I take note of how he's having a hard time looking me in the eyes.

"Pandora has made it her business to draw out our family's very sensitive, very *personal,* situation. So, given what we're facing—"

"You mean your cheating?" I snap, which finally earns me direct eye contact.

I see right away that he's both shocked and angry when I interrupt, when I speak against him, but I've had enough. He doesn't get to tiptoe around this.

"Despite what you may think, Josslyn, you are *not* my equal. I'm still your father and you're still a child," he growls through gritted teeth.

"Actually, I'm nineteen—almost the age you and Mom were when you got married, became parents, so I'm hardly a child. And I'm *definitely* old enough to call B.S. when I hear it."

His eyes widen. Until recently, he'd never heard me so much as whisper a word against him. But since his affairs have been brought to light, my respect for him has dwindled to almost nothing, which has made it difficult to hold my tongue at times.

Visibly angry and running out of patience for this conversation, he stares without blinking. "We've made our decision."

That's it. That's his conclusion.

I pass a look toward my mother. "You're okay with this? Walking away from your career? Letting someone fill your role as hospital chief of staff? After you worked so hard to get there?"

"It's temporary," she insists, but I don't see it that way. Lately, I trust my gut way more than I trust them.

"And your grandmother's been kind enough to open her home to us until renovations are complete," my father adds.

"What renovations?" I'm practically panting when I ask, feeling like the rug's being ripped out from underneath me.

"We've found a home near hers in Pétion-Ville. It's nice, but a bit outdated, so—"

"Wait a second," I cut in, holding my head when the room begins to spin. "You think I'm following you all the way to Haiti?"

He frowns and it's abundantly clear he didn't expect me to fight him on this, but there's no way I'm letting them drag me halfway around the world.

"It's the most logical location," he reasons. "We should be close to family, so it's either we relocate *there* or Havana with your mother's people. Is that the problem? You'd prefer Cuba over Haiti?"

The question is dripping with sarcasm. I know because he doesn't give a shit what I think. No one knows better than me that once my father's mind is made up, there's no changing it.

My head spins again and the filter that prevents thoughts from leaving my mouth as words is beginning to malfunction.

"I'm not going."

"Like hell you're not," he scoffs. "I've already spoken with a contact at one of the best universities and made arrangements for—"

"I'm not... going," I repeat.

His eyes narrow into slits when he glares. "Is this what you want to do tonight? Pick a fight you'll never win?"

I cross both arms over my chest, holding his gaze. He's stubborn and intends to stand his ground, but what he's not banking on is that I've inherited that same stubbornness.

"You've got a week to pack your things," he concludes, thinking that's the end of this conversation, but I strongly disagree.

"My plans aren't changing," I inform him. "In three months, I'll be starting school where I've planned to attend for *years* now. My entire *life* is here in Cypress Pointe, not to mention my internship with Uncle Jon. You can't just expect me to walk away from that, from *everything*."

"Your life is with your family!" he shouts, shaking the entire room when his voice booms in sync with a clap of thunder. "And as far as your internship is concerned, I've already told Jon to contact the next candidate because you're leaving the city."

"You did what?"

"This isn't up for debate, Josslyn."

A wave of defiance swells in me and I feel reckless, like I'm capable of saying anything at this point.

"Maybe I'm not the one who needs reminding about the importance of family," I say to him. "That lecture you just gave *me* would've gone a long way when you stepped out to see those other women."

"Josslyn!"

I ignore my mother's weak attempt at chastising me and stare only at him—this man who's gotten away with far too much for far too long. There's another rumble of thunder and he stands slowly, leaning forward to rest both fists on the surface of his desk. Next, he slices a cold look in my direction.

"Okay, fine," he says through gritted teeth. "You want to be an adult so badly? Have it your way, but know this... if you stay behind, if you defy me, you will be completely alone, in every sense of the word."

There's something dark in his eyes. It isn't quite hatred, but something akin to it. The only thing I can think of is that it's traces of loathing, over having lost control.

Of my decisions.

Of me.

For so many years, I walked a tightrope because he left me no choice. My every move was dictated by him, his lofty expectations. But something about seeing his fall from grace changed me, made me realize that this life is mine to live.

"I'm staying," I say, hoping I at least *sound* brave, because shit... I definitely don't *feel* brave yet.

Staring, he nods, and I feel the weight of his impending words.

"Well, I believe we've both made our decisions."

"Martin, we—"

"The girl's made her choice, now let her live with it," his voice booms, overtalking my mother.

My heart races a million miles a minute and I haven't been able to move yet, not one single step. I'm terrified and have absolutely no plan, but I can't stand the thought of being shoved inside yet another of my father's tiny boxes.

So, I accept that this is really happening and do my best to hold in tears. Praying for a miracle, I turn my back on him—literally, figuratively—sealing my own fate according to him.

I had no idea tonight would mark the moment that I officially become an adult. Nor did I realize it'd be the night that I officially become homeless, but I can't turn back now.

Come hell or high water, I've got to figure this thing out. The last thing on Earth I want is to prove this man right. If that happens, there's no way in hell I'd ever live it down.

Looks like it's time to come up with some sort of plan.

Just wish I knew where to start.

…Fuck my life.

Chapter 3

Dane

"Well, the water pressure's great."

Sterling looks up from his phone when I drop down on the couch in a towel.

"Fuck, dude! Holster that shit!"

Glancing down, I realize why he's complaining—I flashed him a little. I adjust the towel with a laugh, so he'll stop crying about it.

He yawns and I'm eyeing him. "You're seriously tired already? It's not even late."

He shoots me a look then lets his head fall back against the cushion. "We've been moving your shit all day." His eyes close then, but I know just what to say to wake his ass up.

"Too tired for company?"

His head lifts again and I get the exact look I expect from him. "Depends. Who's coming?"

Reaching to where I tossed my phone on the other side of the couch, I pull up a pic. "Her name's Melanie. I met her a couple weeks ago at the gym. She's hanging with her friend Katie and asked what we're getting into tonight."

Sterling takes one look at the pic of the pair hugged up on some recent beach vacation.

"Here's hoping the answer to that question is *'pussy,'*" he laughs.

"They should be here in thirty."

"Sweet."

I relax again and do a bit of math in my head. I should only need about ten minutes to get decent, which means I can afford to chill a while longer.

"And then, there were two."

I open one eye when Sterling speaks. "What the hell are you talking about?"

"West's ass is locked down, now it's just us. Feels weird."

I had the same thought when he and Blue cut out around ten P.M., looking all blissful and shit. Don't get me wrong, I love that they're happy, but Sterling has a point. Shit feels weird.

"We're like Timon and Pumbaa in this bitch, watching Simba and Nala ride off into the sunset without us," he adds with a laugh.

It's at this exact moment that I make an executive decision for us both. "Okay, I'm definitely getting you high tonight."

He laughs, but there's truth to what he said about West. Being closer than most siblings, Sterling feels the loss. We both do.

"Seriously, though. You're gonna be next to get tied down. I feel it."

The joke earns me a hard glare from the one who swears he'll never settle down with just one woman.

"Fuck that and fuck you," he grumbles. "It'll be you and Joss once you two finally get your heads out of your asses."

His words strike me hard, wiping the grin off my face. All because the only two people who seem to know me and Joss will never happen are me and Joss. The fucked up part is… it's not because I wouldn't drop everything and everyone for her in a heartbeat.

We exist in this strange space somewhere between friendship and more, but she keeps her distance. I can't even blame it all on *her*, though. I want her, but know I'd find some way to fuck things up. It's kind of in my DNA. It's the reason my father's currently behind bars. The reason West nearly pushed Blue out of his life before he even had her. The reason Sterling's sworn off commitment altogether. It's also the reason I fight the urge to lay the most solid, non-familial relationship I have on the line.

Although, if I'm being honest, that thought crosses my mind at least once a day.

Joss may be my best friend, but I've thought about *her* more while fucking than whoever I'm actually with. In my head, I've made her come in every position imaginable, in every *way* imaginable—with my mouth, my fingers, my dick. The *real* her may be untouched and innocent, but the version of her that lives in my head?

She's nasty as fuck.

I clear my throat and start thinking about baseball before I pop a boner. Sterling might beat my ass if that happens, seeing as how he's already begged me to put on more than just this towel.

My phone dings and I'm grateful for the distraction.

"Melanie again?"

I shake my head. "Nah, Rose."

"It's almost midnight. Does she ever sleep?"

"Doesn't seem like it," I answer distractedly while reading her text. "Apparently, she's trying to play matchmaker."

"Sounds fun," Sterling chuckles, clearly being sarcastic.

"She's been all up my ass about my image and networking."

"That includes her setting you up with chicks?"

I shrug. "Maybe. She wants me to link up with her daughter, Shawna. She's got a pretty big following from what I saw when I checked out her profile. Plus, Rose says she's got a few promising deals in the works."

"The only promising deal *you* need to be thinking about is Melanie," Sterling concludes. "So, tell Rose to save that shit for tomorrow and take her ass to sleep."

I laugh and set the phone aside. "I'm gonna get dressed."

"How's this supposed to work anyway?"

I halt behind the couch. "How's *what* supposed to work?"

"We've got girls stopping by and this is the only room with furniture. I mean, it wouldn't be the first time we banged two girls in the same room, but… I'd like to think we've evolved since then."

Yeah, sure we have.

"I don't know. Drag the chair into the spare room, I guess." I shrug, this being my only solution.

He considers it for a few seconds, then seems to settle on that being the best option. But then, before he can even drag the thing six inches, the door buzzes.

"Shit, they're early."

He ignores me and continues down the hall with the chair.

"Come on up," I say into the com, not bothering to even check the camera before buzzing the girls in.

My first thought is to rush and grab clothes, but there's not really any point. I'd have them off again in about five minutes anyway. So, instead, I just secure the towel and post near the door to wait.

A minute later there's a knock and Sterling's back in the great room, checking himself out in the mirror. I unlatch the door, but the second I open it, I forget all about Melanie and everything else.

"I'm sorry I didn't call first. I've been driving around for about an hour and didn't even know this was where I was headed until I pulled up outside," Joss sobs.

Seeing her in tears has me thinking irrationally, so the first thing that comes to mind is *Who fucked up, and where the hell can I find them?*

But I hold all that in and close the door behind her. "What happened?" I ask instead, shoving aside thoughts of kicking someone's ass tonight.

She has this bewildered look in her eyes, like she isn't sure how to answer.

"I got this text from my dad that we needed to talk. Then, he and Mom just sprung a bomb at me as soon as I walked through the door," she rambles. "They're leaving for Haiti and he's demanding that I go."

My entire body goes numb hearing her say those words. No, I haven't known her my whole life, but it sure as hell feels like it. Seven years is a long time for someone to be with you almost every single day, to then just be ripped away without warning.

She pushes a mix of tears and rainwater from her eyes, hugging herself while she paces.

A deep breath escapes. It's the only thing that keeps me from spinning out and losing my shit just at the *thought* of her leaving. It's already been one hell of a year, now this. But what she needs right in this moment is someone to listen, someone to be reasonable while she isn't thinking clearly. Seeing me get caught up in my feelings about how her leaving would tear my world to shreds won't help anything.

But... damn.

"I told him I won't go," she states, bringing me instant relief when I hear those words leave her mouth. "But he was so angry," she adds. "Angrier than I think I've ever seen him."

I shoot Sterling a look and don't have to say a word.

"I'm gonna take off so you two can talk," he interjects.

Joss peers up when he speaks, seeming to realize she walked in on the middle of something. "No, I didn't mean to intrude on you guys. Stay. *I'll* go," she insists.

"Stop apologizing. We didn't have anything planned," Sterling lies. "I'll check in on you guys tomorrow."

With a weak smile, Joss nods. "Okay. Be safe, though. It's really coming down out there."

Sterling stops to hug her around her shoulders as he passes. To my brothers, she's been like the sister they never had. But somehow, that entire notion completely missed me. Not once have I ever seen her in that light.

Sterling nods once, then it's just me and Joss.

"Let me grab us *both* some clothes, then you can tell me everything."

The damp curls piled on top of her head quiver a bit when she nods, then I gesture for her to have a seat on the sofa. On the way back to my room to hunt through boxes for a t-shirt for her and a pair of sweats for us both, I flip the switch on the coffee pot, assuming we won't be sleeping anytime soon.

I close my door and if it weren't for the text that comes through, I would've completely forgotten I was expecting company.

Melanie: Pulling up in a sec. Can't wait to see you.

Dane: Actually, something came up. Need to cancel.

Melanie: Well, should we just stop by later? We don't mind.

I hear her offer loud and clear, but don't even consider it. In fact, the second I'm tempted, I envision Joss—soaking wet and crying her eyes out on my couch—and the answer is clear.

Dane: Have to pass for tonight, but now that I'm thinking about it, my brother would still love to hear from you.

I shoot her Sterling's number, deciding that *his* plans shouldn't have to change because mine did. Besides, two girls instead of one? He won't complain.

With that, I've officially traded one form of a sleepless night for another and, apparently... I've also officially got blue-balls.

Just fucking perfect.

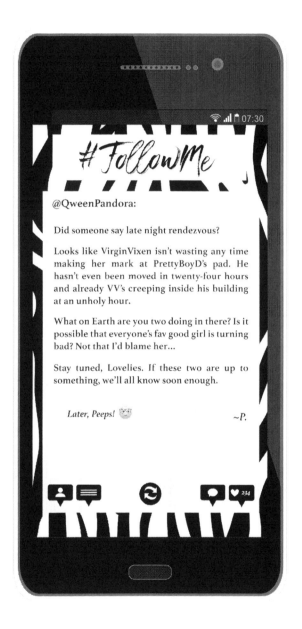

#FollowMe

@QweenPandora:

Did someone say late night rendezvous?

Looks like VirginVixen isn't wasting any time making her mark at PrettyBoyD's pad. He hasn't even been moved in twenty-four hours and already VV's creeping inside his building at an unholy hour.

What on Earth are you two doing in there? Is it possible that everyone's fav good girl is turning bad? Not that I'd blame her...

Stay tuned, Lovelies. If these two are up to something, we'll all know soon enough.

Later, Peeps!   ~P.

Chapter 4

Joss

A warm hand moves slowly up my arm, then back down again. At first, I've got no clue where I am, but then it all rushes back to me.

The argument. Storming out of the house with nothing. Showing up at Dane's door at around midnight.

And now, here I am, locked beneath his arm with my feet propped up on his coffee table beside two empty mugs. He's still asleep beside me or… beneath me? We dozed in a strange position, with my head against his ribs while he leans against the arm rest. One of his feet are propped beside mine, the other planted on the floor.

He's shirtless, so my cheek brushes over his bare skin when I move to sit upright. I notice the smoothness of it, but mostly, I'm trying to ignore how his sweats ride low on the divots in his waist. He's always been fit, but dude's gotten ripped these past few months. Be it out of frustration or as a means of distraction, working out like a beast has turned him *into* one.

My eyes travel up the mountain range that's replaced his abs, and I stall at his pecs—perfectly molded sculptures of tanned flesh. He's obsessive when it comes to manscaping, so he's hairless, completely smooth from the waist up.

Kind of makes me wonder about what his situation is from the waist *down.*

"Morning."

My eyes snap to Dane's with a tiny, inward gasp when he speaks.

He saw me practically drooling over him. No way he missed that. The cheeky, half-grin he shoots me next tells me I'm right.

Shit.

"Sleep okay?"

His morning voice is raspy. Even more so than usual.

"Uh, yeah. Like a baby."

Like a baby? Ugh. I should probably stop talking.

Averting my attention from him now, I push a hand up through the back of my hair, feeling myself tremble when I do. He yawns and stretches, and despite myself, my eyes are on him again. On that lean torso and trim waist. Then, my gaze naturally drifts lower.

Before he has a chance to realize I'm staring at his junk, I stand and head toward the kitchen, hiking the too-big sweats he loaned me last night higher on my waist. While I grab a glass and turn on the faucet, Dane shuffles down the hallway to the bathroom.

It isn't until I'm alone that I'm finally able to breathe and re-center my thoughts. With each year we age, the line between us gets a bit more blurred. At twelve, I only saw him as the boy who mutilated another kid's face for insulting me, but by fourteen, I had a full-blown crush. Who wouldn't though? The Golden boys were at least six inches taller than all the other guys in school, and as natural-born athletes, they never quite looked like boys. They were always bigger and stronger than anyone else in our grade. Every guy wants to be them, every girl wants to be *with* them.

That came out wrong.

Almost every girl wants to be with them.

I'm content being something like a sister to West and Sterling, and BFFs with Dane.

Eventually, by around age sixteen, the crush faded, but the attraction still lingers. Picking up on Dane's occasional lapses into bouts of weakness doesn't help, but I like to think we've mastered the art of resisting. Likely, because we both fear what we'd lose if we didn't.

"Hungry?"

I spin toward the sound of his voice, swallowing the last of my water before nodding.

"Whatcha got?"

He flashes a cheeky grin that says it all. "Cereal, cereal, and more cereal."

I laugh, shaking my head. "Well, cereal it is, I guess."

A breath hitches in my throat when he steps closer, but I realize it's only to reach above my head for two bowls. My eyes are glued to him as he moves around the kitchen, gathering two spoons, milk, and then one enormous box of Cheerios.

He places it all on the counter, then gestures for me to take the stool beside him.

I do. Cautiously, of course. He's still shirtless and it takes so much effort not to stare.

"So, are you good?"

My eyes do flit toward him when he asks, but I glance down into my bowl again right after.

"All things considered, I'm okay."

That's the truth. Last night sucked, but life usually sucks a little less when he's around.

"I did some thinking while you were snoring on me last night," he teases.

Holding in a laugh, I shoot him a look, but he ignores it.

"Since you're staying in the city, regardless of what your parents have decided, my offer only makes sense now."

"Offer?"

Now *I'm* the one getting a look because we both know I know what he's talking about. I was just stalling while I think of a good excuse.

"I've got an extra room, you *need* a room. I need someone to manage my accounts, you need a job. It just makes sense," he reasons.

I glance at him fully this time, staring as he awaits a response.

There are so many reasons to tell him 'no' right now, but I can't seem to remember *any* of them except that doing so could put our friendship on the line. However, I can't exactly say that without exposing that I am, in fact, very attracted to him.

Rock.

Hard place.

Me, stuck right in the middle.

He picks up his phone to check the time. "It's seven. I don't have to return the moving truck until noon. There's time to go to your place, load your things up, and still get it dropped off on time," he says, arching a brow at me. "So, what do you say? Are we gonna be roomies?"

Not sure if he can tell this or not, but the idea of it has me absolutely terrified. Sure, it'll be smooth sailing at first, but what about when it isn't?

I'm pleading with my eyes, but he doesn't let me off the hook.

"Dane, we'd have to set rules. Then, I'd feel like a bitch because this is *your* place, and you shouldn't have to live by—"

"Interesting," he croons, cutting in with a smirk that ends my rant. "What kind of rules?"

I get caught in his stare, feeling the pressure.

"Well, okay. Like, knocking before entering each other's bedrooms or the bathroom," I suggest.

"Done. What else?"

"We'd clean up our own messes," I add.

"Done," he says with that same easy-going tone.

Shit. Think bigger, Joss. Throw something difficult at him.

"No overnight guests of the opposite sex," I add with a dim smile.

Ha! That should do it. No way Dane Golden will go months or potentially longer without the freedom to share his bed with a girl. But I do feel kind of weird about having just said that, especially since we both know that rule only applies to him for now.

He smirks and for a second I think I might have swayed him against this terrible, terrible idea, but then...

"Ok, no sleepovers. Got it. What else?" he counters without thought.

My chest feels tight with the realization that he's not bending. Not even a little.

"I… guess that's it," I concede.

"Good. So, we're doing this?" he asks, shoveling a spoonful of cereal into his mouth.

"Yeah, I guess we are." Despite myself, I smile at him.

"And you'll take the job, too, right?" he adds, striking while the iron is hot.

I give that some thought, but eventually come to my senses. Now that my parents are cutting me off, I'm gonna need the cash. The only solid thing I have right now is that my tuition and book expenses are all covered, thanks to my scholarship. Outside of that? I've got nothing.

Dane's staring when I nod. "I'll take it."

His face lights up and I guess mine does, too. It looks like this is actually happening. With any luck, we'll make it through this adventure unscathed. I mean, it's not like there's gonna be a smoking hot guy sleeping right down the hall every night, right?

Right.

Now, if I can just keep telling myself that lie until I actually start believing it, this should work out great.

#FollowMe

@QweenPandora:

Okay, so... remember last night's post about VirginVixen dropping by PrettyBoyD's place? Well, she stayed parked outside his building all night. If I wasn't suspicious before, I certainly am now.

Not sure about you guys, but where I come from, a guy and a girl claiming to be "just friends" don't do overnight sleepovers.

My guess? These two are coming dangerously close to crossing the point of no return. That is, if they haven't already. Keep you posted.

Later, Peeps!   ~P.

Chapter 5

Joss

"Well, that didn't take long."

I turn the phone toward Dane when we come to a stoplight. Pandora's already starting with the rumors.

"Did you expect anything different?" he asks.

"Guess not, but I thought it'd take her more than eight hours to start running her mouth."

He smirks and it dawns on me how naïve that was. Bitch is relentless. I can only imagine what she'll have to say once it becomes public knowledge that Dane and I are *sharing* his loft.

Damn... we're actually sharing the loft.

It's really hitting me now, as we make our way through the city in the massive moving truck he rented. As much as I hate to say it, it's almost serendipitous the way things worked out. Every single thing I needed, he had within reach—a place to lay my head, a job, this truck.

My gaze shifts toward him when the silver bracelet on his wrist glints in the sunlight. I'm again reminded why this time together won't be easy. I'm a sucker for a guy with nice arms and damn if his aren't amazing. As he grips the steering wheel, I see the results of all the extra weights he's been lifting. Veins protrude beneath his tanned skin and my eyes travel higher, to where a t-shirt squeezes his bicep. I breathe deeply when I force myself to look away.

Why does he have to be so fun to look at?

Guess that's why the internet branded him with Pandora's moniker—Pretty Boy D.

Heaven knows he lives up to it.

We're not too far from my house now and I'm admittedly terrified. Both my parents are at work, so it'll just be us and eventually Sterling. Still, I feel like I'm about to rob the place, even though I'm only grabbing my own things.

We pull into my neighborhood and Dane punches in the gate code when I recite it to him. Then, we're on the move again. The second we pull into the driveway, nausea sets in, but a tight squeeze to my hand has me looking Dane in his eyes. He's smiling a little, and seeing it honestly does settle my nerves a bit.

"You made the right choice," he says, reassuring me.

I nod, hoping like hell he's right.

Before I lose the nerve, I hop out of the truck and move toward the door with my key in hand. Dane's not far behind, trailing with flattened boxes, a roll of tape tucked beneath his arm, and a toolbox. We step inside and a wave of sadness hits me while disarming the alarm. Not because I regret the decision to remain in the city while my parents flee the country, but because the illusion has faded.

Not so long ago, I fell for it, believing we were a happy family. It made me blind to how hard my dad pushed me, how he wanted to dictate every single aspect of my life. But now that the smoke has cleared and I see our bullshit life for exactly what it is, the hole it's left in my soul is hard to bear.

"Let's get this over with," I sigh, already needing to get out of here.

"Point the way."

I smile a bit at Dane's response, thinking how strange it is that he's seeing my bedroom for the first time, after being friends for so long. The few instances Mom's allowed him to visit when my dad was out of town, we only hung out in common spaces.

The privacy aspect of our friendship is grossly disproportionate. I've always been welcome inside Dane's living spaces without restriction, but my father's rules meant I had to keep *him* at arm's length. But now that we'll have the same address, I guess that's sort of gone out the window.

"I heard a rumor about your bedroom once," he says as we climb the stairs.

"This should be good. Tell me."

"It is, actually. Apparently, you have a gold bust of yourself on a pedestal in the corner. That true?"

Smiling, I glance at him over my shoulder. "Well, I guess you're about to find out."

Not sure why, but my heart thuds harder inside my chest as I speak the words. It only quickens when we finally reach the end of the hallway and cross the threshold into my room.

It's only been about a year since I updated the space. I swapped out my comforter, got rid of the frilly valences on both windows, added a large, vintage-style rug, and painted over the pink walls with a subtle gray. Now, with Dane standing beside me, I'm grateful I made those changes. Seeing as how it basically looked like a ten-year-old slept here before that.

"See? No bust. Just this watercolor portrait, but that doesn't count. It was a gift."

A gift from Carlos that he painted himself, but I don't mention that part.

Dane takes slow steps, taking it all in.

"So, this is where all the magic happens," I tease. "Or, where exactly *no* magic happens."

He laughs at the obviously self-deprecating joke.

"Where should we start?" I ask.

He answers by handing me a few boxes. "If you want to assemble these and start filling them, I'll work on taking apart some of the big stuff. Might take me a while."

"Or I can help with *that* until Sterling shows up," I offer, which has Dane's brow shooting up.

With this whole thing being completely spur of the moment, West had plans, but Sterling's supposedly on his way. Still, I don't see the point in waiting.

Dane eyes me and, for a second, I think he's about to say I'm not strong enough, but he only smiles.

"Up to you," he says, popping his toolbox open to grab a screwdriver.

We work our way around the room—removing the mirror off my dresser and disassembling my bed. Then, I start taking my clothes from the closet and transferring them out to the rental, hanging them on the handy little racks across the back. Sterling pulls up right as I jump down from the truck bed, and the dark shades he wears are a dead giveaway of the turn his night took after leaving Dane's.

He climbs out of his SUV and I have a super annoying idea.

"Hangover?" I ask as loudly and as close to his ear as possible.

"Fuck, Joss!" he barks back.

Laughing, I loop my arm with his and lead us toward the door. Tall as he is, what's a slow pace for him is *normal* pace for me. We enter the house and I gaze up at him with a grin.

"What's wrong? Too loud?"

"Real fucking cute," he grumbles.

"Yeah, well, I try."

If looks could kill, the one he just gave would've done me in.

"What'd you do? Throw a rager after you left the loft?"

"You could call it that," he says with a grin. "Got a call on my way home and made a little detour. There were drinks involved. Lots and lots of drinks."

He's vague and I have a feeling I don't want the details he's holding back, so I don't ask.

"Dane's upstairs. I helped him take everything apart, so you should only have to help him bring it down."

"Cool," he says with a nod, walking the steps in sync with me. "So, you guys ready for this? Most couples don't move in together until they've been official for a few months."

He laughs and I shove him.

"Not funny."

"I'd say it's about as funny as your loud ass yelling in my ear, so I guess we're even," he gripes.

We make it to my room, and after a brief, vague conversation between him and Dane about whatever weirdness Sterling got into last night, we get back to work. I start by packing boxes, while the guys walk the furniture out. It doesn't take long before the room begins to look empty. I try not to think too much about how strange it all feels. Besides, I only planned to live at home for the first semester anyway. After that, I would've made the shift to living on campus. Seeing as how my school of choice is still within the city, my parents eventually caved, coming around to the idea.

Still, knowing I'm leaving under these circumstances, with bad blood between me and them, it's not easy.

I pass Dane on my way down with a box of books and he flashes a half-smile that's right on time, right as my mood was beginning to dip. I don't miss that he's really excited about this, which has me thinking I was worried for nothing.

We can do this.

We've been friends for years and never crossed a line. This is no different.

I climb the ramp into the truck and set the books down before heading back inside. After stopping in the kitchen for a glass of water, I'm on my way upstairs again. My legs are definitely starting to get fatigued, but we're nearly done. Too close to complain anyway.

I hear the guys shuffling around inside my room, likely still gathering stray items like they were when I'd last left them. I make it back just as Sterling's reaching to the top shelf of my closet, grabbing down a box that instantly has my heart palpitating.

Because it's not just *any* box.

It's *the* box.

I try not to panic and call more attention to myself, try to fight the urge to lunge at Sterling, but OMG! This *cannot* be happening!

He shakes the black shoebox a bit, hearing the contents roll around inside. Contents that sound nothing like a pair of shoes. There's a curious look on both his and Dane's faces when he grips the lid, intending to peek inside, but that cannot happen. It's like I'm having an out of body experience, leaping several feet across the room to grab it before he has the chance, but I'm completely out of my head right now, clumsy, uncoordinated.

Dane's staring as the whole thing plays out, and I'm sure that, to him, it looks like I'm freaking out over absolutely nothing, but he's so wrong about that. It's definitely something.

Just at the *idea* of these two seeing what's inside, I want to die a little. But the moment I have the box in my hands, just when I think I'm in the clear, the absolute worst thing that *could* happen *does* happen. I fumble it and can only stare in horror as it falls to the floor, landing upside down with a thud.

No, the guys don't *see* what's inside, but... they sure as hell can *hear* it, vibrating too loudly to deny whatever these two are thinking right now.

My hands fly to my face, hiding my shame. Or at least I'm trying to, but Sterling's deep chuckle makes that impossible. I don't hear Dane, but imagine he's laughing, too.

"Damn, Joss. What kind of motor you got in that thing?" Sterling asks, barely able to get the words out as he laughs.

Kill.

Me.

Now.

Feeling like my face might actually go up in flames, I quickly stoop down to retrieve the box. Then, I turn my back to hit the off switch on the vibrator that's just thoroughly ruined my life.

Thanks a lot, Victor.

Yes, I fucking named it.

The damage is already done, though. And if *two* Golden boys know my secret, the third will soon enough.

"Don't be embarrassed," Sterling croons, his words slow and suggestive. "We all practice a little self-love every now and then, just... maybe not with power tools," he adds, chuckling again, but a bit more subdued this time.

I'd never explain this to *them*, but Victor's far from power-tool-status. Measuring at about the size of a finger, I like to think of him as small but mighty.

Sterling rests his arm around my shoulders, and I shrug from beneath it, following the action with a hateful glare. Somehow, that look morphs into a smile the longer I try holding it in.

Asshole.

"All right. Lay off," Dane cuts in, scolding Sterling on my behalf—the guy who's usually the mature one of the crew.

God, help us all if that's true.

I finally look up at Dane just to see if his defending me was sincere or just to mask that he, too, had gotten a good laugh, but there's no sign that he's found anything amusing, which I do appreciate.

This is not the start I wanted us to have. I thought it'd be at least a few months before we had any embarrassing moments between us, but leave it to me to kick things off with a bang.

Or... a buzz.

Doing my own version of the *walk of shame,* I cradle the box to my chest and traipse down the stairs. Once I'm at the truck, I hide Victor deep underneath the passenger seat where he can't get me into more trouble.

We finish up the job—mostly with me not looking either of them in the eyes—then I lock up and accept that it's really time to move on.

Breathing deep, I stare at the front door. This is really happening. I'm really on my own.

Dane steps up beside me and slips his arm around my shoulder. Unlike with Sterling, I don't shrug him off. Actually, I lean into him, accepting the comfort he offers. Seeing as how it felt like I'd fall apart a second ago.

He squeezes me a bit and I find myself feeling more grateful for his presence than usual. The look I get from him is one I don't expect. It's filled with emotion—sympathy, concern, warmth. Now, despite knowing I *should* turn away, I can't.

"Thanks for making room for me," I say, peering up at him.

That feeling he gave me a moment ago only deepens when he speaks, and I swear the words reach all the way down into my soul.

"I didn't have to make room for you, Joss. You just fit. Always have."

That settles on my heart, hitting me harder than expected. I finally understand the full scope of why we can't afford to mess this up. What Dane just admitted was absolutely true. He and I are kind of perfect together, a perfect fit.

Just the way we are.

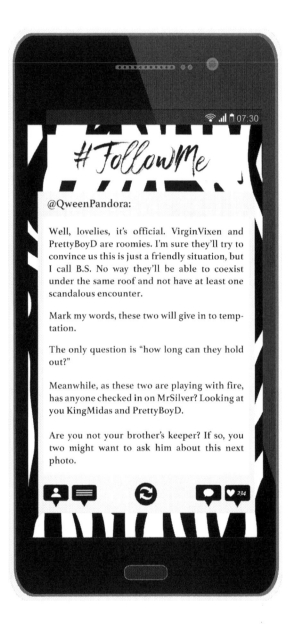

#FollowMe

@QweenPandora:

Well, lovelies, it's official. VirginVixen and PrettyBoyD are roomies. I'm sure they'll try to convince us this is just a friendly situation, but I call B.S. No way they'll be able to coexist under the same roof and not have at least one scandalous encounter.

Mark my words, these two will give in to temptation.

The only question is "how long can they hold out?"

Meanwhile, as these two are playing with fire, has anyone checked in on MrSilver? Looking at you KingMidas and PrettyBoyD.

Are you not your brother's keeper? If so, you two might want to ask him about this next photo.

#FollowMe

@QweenPandora:

The handsome gent seen headed into the Harrison residence sometime last week looks an awful lot like the youngest Golden triplet.

Speaking of scandalous, sneaking around with your new dean? The wife of your former headmaster? Well, it ranks right up there, doesn't it? Shame on you, MrSilver. And to think, the ink isn't even dry on her divorce papers yet.

Later, Peeps!   ~P.

Chapter 6

Joss

Despite the small measure of help she offered the triplets in months past, Pandora is toxic as fuck. I muted her posts for the last couple days, hoping to drown out whatever negativity she might get circulating, and I couldn't have been more right about that.

I caved this morning, peeking in to see what she had to say and, of course, she's feeding the rumor mill big time. This shit about Sterling is sure to cause a stir, and she hasn't been shy about calling massive attention to me living here with Dane, speculating that we'd cross the line eventually.

As of today, two days in, we've had no drama and no awkwardness.

So, suck it, Pandora.

I lift my head from the mattress to peek at the door. Seeing that I hadn't forgotten to lock it after coming back from the shower, my head falls to the mattress again, letting my feet dangle off the edge.

Maybe moving in together wasn't a mistake. Although, it might still be too early to tell.

The phone sounds off and I glance that way before reaching across the comforter to grab it.

Carlos.

I answer and he smiles at me through the screen.

"Good morning," he greets me, his accent lacing through every syllable.

"Good morning." I smile up at him after rolling onto my back again.

"Did I catch you at a bad time?"

"Nope. Just finished showering, so my day hasn't really started yet."

I sit upright, adjusting the towel around my chest with my free hand. At first, I'm unsure why his expression has just changed, going from being happy to see me, to confused.

"Are you… vacationing?"

It takes a second to realize he's noticed my backdrop is different than usual. Instead of seeing the gray painted walls of my bedroom, he's staring at a wall of exposed brick and a huge window behind me.

"Um, not exactly. I moved," I share.

"Oh." His brow quirks with that one word, but I know he has more to say. "Are you in the dorms already? I thought you were holding off until next semester."

There goes that sensation again. The one where it feels like my stomach's bottoming out. It comes from feeling like I live in two worlds and they've just collided.

"Actually, I moved in with a friend a couple days ago. My parents decided to leave the country for a bit, and I stayed behind."

It feels strange dumbing that entire fiasco down to so few words, but I'm not in the mood to rehash the entire, painful ordeal.

"Hm. Well, I'm sure it'll be fun," he says with a smile. "Is this your friend Blue?"

My stomach churns again. "Nope. Dane." I say it quickly, leaving little room for my words and tone to be analyzed.

He's seen Dane before. Granted, it was only through pics of us I posted on social media, but it was enough to make him ask questions about the nature of the relationship early on. Nothing that felt too possessive, just him wanting clarity as to whether Dane and I were involved or just friends. Only, even *after* I explained that we'd been tight since sixth grade, I sensed his lingering suspicion, his discomfort with the idea of me being close friends with a guy.

It's always evident in the slight changes in his expression whenever I talk about Dane, or how he quickly rushes off the phone when he happens to call while Dane and I are hanging out. Basically, I know he subscribes to the same theory as everyone else.

That there's absolutely no way a guy and a girl can keep a relationship clean without lines getting crossed. Guess we'll just have to let our actions speak for us.

"Oh," Carlos finally says, unable to hide that look on his face.

"He got a loft downtown and offered to let me stay," I add nervously. "It's big enough that I have my own room and everything."

Dead silence. In fact, the only feedback I'm getting is that stiff head nod that makes it clear he isn't believing a single word I've just said.

"It won't be too far a drive from school, either. Which will be nice when cheer practice starts in a couple weeks, and especially when winter hits."

Still nothing.

I fidget with one of my damp curls and let my gaze drift to the wall, feeling super uncomfortable with his reaction. It's put me in a position to keep explaining why I decided to do this, but I don't owe him that. We're not together and I haven't made any type of commitment. Honestly, yeah, there's some pretty strong physical attraction between us, but I don't think this is going anywhere. If it were, after keeping in touch for a year, I think I'd know.

"You'll… have to give me a virtual tour sometime," he finally says, flashing what seems like a tight smile that leaves him a little too quickly.

"Sure. Whenever you're ready."

I'm anxious to end our call, so I take this next bout of silence as an opportunity.

"Well, I should get ready. I've got a few things to knock off my to-do list this morning."

"Of course. We'll talk later."

"Bye," I say with a wave, feeling super relieved to be ending this.

The moment my screen goes dark, I breathe a sigh of relief. I've got enough to worry about without adding Carlos' feelings to the list.

Starting with the fact that my parents are leaving soon, and I have yet to hear from either of them. I'm sure Mom would've, but she's likely been super busy tying up loose ends. Still, the radio silence hurts a little.

Don't do it, Joss. Don't let the sadness in. Focus.

With that, I stand from the bed and throw on the khaki shorts and white tank I laid out for the day. Then, I work a bit of product through my hair and pull it up into a bun. After that, I open my bedroom door and settle in to start my first day of work. I'll mostly be on my phone and iPad, but it seems fitting to be at my desk, so that's where I sit, providing a bit of structure.

"Let's see what we have here," I sigh to myself, pulling up Dane's Instagram account. His login info is the same for everything, which has me making a mental note to encourage him to change that.

Right away, I see where I need to start, but there's some serious hesitation as I stare at his jam-packed DMs. I'm guessing he's gone through them this week, but there are still nearly a hundred staring me in the face right now. So, pulling up my big girl britches, I go in with caution.

Right away, I feel like I need a body condom just reading this shit. Photo after photo of naked chicks trying to *give* their vaginas away. I mean, straight up handing them over on a silver platter for Dane to do with them as he pleases.

"Thirsty bitches," I grumble to myself.

Delete. Delete. Delete.

Boob shot.

Delete.

I should've waited to shower after I finished with this shit, because *now* I feel dirty all over again.

I keep scrolling into some of the older messages and don't see what I expect. There's very little engagement on Dane's part. As in, he doesn't respond to most of this B.S. From the looks of it, he only replies to people he actually knows.

Interesting.

"Find anything good?"

I nearly leap out of my chair when he wanders in with coffee, smiling behind the mug when he sips. At first, I'm focused there, on his smile. Then, I notice he's shirtless, wearing nothing but plaid pajama pants. The long, thick, and very distinct outline between his legs tells me he's likely not wearing anything underneath them.

"I… no, actually," I say once I finally remember 'how to English'.

Damn abs.

"Looks like Rose was worried for nothing. I mean, yeah, these girls reach out, but you haven't done or said anything stupid. Not from what I can see anyway."

He smiles again. "This should be an easy job for you, then."

I shrug and glance back toward the screen, scrolling to the top again. That's when I notice one I missed. Surprisingly, I'm not accosted by body parts when I open it.

"You know something about a girl named Shawna?"

Dane's eyes slam shut when he nods. "Shit. Yeah. Rose mentioned that she'd be in touch. It's her daughter. She sent something?"

I nod. "Yep, just to introduce herself. Nothing specific."

He sips again and shrugs. "Maybe I'll get to it when I'm done at the gym. Need anything before I go? There's coffee," he adds, lifting his own into the air.

I glance up at him for a sec, being mindful not to stare. "Uh, nope. I think I'm good. Have fun."

"Will do."

I don't look up again until he's gone. Mostly because I don't trust myself. It's only day two and I'm already thinking we should add another rule to our list.

Dane shalt not go shirtless.

Signed, my ovaries.

Chapter 7

Joss

After "work"—if I can even call it that yet—I finished unpacking my things, put Victor someplace safer than a shoebox in the closet, then broke down all the boxes and took them out to the dumpster. I even got up the nerve to call my uncle, only to have him confirm that he did in fact give my internship spot to whoever was next in line. He apologized profusely, but then explained that he had to act quickly. With plans to spend the summer in Europe, as soon as my father reached out, the runner up got the call.

It burns knowing that my father—someone I thought had my best interest at heart—would do something so underhanded. But I'm starting to see the man for who he really is.

Selfish. Mean. The asshole of all assholes.

Shake it off, Joss. You were doing great. Just move forward.

On a lighter note, with all the boxes gone, my room feels a bit homier and less like a storage room. With so much time on my hands, I even got some of Dane's things put away. He's a guy and it would've sat there forever otherwise.

Now, as I stand at the stove, preparing dinner, I'm hoping this gesture doesn't give the wrong impression. The point is to show my gratitude for Dane opening his place to me, but now that I'm thinking about it, unpacking his things and cooking for him might come across a bit too… girlfriend-y.

Well, shit. I've already spent my last dime on chicken, rice, and roasted carrots. No turning back now.

Bored and waiting for the timer to go off, I grab my phone from the counter and scroll through my feed, seeing what I've missed after keeping busy all day. Mostly, it's pics of people's meals, mixed drinks, and pets, but an image posted an hour ago has my full attention.

A lean torso covered in sweat, biceps far more stacked than even just a few months ago, and a face that's handsome, but not *too* handsome. Rugged is a good word. The look he's giving is anything but innocent. It's lethal.

Yeah, he definitely lives up to the name Pretty Boy D.

I haven't blinked in a full minute because I'm stuck gawking at him, imagining what my best friend looks like without clothes.

Not my proudest moment.

This lapse reminds me of the one I had when he came into my room this morning, half-naked. So, I check the reaction quickly this time, opting to peek at the comments instead since doing so is officially my job now.

As expected, the reactions are about as explicit as what I found in his private messages earlier, only no nudes. If I didn't already know it, I would after such a close look at his account—these women want him.

Bad.

"You cooked?"

Shocked, my eyes flash toward Dane at the sound of his voice. I was so engrossed in his update I hadn't even heard him come in. He can't see my screen, but that doesn't stop me from feeling like a kid caught sneaking cookies.

"I... I um... yeah," I finally force out, fumbling to shove the phone inside my pocket.

His eyes narrow with suspicion. "Shit, was that porn or something?"

He flashes a wicked smirk when asking and, naturally, the sight of it makes me even *more* jumpy.

"What? No."

He's still giving me that look. "Let me see your phone then," he teases, coming closer.

"It wasn't that. I was just—"

You were what, exactly? Staring at his pic? Staring at the waistline of his shorts, wishing you had magical powers to see what he's hiding beneath them?

He's laughing now, letting his gaze slip over me. "Damn, was it that kinky?"

I'm positive my face is red now. The heat blooming upward from my neck tells me so.

"It was just something personal," I lie, which I normally hate to do, but this doesn't count.

His glare stays trained on me for a bit, then he backs off, allowing my heart to settle again.

Finally.

"Now that the interrogation's over, you hungry?" I ask, still trying to mask my own guilt.

"Starving." After answering, he watches as I move to the oven to peek inside.

"Well, the chicken's almost done."

"Good thing I showered at the gym then. Just let me put my stuff away."

I nod as he walks off, pretending I didn't just picture that—him covered in lather, rinsing it down the drain until all I see is smooth, bare skin.

By the time he makes it back, I've plated the food and gotten us set up on the fire escape. It's a perfect night to dine outside, so we'll make use of the small, wrought-iron table and matching chairs the previous renter left behind.

"Out here."

Dane diverts his path when I call out, then drops down into the seat across from mine. As I stare at his tousled hair, the way the faint rays of the summer sunset touch his skin, I realize I was right.

Cooking him dinner does feel extremely girlfriend-y.

Not even sure that's a word, but I've used it twice now, so I'm gonna pretend it's a thing.

"I saw that you put some of my shit away. I owe you," he says, glancing up from his plate to flash a smile.

"I hope that wasn't invasive. I just had extra time and thought I'd help you out. Having extra time is also the reason I cooked," I add with a nervous laugh. "Well, that and because I wanted to show my appreciation."

"For?" he asks, popping a carrot into his mouth.

"For letting me stay here. For being a good friend. All of it."

Chewing, he shrugs casually. "You never have to thank me for anything, Joss, but… you're welcome."

God, he's perfect.

I'm failing at this whole keep-things-in-perspective plan, so I try to make light conversation.

"You know, I was thinking. We should decorate out here. I mean, it's bigger than most fire escapes, so we could totally string some lights around the rail, get some clay pots out here, a few plants…"

Sunlight makes the green centers of his eyes burn when he peers up, cutting his chicken while smiling.

"What? You hate it?"

He shakes his head, taking a bite. "Nope. Opposite. I like that you're making plans, feeling at home."

I suppress a grin by sipping from my glass.

"Been sleeping okay?" he asks. "I know being in a new place can be weird."

I shrug. "Actually, it's been fine. How about you?"

He shrugs, too. "Pretty sure I'll rest better once I have an actual bed."

When he mentions it, I feel kind of bad his new one—a custom-made California king—won't be delivered for a little while yet.

"Not to mention how sore I'll be once practice starts next week. Should be fun," he jokes. "Aren't you starting cheer soon?"

"Yeah, but we won't be meeting as often as you guys. Thank God," I add with a laugh.

"You nervous?"

"About being on the squad? Nah, not really. Won't be too different from dance as far as conditioning is concerned."

He nods, agreeing. Then, my phone vibrates for about the third time in the last sixty seconds. It's still in my pocket from when I tried hiding it, so it rumbles against the wrought-iron seat, loud and obnoxious.

"Need to get that?"

I meet his gaze when he acknowledges it this time. I set my fork down to silence it. "Sorry. It's Carlos. I can call him back."

"Ah, Carlos," he says in a tone I find extremely hard to read. "So… what are you two exactly? Friends? More?"

I glance up at him, unable to hide my smile. "Funny you should ask. He was wondering the same about me and you."

There's a pleased smirk on his lips now. "Interesting."

"Yup. As soon as I told him we're sharing this place, he gave me *the look.*"

He knows exactly what I'm talking about. It's the same look we've been getting since we were young. That look of disbelief when we tell *anyone* that the only thing between us is friendship.

"Your *guy friends* always feel threatened," he adds with a cocky air to his tone, letting me know he isn't completely oblivious as to why. I mean, he's seen himself in the mirror.

"Well, he can feel however he wants about it. I'm pretty sure whatever we've got going on is dead in the water. We live a world apart."

I spoon rice into my mouth before looking at Dane again. He's kind of picking over his food now, which is a far cry from how he'd been enjoying it a moment ago.

"What is it? Does something not taste right?" I ask, but he shakes his head.

"No, everything's great." That answer leaves me even more confused, which is why I set my fork down and reach for my napkin.

"Then, what is it?"

It takes a bit for him to even look at me, but when he does, I see more than I think he means for me to see.

"I'm just wondering… is that the only reason it's not working between you two? Distance?"

The question seems simple enough, but it feels loaded. Like, he's asking a question wrapped inside another question.

One I'm not sure I want to answer.

Scrambling for a response, I shrug. "I mean, I suppose that's had a lot to do with it. Our only means of communication is video chat, and we can't build much of a foundation with thousands of miles between us."

When I finish, Dane nods slowly, thoughtfully, but his eyes never leave me. My heart flutters, and now I'm worried that *I'm* the one being too transparent.

So, I scramble again.

"But this Shawna thing should be good, right? I mean, from the looks of it, she's got a pretty big following. That'll lead to some cross-over once you two start making appearances together. Assuming that's Rose's agenda, that is."

The next look I get from him hits me right in the chest. It's like he's confused and wounded at the same time, maybe wondering why I'd bring that up now.

Don't bend on this. You know the lines have to stay clean. No blurring whatsoever.

"I'll reach out to her first thing in the morning to set something up for you guys," I say quickly, before I change my mind altogether.

I still have his attention, and it's incredibly uncomfortable. Mostly, because he has yet to respond to my announcement. But then he swallows hard and seems to snap out of… *whatever* that was.

"Yeah, of course. Sounds good."

We finish eating in silence, and I gather our dishes when we're done, needing an excuse to put space between us.

You're doing the right thing, Joss.

I mean, aren't I? Not only is setting him up with Shawna good for his career and good for strengthening his rapport with Rose, but I'm beginning to think it's good for our friendship, too. Maybe if we

aren't so focused on each other things won't get so confusing. So...
overwhelming.

I set our dishes on the edge of the sink and start rinsing them to
load into the dishwasher. Meanwhile, my thoughts are a mess,
wondering if I just made a stupid move. I feel so torn I'm sick to my
stomach, but only until I give myself a reality check.

Mom and Dad were best friends once. Then, they gave into their
feelings and, from there, the relationship went to shit. I've seen that
scenario play out with my own eyes, so it's decided. No matter what
my heart says, I have to think with my head. Dane and I can never be
more than what we already are.

Period.

Chapter 8

Joss

"Cool if I take fifteen?"

My knee bounces beneath the table while Blue gets permission from her uncle, Dusty, to go on break a little early. They're not super busy, so I'm hopeful. Heaven knows I need her advice right now.

Dusty glances up from the grill where he's hard at work. "Sure thing. Fix you and Joss a milkshake first. On the house," he adds with a nod.

I wave when he flashes a smile my way. Somehow, he's not sick of seeing my face, despite how much time me and the guys spend here. Now that Blue and West have gotten things sorted out, Dusty's Diner has kind of become our hang out, which Dusty doesn't hate. According to him, people in this city look at our crew as local royalty, so business has been booming lately. If you ask me, we all have *way* too much baggage for anyone to envy us. I suppose they're only considering what they assume is in our bank accounts, though, instead of the drama surrounding our actual lives.

Which is pretty damn shallow, but not a surprise.

Wonder what they'd think of me if they knew my father had completely cut me off? Would they still think it's cool to be me?

Sighing, I go over all the shit I need to vent about. Blue makes two strawberry milkshakes, removes her apron, then joins me in the booth. She shoots me a grin and slides one of the tall glasses my way.

"Ok, so tell me what you think you screwed up," she says, quoting the desperate text I sent a few hours ago.

Sighing, I stir the shake a bit, still getting my words together.

"Or we could start with something lighter," I suggest, in no hurry to spill my guts.

"Oookay, what do you consider lighter?"

I shrug. "Anything. Tell me how Scar's doing. She and your dad getting along okay without you?"

The first indicator that things have done a complete turnaround is that smile Blue's wearing. Months ago, she'd been so hellbent on hating her father for the rest of her life. But now? She's actually entrusted him with the one thing she loves on this planet as much as she loves West Golden.

Her sister, Scarlett.

"They're good. She sent me a pic last night of their first homemade pizza together."

"Did you go over for dinner?"

I know the answer before she even speaks, judging based on how her face is scrunched.

"Not exactly. I told them to get a bit more practice, *then* invite me," she laughs. "I'd rather not be turned off from pizza for the rest of my life."

A smile touches my lips, but there's pain beneath it. Hearing how Scar is building a relationship with their once-estranged father is a reminder of how things with mine are falling apart.

"Enough about that stuff, though. What's up with you?"

Hearing her ask, I accept that it's time to get to the real reason I came seeking her advice today.

"I already know I did the right thing, but I guess I just need to tell someone," I sigh. "Honestly, I'm not even sure why I texted you."

"Is it about Dane?"

I nod. "Yeah."

"...I'm listening," she teases when I don't elaborate.

I suck down some of the shake to buy myself a few more seconds, because I know how this is going to sound.

"Well, I'm managing Dane's social accounts. Which, for now, just means I engage with his followers, respond to DMs, stuff like that. So, I officially started yesterday morning, and as I was wrapping things up, I came across a message from Rose's daughter, Shawna. Apparently, Rose wants them to link up and—"

"Wait," she cuts in. "When you say *link up,* what does that mean exactly?"

"It's supposed to be a networking thing, but it seems kind of like a publicity stunt? Almost? Kind of?"

"So, Rose wants them to start dating—or at least *look* like they're dating—to get people talking?" she asks.

"Yes, exactly. And when I mentioned to Dane that she'd reached out, he was casual about it, not all that interested. But then *my* dumb ass had to push," I admit, hearing my own voice in my head from last night.

Blue pauses mid-sip to glare at me. "Joss, what the fuck did you do?"

I can't even look her in the eyes, because more than anyone, she knows. Knows there's a hidden layer to mine and Dane's relationship. A layer that—if left unchecked—would turn into something it shouldn't.

"I told him I'd set everything up."

"As in, set up the date?" When she asks, her eyes nearly bug out of her skull.

"It was the right thing to do," I say again, aware of how it sounds like I'm trying to convince myself.

Blue's only response is to continue glaring at me.

"I know what you're thinking, but you're not there in that loft. It's only been three days, and *already* I feel the pull," I admit.

"Then don't fight it!"

When I roll my eyes, she grabs my hand.

"Remember what you said to me when we were in Louisiana last Christmas?"

A deep breath fills my lungs and I hate that I do, in fact, know what she's about to say.

"You told me there's a type of love between you and Dane, even if it isn't romantic love—which I'd beg to differ—but the point is that you like him. And you trust him. So, I fail to see the harm in, you know, getting a little closer," she adds wiggling her shoulders until I laugh.

"I hate you."

"You try."

My gaze slips out the window and I know the damage is done. I've already backed myself into a corner with what I promised Dane over dinner. If I renege on my word now, he'll know.

He'll know I'm confused about my feelings for him about fifty percent of the time.

He'll know I've considered throwing caution to the wind on many occasions, just to see what it'd be like to be with him. In every way imaginable.

"What're you doing?" Blue's eyes are fixed on my phone when I pull it from my pocket.

I finish the task at hand before answering, knowing she'll only try to talk me out of this. It isn't until I hit 'send' that I finally meet her gaze.

"I messaged Shawna back. Like I said I would."

I'm getting that look again but turn away from it because I hear Blue's thoughts now, too.

She thinks I'm being stubborn, thinks I'm digging myself in a deeper hole, thinks I'm doing something I'll regret later.

How do I know this?

Because I'm thinking the same thing.

My phone sounds off in my hand and my heart sinks.

"That her?"

"It is," I nod, trying to hold to the notion that this was all done in the name of preserving me and Dane's friendship.

"Well? What'd she say?" Blue asks.

I meet her gaze and feel nauseated, knowing it's now a done deal.

"She said what I expected her to. It's a date."

Chapter 9

Dane

Well, I definitely didn't see this coming. Not from a mile away.

If Joss wanted me to see she's hellbent on keeping me in the friendzone forever, message received.

Nothing screams *'it's never happening'* louder than the girl you want appointing herself as your wingman.

Point taken.

Shawna's late and I'm half a second from leaving when a light touch squeezes my shoulder.

"Hey."

I turn and we lock eyes, recognizing her from her profile. I honestly hadn't glanced at it before tonight. Figured I'd need to know what she looks like, so I don't end up approaching a stranger by accident.

"I was just starting to think you wouldn't show," I say, lightheartedly enough that she knows I'm not upset.

"Yeah, sorry about that. My cat, GG, slipped out of my apartment when I was leaving. Which means I had to chase after her for like ten minutes before finally wrangling her in. It was just… a whole thing," she adds, sighing as she relives the stress of it.

When she looks up, she finds me smiling.

"What?"

"Your excuse is that you had to go chase your cat?"

She shrugs, grinning. "Well, what excuse would you accept? That I was washing my hair and lost track of time?"

A laugh slips and we're moving now, taking slow steps down the sidewalk. Meeting up downtown—not too far from my place—seemed like the best idea.

Glancing over, I actually look at her now, instead of just scanning her features through the barrage of selfies on her IG.

She's good-looking, definitely fuckable, and bears no physical resemblance to her mother. Thank God for small favors. Long hair stretches almost to her waist, the dark color contrasting her stark-blue eyes. I'm six-foot-three and, with the yellow heels she's wearing, she nearly matches my height. Tight jeans hug the length of her legs and she's curvier than expected. Another plus. Her hips and ass complement the nice rack her crop top's showing off.

All-in-all, I'm not disappointed.

"Your messages were a little vague. I kind of thought the same thing you did, that you might not show."

I push a hand through my hair, preparing to confess something. "Actually, I'm not the one who hit you up, so I'm not really sure how the conversation went."

She grabs her chest, feigning offense. "I'm gutted! You mean to tell me I had a whole conversation thread with your secretary or some shit? That burns," she adds with a laugh.

Okay, so she's chill. Another plus.

"It wasn't like that. Your mom suggested that I hire someone I trust to manage my accounts, so I tend to not do much on them myself anymore. You know, aside from posting pics and updates."

"Ah, Rose," she sighs. "She's just the right amount of pushy to make me resent her, but good enough at her job that I don't fire her ass. Blood or not."

"I see you're on a first-name basis with one of your parents, too."

Shawna shrugs. "It was her idea, not mine. I turned ten, and she said being called Mom gave people the impression that she's old, so she's been Rose to me ever since."

I flash Shawna a look, weighing my words carefully. "She's… different."

"Are you kidding me? The woman's batshit crazy. I grew up with her, so I should know! Not to mention all the pressure to uphold this damn picture-perfect image she expects us to adhere to. Plus, on top of all the *social* pressure, she wants us *physically* perfect, too. I got so fed up with her last month, telling me I needed to find my way into the gym one extra day a week, I bought a double fudge sundae and vegged out on the couch in protest. It was the only way I could steal back that last bit of my soul she tried to take from me. Thank God I have my own place and can shut her out when I need to."

Shaking my head, I have an epiphany. "You're officially the only person who understands this side of my life. My brothers think I'm in the gym so much because I'm vain, and my friend, Joss, thinks it's to stave off depression, but the truth of it is, I'd rather not have your mom rip me a new one if I *don't* go."

"Exactly! The woman either needs a stiff drink, or a stiff cock. I'm betting either one would chill her the fuck out. It becomes clearer every day why my dad bailed."

On that note, it's time to change the subject. I know better than to involve myself in other people's family drama.

"Ice cream?"

Shawna's gaze follows when I point across the street to the shop on the corner.

"You teasing me because of the story I just told you?"

I laugh a bit. "Total coincidence. This was part of the plan even before you shared."

"We can go, but if you tell Rose I ate this, I'll hunt you down."

I raise my hands in surrender. "Your secret's safe with me."

She eyes me playfully, then nods.

I lead the way, stretching my arm in front of her when some asshole on a motorcycle runs a light and almost hits us. Once we finally make it to the window to order, I get yet another shock tonight.

"Hey, Shawna. The usual?"

Shawna glances at me and I hold in a laugh. "The usual?"

"Ok, so maybe I come here a lot. Sue me," she whispers, and then gives her order to the cashier. I tell them to make it a double, then we stand off to the side while we wait.

"If you're a regular, I take it you live close."

Her gaze meets mine when she points. "Just up the street, actually. You far?"

I point in the opposite direction. "A few blocks and a couple turns that way."

"That's right. You just moved into a loft, didn't you?"

My brow quirks. "You stalking me?"

Laughing, she shrugs. "Only on days Rose doesn't have me busting my ass in the gym. But in my defense, social media makes it super easy to unearth shit about, well... *anyone.*"

Our order comes up before I can respond, but I don't disagree with her.

We're on the move again, both with fudge sundaes.

"I know your mom's been here a few years, but what about you?"

"Just moved to CP about six months ago, actually. Speaking of, how the hell do you guys deal with Pandora? Thank God I'm not on her radar. That bitch is relentless!"

I shoot her a look when we near the front of the theater. The plan is to catch a movie, but first I need to burst her fucking bubble. When I smirk, she seems confused.

"You mean you *weren't* on her radar. Because after tonight, she'll definitely know who you are."

Shawna's steps halt with the realization. "Shit."

"Yep, welcome to the dark side."

"Gee, thanks."

We finish the sundaes, take a few obligatory photos in front of the fountain so Rose stays off our backs. Then, once those are posted, we get in line to buy tickets.

"Ok, I have a confession," Shawna pipes up.

"I'm listening."

"So, we both know Rose makes a lot of overbearing, over-the-top suggestions, but… hanging out with you is one I wasn't opposed to."

She flashes me a blue stare and I don't hate that I'm here with her either. The night could definitely be going worse.

"Who knows? That woman might have actually gotten something right this time."

I feel when she glances at me again and I meet her stare.

"Yeah. Maybe she did."

@QweenPandora:

Well, what have we here, lovelies? PrettyBoyD's been spotted with a brunette beauty on his arm and the two look cozy AF if you ask me.

Eating ice cream.

Turning the sidewalks of Downtown Cypress into their runway.

We all know our boy gets around, which is why I've come to think of him as the king of random hookups, but a date? Not quite his style, is it?

Until now, the only girl he's seen with in public, actually enjoying her company, is VirginVixen.

Could it be we jumped the gun thinking the roomies would make a quick love connection?

Chapter 10

Dane

"I'll call you back in a few. Dane's home," Joss says in a rush just as I hear movement coming from her room.

"Can't you two talk when we're done?" a guy asks through her speakerphone. I can only assume it's Carlos.

"He's coming back from a... work thing, so I need to check in and see how it went," Joss reasons, which is I guess how she sums up me being out with Shawna.

I slide off my sneakers and walk away, but then double back to put them on the rack when her request that I don't leave them in the doorway rings in my ears. By the time I make it to the hall, she's ended her call and the door to her bedroom flies open.

She's smiling, but I know her. It's not a real smile. It's the kind she puts on to save face.

Something's up.

"So, how was it?"

I pause, trying to find the right words. "It was... nice. Definitely went better than expected."

A long, awkward silence fills the space between us, and Joss slips her hands into the pockets of her shorts.

"Oh, cool. I hoped you'd have fun."

Real fucking nice. What I want is you, and what you want is for me to have fun with another girl.

75

Just what I wanted to hear.

"Well, I should turn in. I have a photoshoot tomorrow afternoon and I need to hit the gym before that, so…"

"Oh, right." She laughs and I don't miss that it's almost as forced as that smile from a moment ago.

I take three steps before a breathy, "Wait," makes me pause, then I glance over my shoulder. "Can't you hang out for a few?" she asks. "I'd like to hear more about your night."

I let that sink in, her wanting more details about the date. If the shoe were on the other foot, the last damn thing I'd want is to hear about her and some other guy. That's where we're different, though. I know she feels something, but she's determined to suffocate the hell out of it until it dies. My guess? Convincing herself that I'm even *half* as interested in Shawna as I am in *her* will only help her believe that lie.

So, no fucking way. I won't indulge her just to ease her damn conscience.

"I'm beat. Maybe tomorrow."

I turn my back to her like before, after seeing proof that she's visibly disappointed from having been shot down. Still, no one's more disappointed than I am.

"I'm sorry."

Those words hit me and despite myself, I stop again. And this time, I hear her take steps toward me.

"I know I fucked up," she admits. "I should've… I should've asked if you were okay with this, going out with her."

"It's not all on you. You told me you were sending the message and I didn't stop you," I say back, thinking to myself that one reason I hadn't protested was because I didn't actually think she'd go through with it.

"I know, I just… haven't felt right about it since," she admits. "We're friends, but damn it, Dane."

There's a long pause that follows. One that has me tempted to face her, but I'm certain she'd lose her nerve to continue the second we make eye contact.

"We've entered some kind of weird, gray area that has my head all fucked up, and my nerves are shot to hell." She's breathless now and I don't miss how her voice quivers with each syllable.

My heart races and I'm shocked she's said so much. No, it's not an admission of love or anything like that, but it's more than what I've been given in the past. More than being made to feel like I'm losing my mind thinking there's more to us than friendship.

I let out a breath and finally face her, feeling the tug in my chest when I meet her dark eyes. With so much emotion swimming in them, it guts me knowing she might always keep me at arm's length. The thought of never having her like I want her feels like hell on Earth.

She lifts her hands, fidgeting with her nails, but doesn't look away.

"Dane, both our lives are all over the place right now, so I know I don't need to explain what that feels like, but I don't have family a few miles away. So, for me, you're the only stable thing I've got, which means I can't afford to mess this up."

Without saying much, she's said it all—admitted that I'm not the only one who has a hard time keeping my distance. It hits me that I've only been looking at this from one angle, and none of them were *her* angle. Aside from having me—or people connected to me—she's alone in this city.

Another breath rushes from my lungs, and guilt sets in for only seeing what I wanted to see.

"Let me change, then I'll come to your room."

She smiles a little, then nods. "Okay."

We part ways and I do exactly what I said I would, swapping out ripped jeans and a tee-shirt for a pair of dark basketball shorts and a white tank. When I pop into Joss's room, she peers up through thick, long lashes, sitting cross legged on her bed.

She's got the face of an angel, and the body of a goddess. I take in how the tightness of her waist draws attention to the flare of her round hips. The shorts she wears are tiny and don't hide much, sort of like the cut-off hoodie that stops right beneath her tits. When I drop down near the edge of her bed and rest my back against the post, I pretend not to notice any of that.

"So, tell me about Shawna," she says, but there's an air of sadness within the request that isn't lost on me.

"She seems cool, I guess. It was nice talking to her about things no one else really understands where work is concerned, but other than that, it's still kind of early to tell."

Joss smiles and it's more sincere this time. "Did you two make plans to meet up again?"

"Not yet. I might message her in a few days. Might not."

She holds my gaze and neither of us blinks. "Well, it sounds like you two hit it off. Pandora seems to think so, at least."

It's not until she says this that I even realize something's already been posted. I shouldn't be surprised, though. Nothing's a secret in this city. Guess Shawna's figuring that out as we speak.

"What about you? Having a good night?" I ask, turning the spotlight off myself and onto her.

She sighs before answering. "Guess you could say that. I got some reading done."

My eyes flicker to the book left open, face down on her comforter.

"And… you were talking to Carlos when I came in, right?" I try to say that as chill as possible, but it doesn't matter. She knows I hate the guy by default. Simply because they have some sort of connection.

I leave out that I overheard his reaction when she blew him off so we could talk. Little does he know, I'm not a threat to whatever he's trying to build with her.

Not that I don't wish otherwise.

"He wants to come here."

I shoot her a look. "To the city?"

She nods. "Yeah, despite me telling him not to."

My gaze lowers to the floorboards and I don't really know what to say to that.

"What's that look mean?" She laughs a bit when asking.

I fix whatever facial expression just gave me away and meet her gaze. "It doesn't mean anything. It's just that, the other night, you seemed pretty certain there's nothing between you and him. Guess I'm just wondering when that changed."

Damn, dude. Wrangle it in a bit. You sound like some jealous, possessive asshole and she'll hear it if you're not careful. She wants to just be friends, so just be a friend.

"I *am* certain," she sighs. "But he seems to think time apart has just dulled what sparked between us when we met in Cuba last summer. I, on the other hand, think that spark is dead in the water. I'm gonna keep working on him, trying to convince him not to waste his time or money."

It's hard not to relate to the guy, maybe even feel a little sorry for him. Joss is incredibly hard to pin down. I should know. I've been trying since we were twelve.

I'm still watching when her gaze drifts to the nightstand. Then, I'm confused when her eyes land on a sheet of paper there, and she snatches it up before I can read any of the words written out in bold, purple marker.

"What the hell is that?" I ask with a laugh.

Well, I'll be damned. If how red she just turned is any indicator, whatever she's hiding must be pretty fucking good.

"It's not—"

"You're about to lie to me and we've been friends way too long for that shit. Tell me what you're hiding."

She stares at my hand where it lingers in the air, then one of the hardest eye rolls I've ever seen is aimed right at me.

"Fine, but keep in mind that I was *super* bored tonight, and I might've gotten into whatever alcohol that is in that bottle you keep in the cabinet over the fridge. So, I can't be held responsible for anything that paper says."

She unfolds it a little but doesn't hand it over. My confusion surrounding whatever this is I'm looking at must be evident, because the next second, she explains.

"Like I said, I had a little too much time on my hands tonight, so I may or may not have made a list of all the things I've never done. You know, because my dad would've freaked-the-fuck-out if I had," she adds.

I keep scanning and an idea hits me.

"Well, shit! Let's cross some of this stuff off," I say with a grin. "Pick your top three and we'll have them done before summer ends."

She eyes me and I see her wavering.

"Where's the marker?"

I don't get an actual answer, just her digging in the drawer to hand it over. Then, she grabs her book and lays the sheet flat on top of it.

"Ok, so we're circling *'smoke weed'.* You know I'm good for that one," I say with a laugh.

"But you don't smoke during football," she speaks up, knowing I swear off anything I think might impair my game during the season, including weed.

"It'll just be once. I'll be fine," I say distractedly, scanning for something else to circle. "How about this one—a tattoo. I'll take you to the place my brothers and I go. They'll hook you up."

She's watching as I move down the list, glancing up at her when I find the third thing. "You never mentioned wanting another piercing. Where?"

"My ear. The cartilage," she clarifies. "My dad said it was tacky, so I just figured I'd live without it."

Her eyes are on me when I mark that as the third and final thing on the list. "Well, get ready, because that shit's happening."

She laughs a little—a clear sign the mood has lightened since the tense moment in the hallway. But as I stare at the sheet, I notice more of the deep-purple ink bleeding through from the back.

"What are you doing? We already have three," she speaks up when I snatch the sheet from her hand, realizing part of the list was hidden.

I don't fully understand why she's redder and suddenly leaping all over me, trying to snatch the paper away. That is, until I see what's made number eleven on the list, apart from the original ten. There, printed on the back, is an addition I didn't expect to see.

She wants to lose her virginity.

Burying her face, it looks like she's holding her breath. "I only made the list to vent," she rambles, speaking muffled words from behind her hands. "It wasn't real, I was just getting my feelings down on paper, and—"

"Joss… you don't have to explain," I cut in, holding back a smile. If she saw it, she'd only feel more embarrassed.

"It didn't mean anything," she continues to say, probably wishing she could crawl underneath a rock.

My thoughts drift back to the day Sterling and I helped her move, back to the sex toy hidden in the black shoebox. It isn't a surprise that she owns one, but between that discovery and now this, I'm pretty sure I'm reading the signs right.

She's held out her whole life, been a good girl because she thought she had to be. But now, after years of waiting… she's ready to fuck.

Something inside me awakens—the part of me that's always been more protective of her than anyone else. All at the thought of the many ways this could go, now that I know she's given this some thought. It wouldn't take much for her to fall for someone this summer, then think *that* asshole's worthy of staking his claim. I don't say this out loud, but I'll be damned if I'm not thinking it.

Something I really have no right to think.

That, if she's going to trust *anyone* with her body, her *heart*… it should be me.

At the sound of the marker moving over the paper, Joss peeks through her fingers, seeing that I've just circled number eleven. There's confusion in her eyes when she looks up again.

"It's contingent," I say, weighing my words. "If you don't meet someone, or if you change your mind, we'll still get your top three picks crossed off the list."

I stay unnaturally still, hoping I made that part about her finding someone sound like a real option, something I'd actually allow.

After the shock of me being in on her secret starts wearing off, Joss and I lock eyes right before she nods, letting me know she's in.

"…Okay," she says with a deep sigh that turns into a smile.

I return the paper and she tucks it inside her drawer before meeting my gaze again. She doesn't speak, but the air in the room is charged with sexual tension. I suppose we've said a lot tonight without actually saying it. So, the only thing left to do from here is to find out if she knows what I know.

That she is now, and was always meant to be, mine.

Chapter 11

Joss

"Just hang in there a few more seconds and…. Done."

I breathe easy for the first time in an hour, glancing up at the artist who just permanently marked my skin. Dane insisted on coming straight here, not even twelve hours after learning about my list. He thought I'd chicken out if too much time passed, so here we are.

"You good?" he asks, drawing my attention to him and away from Max, the artist.

"Hurts like hell, but I'm good."

Dane glances down at the daisy inked on top of my foot and laughs. "Probably wasn't a good idea to get your first one right over bone."

When he warned me of this over breakfast, it hadn't fallen on deaf ears. However, I wanted something that won't be the first thing someone notices when meeting me. Or the first thing my parents see when I finally lay eyes on them again.

I brush off that thought before it can make me sad and glance up to thank Max for his work. He tops the tattoo with ointment, wraps my foot, then I hop down from the chair. Dane insists on paying since he was the one who suggested I knock a few things off what I've officially dubbed the *'Never Have I Ever'* list. Then, once he's done, we cross the parking lot to his car.

"You gonna be all right?" he asks with a smirk, watching me wince with every step I take.

When I give him the finger instead of an actual response, his smirk turns into laughter.

"Here. Hop on."

He says those words, but it takes time for them to register. Even when he stands in front of me and reaches back, drawing me closer by my wrist. I'm trying not to overthink things as I'm hoisted up onto his back, with his rock-solid arms wrapped around my legs as I cling to him.

My cheek presses against his hair and it's hard to ignore the closeness. His scent is something I think of often, following a close call we had this past Christmas. Visiting his family in Louisiana led to a game of Truth-or-Dare with his rowdy cousins, and that game ended up being the closest Dane and I ever came to crossing the line. It began with a dare to kiss him, and it ended with me being mortified when I couldn't follow through.

Now, as my arms rest over his broad shoulders, as I squeeze him between my legs, it's on my mind again, and so is last night's conversation. I hardly slept because it was *all* I could think about. When Dane added the fourth item to the list, I was admittedly confused.

Did he mean he'd help me find some random guy to lose my virginity to? Or… did he *mean* to make it sound like it should be him?

If I'm being honest, I only agreed to it because I assumed he meant the latter, but I know that makes me sound like a walking contradiction—agreeing to sleep with him when I've spent so much time and energy trying to convince us *both* I don't want that.

But as the sun breathes its sweltering heat over us, and as Dane's muscles flex and roll beneath his skin, I feel him everywhere. When I exhale a breath near his ear, he responds by lightly brushing his thumb down my thigh.

Resisting him sure as hell won't be easy.

He carries me all the way to the passenger-side door and doesn't put me down until he opens it. When I slip off his back, the action of my body moving against his has me letting out another of those ragged breaths. Especially when I climb into the seat and meet his green stare. It tells me I wasn't the only one thinking things I shouldn't have been.

He keeps that look trained on me as he closes me in, not averting his stare until he rounds the hood of his car. By the time he gets in, I've decided it's probably best that I focus my gaze out the window, but that lasts for all of ten seconds. We're not moving, so I peek over to see why and find Dane posting the pics from today's adventure. Including the one of me crying actual tears.

"You dick! Did you seriously just share that?"

I'm yelling, but laughing as hard as I am, he doesn't take me seriously.

"Sure did. And it's my favorite one of the day."

"Of course, it is. Because it's the one I hate most." When I roll my eyes, he nudges me playfully.

"Relax. You still look good in it."

The compliment makes my heart flutter even though its innocent enough. It's just that, coming from him, things like that always feel so much more weighted.

"You should come with me to my shoot. It starts in an hour, but I like to get there a bit early. You down?"

I've never tagged along for one of these gigs, but I *have* been curious about how they go.

"You sure that's okay?"

He laughs a bit. "Why the hell wouldn't it be?"

I shrug, imagining I'd be in the way, making him uncomfortable in front of the camera.

"Just say yes," he croons with a smirk. "It'll be fun."

I blink into the sunlight, weighing my options—chill at home alone, or hang with my best friend the rest of the day. It's kind of a no-brainer.

"Can we stop for food first?"

He glances down at the clock before answering. "We should have time, but I'll just get something for you. Rose insists we show up to shoots on an empty stomach. And seeing as how I already cheated and had breakfast, I probably shouldn't push it."

He smiles after that, but I don't. The more I hear about her, the more I hate the woman's guts. However, I keep my thoughts to myself.

"Sure, okay. I'm in."

"Good."

His gaze slips to my lips when he wets his own and I feel heat from more than just the blazing sun when he scans me with a look. Hopefully, this shoot is rated-PG, but... is it bad that I'm secretly hoping it isn't?

Damn. On second thought, maybe this isn't such a good idea after all.

Chapter 12

Joss

We hit a drive-through quickly, and I eat while Dane drives. I'm done by the time we pull into the small lot of a brick building that looks like a scaled-down version of the one that houses our loft.

We step back out into the heat, and I trail behind him, moving toward the entrance. We're hit with a blast of cool air the moment we step inside, and my sandals glide over the smooth, polished concrete floors. Hanging back while Dane checks in with the woman at the front desk, I take in the beautiful black and white portraits hung high on the brick wall near the door. This place has a whole vibe going on. From the minimalist décor, to the low-fi instrumental pumping from mounted speakers. The whole thing makes me wish I'd worn more than jean shorts and a pink tank top, something posh.

Heat from Dane's palm when it rests against my lower back is jarring, but only because he doesn't usually touch me that way. Meeting his gaze, he seems to notice I'm hyper-aware of the contact, and he casually pulls away.

"She said it should only be a few minutes, so it sounds like they're taking me back early."

The smile I offer feels tight and awkward. "Cool. Should I just wait here? Or…"

He shakes his head. "Nah, you're allowed to come back. I'd *like* for you to come back," he adds, amending his first answer.

I face forward again when I realize I'm staring, secretly hoping this energy between us chills the fuck out before it burns me alive.

"Dane Golden?"

We both glance behind us when a woman pops her head out of a door. She's smiling and gesturing for Dane to join her, and per his request, I follow.

"The clothes Dom wants you in are hanging up right behind the screen. There's also a shelf back there to hold your things."

Dane nods graciously, looking completely relaxed. If it were me, I'd probably be anything but.

"Be right back," he says, before disappearing behind the screen where he was told to prepare.

I cross both arms over my chest and look around.

The tall ceiling and three walls are painted pure white, the fourth being nothing but windows. Unlike the floors found in the lobby, restored wood slats glisten with a fresh coat of wax. Near a black backdrop, tall lights mounted on stands aim right where I imagine Dane will be standing in a moment.

It all feels a bit sterile, intimidating.

You'd never guess that by looking at Dane, though. He steps out from behind the screen, the picture of confidence in jeans and a white tank that hugs his abs in just the right way.

He chats with the photographer for a bit, smiling like the pro he's become over the last few months, but my attention's drawn behind me when the door opens. I glance that way as a tall, sophisticated woman strolls in. She's middle aged and dressed in what looks to be an expensive silk blouse, paired with a black pencil skirt. Her blonde hair is smoothed into a bun so tight I swear it's given her a mini facelift. She clicks across the floor in bright red heels that match her lipstick and the frames of her glasses. I smile at her a little, but her only response is the dismissive, sweeping look that passes over me. She saunters forward, not stopping until she makes it to Dane and the photographer. I'm not entirely sure what to make of it, but it's clear she's not exactly friendly.

My heart sinks when Dane gestures toward me and says something to the woman. She levels that same cold glare on me and I'm starting to think I should've waited in the car after all.

Unfortunately, Dane's bringing her closer and it looks like I'll have to speak.

"Joss, I'd like you to meet Rose. Rose, my best friend, Joss."

Ah, that explains it.

I force a smile. "Nice meeting you."

At first, when I offer her my hand, she just stares at it. But then, she must realize she can't be that outrightly rude to someone and get away with it and presses her palm to mine.

"Pleasure."

That's all she says, so I shut down too after that.

Dane passes a questioning look my way, but I force a smile so he's not tipped off that I'm really not feeling Rose all that much.

"Guess you two can keep each other company while you wait. I should get over there," he says, aiming his thumb over his shoulder to where the photographer's just about done setting up.

"Go, dear. We'll be fine," Rose croons. Like the silver-tongued devil I imagine her to be.

Dane heads over and now it's just me and Rose. Who, legit, gives me Cruella de Vil vibes.

And now I'm humming the song to myself, because I'm so fucking mature.

"So, you're Dane's beloved Joss," she says with a tight smile. Despite addressing *me*, her eyes never leave him, staring as an assistant oils his arms.

"Guess so."

"Hmm."

What the fuck is that *supposed to mean?*

"The images he shared at the tattoo parlor are already creating quite a bit of buzz," she comments.

I wait for her to get to the point, but I guess that *is* the point.

"Yep, Dane's followers love him."

"That they do," she agrees.

I'm tempted to move away from her because she's negative AF, but I don't want to make a scene.

"Several of his commenters seem to be wondering what's kept you two stuck on just being friends throughout the years. And, if I do say so myself, I'm admittedly curious as well," she says.

What I *want* to do is tell this nosey bitch to kiss my ass, but I don't. For Dane.

"Well, we've been friends a long time, so it's just what works for us, I suppose."

She casts a look down on me, towering over me in those red heels. "Yes, I suppose," she replies, echoing my words.

When she looks away, I decide to pretend she's not even here, focusing only on Dane. He's a different guy in front of the camera. I know him as the funny, sometimes weird, loyal friend I wouldn't trade for the world. Behind the lens, he's a sex symbol.

Pretty Boy D.

Damn, did it just get hot in here?

I swallow deeply when I realize how I'm gawking, but a quick glance to the right reveals I'm not the *only* one who noticed how I watched him. Rose is all over it, scanning me with a look that makes it clear she wishes there was an ocean between me and Dane, likely because me being around has thrown some sort of wrench in her marketing plan.

Or… in her plan to help her daughter sink her claws into him.

Facing forward again, Dane's pulled off his tank and, from the looks of things, the assistant has oiled his chest and abs now. Girl's got a sweet job if you ask me. He poses for pic after pic, then the photographer gives him a thumbs up.

"Change and we'll continue."

Dane nods at the guy, then heads back toward the screen, halting when his name's called.

"Oh, and Dane? Lose the boxers. We're going sexier this go-round."

Dane nods and I resist the urge to swallow again, knowing Cruella's watching. So, instead, I take out my phone to see what kind of attention those pics she mentioned are getting. She hadn't lied. It's been maybe an hour and, already, they've gotten tens of thousands of likes.

"Enjoying your new position on the team? Social Media Manager is a pretty important role," Rose comments, prompting me to meet her stoic expression.

"So far, so good. Dane's an easy guy to work for, though."

She nods, agreeing. "That he is. My only gripe is that he's a bit naïve, blind to potential pitfalls. It isn't his fault, though," she sighs. "He's got a big heart and has this notion that he can take everyone with him as he rises. He'll realize that isn't so one day. Not everyone's destined to climb Everest, and he won't be either if he doesn't cut some of the dead weight."

Shots fired.

No, she doesn't *say* she's talking about me, but this bitch is talking about me. I know it. She knows it.

Not sure what I've done to get on her bad side, but the feeling's mutual.

Dane's back, and seeing him wipes my mind clean of Rose and her bullshit. Why? Because he looks like sex on legs right now. A pair of black, silky pants that tie at the waist hang low on his hips. And thanks to the photographer's request that he remove his boxers, I see more of him than I probably need to—particularly, the outline of his dick beneath the thin material.

He once teasingly told me he was huge. Honestly, I figure all guys say that, so I didn't pay it much attention at the time, but… I'm paying attention now.

It certainly was *not* a lie.

He gets into position, then the camera begins to flash. I'm already imagining the filthy comments I'll have to wade through when he posts highlights from today's shoot. Mostly because his fans will only be typing out the exact things I'm thinking to myself right now.

One thought in particular stands out—item number eleven on the *'Never Have I Ever'* list.

Focus, girl. It's Dane. Your friend, remember?

"He's a natural," Rose comments, reminding me of her presence. I'd tried so hard to forget she was even here.

"He is," I say with a nod, agreeing.

"He and Shawna truly do make an attractive couple," she adds, being blatantly catty, and then she steps away to take a call.

My stomach turns as the statement begins to take effect. They serve as a reminder that Dane had just been out with Shawna the night before, not even twenty-four hours ago, actually. After he and I hung together all morning, I'd nearly forgotten how I spent most of the evening wondering where he'd take her, wondering if they were having fun, wondering if he was falling for her.

I pretend not to be annoyed by this woman and her snide comment, blinking an admittedly thirsty glance toward Dane.

Please let this wrap up soon. I'm not sure how much longer I can stare at him like this and not get weak.

Well... *weaker.*

As if to answer my prayers, the photographer shoots one last pic and gives Dane another thumbs up. This time, the assistant starts switching off the bright lights and straightening up. Within a few minutes, Dane's changed and coming toward me, right as Rose's call ends.

"You did wonderful," she gushes, squeezing him with a dainty hug.

"Thanks." He's gracious as usual.

"I've got a few things lined up for you. For starters, there's a carnival coming to the city next weekend, so I'll tell Shawna to clear her schedule. It'd be a great photo op for you two," she adds with a smirk. "At any rate, I'll be in touch to chat about some other thoughts I have. Maybe next time I can get you and Shawna lined up for a joint shoot. Sound good?"

Dane nods. "Sure."

"Of course, it does. That's why you want me on your team," she says with a wink. "Take care. Talk soon."

And just like that, Hurricane Rose blows her ass out of the studio.

I'm quiet as Dane and I make our own unhurried exit—thanks to my sore foot—but I know he notices I'm not saying much.

"Everything good?"

I hate that he even has to ask. Hate that he noticed. Today was a good day for him, and I don't want to ruin it. So, I don't.

"Yup! You did great. It was fun getting to see you work."

If he were the type to blush, he probably would have right there. Judging by how he smiles.

"Honestly, I thought you'd be bored."

I shoot him a look. "Not at all. It's cool getting to see you in your element."

"I know you'll have practice starting soon, too, but if you like this sort of thing, you're welcome to join me whenever."

I smile up at him. "Thanks. I'll take you up on that."

In the lot, he comes around to open my door again and I climb in, waiting for him to join me.

Today was... eye-opening. For *many* reasons. But what's obvious is that Rose is every bit as toxic as I imagined. If she made one thing clear with our first meeting, it's that she definitely has a vision for Dane's future.

And if she has anything to do with it, I'll be shoved way, *way* out of the frame.

Chapter 13

Dane

My head lifts off the pillow when the phone rings. With one eye open, I reach to where I've left it on the coffee table and stare at the screen.

Rose.

She mentioned earlier at the shoot that she wanted to talk, but I thought she'd call at a decent hour. Not at fucking one a.m.

"Yeah?"

"Good, you're up," she replies, completely missing that I'm groggy and still half asleep. "I thought we might have our little chat now?"

This woman's a damn psychopath.

"Sure, what's going on?" I force myself to sit up, then stand from where I'd been sprawled out on the couch. Otherwise, I'd doze back off mid-conversation.

"Well, this isn't easy to say, but… I have concerns," she says.

"Okay, like what?" I slip out onto the fire escape, so I don't wake Joss.

"If I can be frank with you, it's about your friend. Or, rather, it's about the image you two portray and how it's hurting *your* image in particular."

I'm beyond confused, which is probably why my next question is kind of a stupid one. "You mean Joss?"

Of course, she means Joss, but how in the world can she possibly be bad for my image?

"Here's the thing," Rose sighs. "You're sending your followers very mixed messages. One day you're seen in photos with Joss, all over each other, looking like a happy couple. Then, that very night, there were pictures of your outing with Shawna—which she enjoyed very much, by the way."

I don't miss the shameless plug.

"It's no secret you and Joss are sharing a place now, and they of course know you two are close friends and have been for quite some time, but... if you allow things to continue this way, people will never believe you and Shawna are anything more than friends. I think you understand that the idea of a relationship developing between you two benefits you *both*. Just one date and both your follower counts have gotten quite the boost."

My brow gathers and I stare down on the street several floors below, wondering what her angle is here.

"Shawna *is* just a friend," I point out.

Rose makes a strange sound on the other end of the line as she searches for the right words.

"Yes, maybe, but I think we both know there's potential there for her to be much, much more than that. That is, if you make a few changes."

"Changes," I repeat. "Like cutting Joss out of my life."

"Let me be clear," Rose jumps in again. "I've got no personal quarrel with this girl. She seems lovely enough, but this is a dual issue, Dane. Yes, having people assume she's a love interest is an inconvenience, but the *real* problem is that she comes with a bit of baggage."

Those words have heat flashing up my neck, to my face. It's way too late for this shit.

"What the hell is that supposed to mean?"

Rose is silent, maybe processing having been talked to this way, but she crossed the fucking line way before I did.

"I see I've hit a nerve," she says in a hushed voice. "While I certainly didn't mean to ruffle your feathers, I won't take back what I've said. As your brand manager, it'd be remiss of me not to warn you when I see you making mistakes. And like it or not, your close ties with Josslyn Francois are a mistake."

"I—"

"Her father's recent affair—or should I say affairs—have painted their family in a very unfavorable light," she cuts in to say. "And as I'm sure you know, I have worked very hard to make sure the public separates you from your father's misfortune. Have I not?"

I don't say a word, because if I do, it'll only be to cuss her out.

"Now, while you're thinking on *that,* imagine how being associated with Joss might cause people to again associate you with scandal, at which point it would be very easy for them to recall your father's misgivings, and let us not forget your ties to the notorious Ruiz family."

My blood's boiling. She's pulling at threads now. Yes, my father is the illegitimate son of Augustin Ruiz—the city's most nefarious kingpin—but most are either unaware of or unconcerned about that connection because my brothers and I don't bare that last name.

"Speaking of, that missing cousin of yours—Ricky, is it? Has he turned up?"

She doesn't ask out of concern. Instead, this is another attempt to remind me of all the shit she's covered for me, in the name of rebirthing my public persona.

"He's not missing," I say through gritted teeth. What I won't tell her is that we know exactly where he is and will never breathe a word of it. He went away to avoid the fallout after my father got caught, but I'm sure he'll return when the heat's off him and the rest of the Ruiz family.

Until then, I ain't saying shit.

"You'll have to forgive me if I've crossed the line," Rose says, trying to sound sweet, but failing. "I only mean to help you put things into perspective, see them from angles you aren't accustomed to."

"I've heard you," is all I say.

She's quiet, maybe holding out hope for more of a response than that, but that's all she'll get out of me. She's lucky I didn't just tell her to kiss my ass and then end the call. That's sure as hell what I *should've* done. What stops me is remembering her reputation of being a juggernaut in the industry.

She's so focused on me coming across as wholesome and stable, she's lost sight of what matters most. That people remember I'm human. And being human means there are imperfections, mistakes to be made, corrected, and learned from. I won't let her turn me into a robot, but she'll find that out soon enough.

"We done here?" I ask, hearing the frustration in my own voice.

Rose clears her throat a little and I imagine that pinched mouth of hers turning down.

"Yes, I suppose we are, but let me leave you with this. Sometimes, people have to choose, Dane. They can either cling to what's important to them *now* or embrace what will certainly be important to them in the future. It's rare that anyone can have both."

In this scenario, my friendship with Joss is clearly that thing Rose believes I'll have to eventually let go of, but that just proves she doesn't know shit about me. Joss is the one and only thing in this life I've wanted consistently. Every single moment of every single day, since I first laid eyes on her when we were twelve.

"I've gotta go."

I end the call there, not giving a shit if she's upset, because I'm disgusted—with her, our conversation. I'd never leave Joss or anyone else in the dust to protect my image, to get endorsements, or *any* of that shit Rose gets wet for. It's fucking ridiculous to even think about it.

What kind of asshole does she take me for? A gullible one, I guess. Which is probably why she thought her lame speech would work on me.

If Rose wants me to choose, then the fucking joke's on her.

Because I'll always choose Joss. I did back when we were kids, and I still choose her today.

End of story.

Chapter 14

Dane

Never imagined I'd be putting my football training to use like this—dodging screaming kids with their sticky, cotton-candy-covered fingers aimed right at me. All so they can be the first to get to the next ride.

Beside me, with a giant stuffed bear tucked beneath her arm, Shawna belts out a laugh.

"Something funny?"

When I ask, she laughs harder. "Nope. Just watching one of our city's Golden boys freak the fuck out over his sneakers getting stepped on. Nothing out of the ordinary."

"It's like the streets are infested with them," I scoff.

"Yeah, fairs tend to draw the wildlife out of their natural habitat," she says with sarcasm. "Not big on kids, I see."

"Didn't say that. I just prefer the clean, well-behaved, quiet ones."

Her brow shoots up. "So… you're not big on kids."

I laugh instead of defending my point. "You know what I mean."

We take slow strides, drinking in the scenery as skyscrapers tower above us. The fair comes to downtown Cypress once a year, and it transforms the entire city. The shops that line the streets are all well-lit and decorated with festive lights. It's like, for these few days, we're in another world.

Passing a funnel cake cart, I don't miss how Shawna glances over.

When she doesn't ask to stop, I guess she's decided to skip it. Girl's got one hell of a sweet tooth.

She catches me smiling at her and blushes a bit. "What?"

"Nothing. Just expected you to give in. You damn-near hulked out a few minutes ago when you smelled elephant ears."

She rolls her eyes with a smile. "I do have willpower, you know. And by willpower, I mean there's a tiny version of Rose living inside my head. She screams at me whenever I'm tempted to eat bad things. She wins most of our arguments, by the way."

"Sounds about right."

Mention of Rose brings tension to my shoulders, recalling the phone call I got after the shoot last week. We hadn't talked much since then, other than me answering her text when she reminded me about the photo op here with Shawna tonight.

"Isn't that your brother?"

Shawna nods toward the merry-go-round and I scan the crowd until I spot West and Blue, arm-in-arm, waiting in line for the ring toss game. Judging by the stuffed alligator, giraffe, and turtle he's hauling around, I'm guessing they've been making their rounds.

On cue, he spots me and does a doubletake. I don't miss how his gaze flashes to my right where Shawna's walking beside me. He knows we've been hanging out, knows it's Rose's doing, but I imagine this is still a surprise.

The last one to notice we're all here together is Blue. When her eyes widen and she forces a smile, I have a pretty good idea what's going through her head. We approach and I'm curious to see how this will play out.

"West, Blue, this is Shawna," I say with a sigh.

"Nice to meet you," West says with a subdued smile.

With what we've been through, we're all very anti-new people, so I'm not shocked he isn't friendlier. Blue's no different. She sweeps over Shawna with a look of reservation. Yeah, she's skeptical of people, too, but I get the feeling it's about more than that with her.

"Hey," Blue says in a clipped tone.

Shawna seems to notice the less-than-friendly greeting and offers nothing but a dim smile and a wave.

Blue's icy stare slices to me just before West speaks up. "You guys having a good time?"

"Mostly, I've been laughing at your brother dodging filthy kids, so that in and of itself has been entertaining," Shawna answers with a laugh. "What about you two? Looks like someone's on a winning streak."

She points toward the stuffed toys West is toting.

"We might've dominated a game or two," he gloats.

Once a cocky dickhead, always a cocky dickhead.

I laugh a bit, knowing he likely beat out some hopeful kid to win all this shit, and I'm also guessing he felt zero remorse about that.

"We've only won once, so I guess we have some catching up to do," Shawna says with a laugh, lifting her bear a few inches into the air.

When she finishes speaking, instead of her arms falling back to her sides, the one not clutching the bear slips around my bicep.

Blue's gaze lasers in on the contact and she arches a brow.

"Joss around somewhere?" she asks suddenly, taking a play straight out of the *'Cock Block Handbook'*.

If this were an actual date, I might be pissed with what she just pulled, but instead I'm only amused, holding in a laugh when I lower my head.

"Um, nope. She was at the loft last I checked."

I glance up after answering, fully expecting that look Blue's giving me right now. It reminds me of the one my great-aunt, Cheryl, gives when one of us has done or said something she doesn't approve of.

Blue's tried to be subtle about rooting for me and Joss to break through the wall of friendship, anxious for us to discover what's on the other side. But even with her trying to play it cool tonight, it's clear how badly she wants it to happen.

Almost as badly as I do.

Almost.

"She's home alone on a Friday night? That sucks. Maybe I should call and see if she wants to come hang out?"

There's genuine sympathy in Blue's tone as she mentions it. When she looks up at my brother, waiting for a response, it's clear this isn't just some ploy to rub Joss in Shawna's face.

Well, not entirely anyway.

"I'm sure she's fine," West reasons. "Besides, I have practice in the morning, so I don't plan to be out much longer."

When he leans in to whisper something into Blue's ear that has her smiling, I'm guessing an early practice isn't the *only* reason he wants to head home soon. Still, his answer reminds me I should probably call it an early night, too.

West draws Blue close by her shoulders when he speaks again. "Well, it was nice meeting you, Shawna. Pretty sure we'll see you again soon."

Blue doesn't say anything else about Joss missing from the picture tonight, but one final glance in my direction tells me it's still on her mind.

Shawna offers a polite smile and waves at West and Blue again. "Great meeting you both."

With that, they're gone and it's just us again.

We continue our slow trek toward the Ferris wheel, but she's noticeably quieter than she was a moment ago.

"Getting bored?"

One of her bright grins flashes up at me. "No. It's not that."

"What is it then?"

She hesitates, taking time to gather the right words, I guess. "Meeting them just went a bit differently than I thought it would."

I glance over, observing as she watches the crowd. "What were you expecting?"

She shrugs and I wonder if she's not as impervious to being snubbed by Blue as I thought.

"I guess it's just one thing getting to know all of you through Pandora's posts, and something completely different seeing that you're actually real people."

A laugh slips out. Not quite the answer I was expecting.

"That came out wrong," she mumbles to herself. "I mean, I knew you all were real people, but I guess I bought into the hype that there wasn't any depth beyond the captions beneath your pictures, you know? There's a lot more to your crew than most of us realize. You guys are solid, and… it makes me think."

When she adds that, I glance at her again. "Makes you think about what?"

Her gaze lowers and she's gently twisting the ear of her bear, hesitating like she'd done before.

"About… you and Joss," she finally admits. "I thought the pics of you and *her* were just that, pics, but I guess I'm wondering if everyone's right about you two."

I don't have to ask what she means. I've read the comments, know what people assume.

"You don't have to explain anything to me," Shawna rushes to say. "I know we're not a thing and we only meet up because this is what Rose wants. These are just my thoughts."

Most girls wouldn't have said any of this out loud, wouldn't have been so transparent. Especially ones who look like her. The hot ones don't usually have vulnerable moments like this, ones in which they acknowledge that they don't just have their pick of any guy they want, that there's competition.

"We're all close," I say first, laying the foundation for where I see this conversation heading.

"Which is pretty dope," Shawna adds with a smile.

"I'm sure you kept up with all the stuff that got shared on Pandora's app these past few months, so it's no secret that Joss' homelife went to shit around the same time mine did."

Shawna nods. "Yeah, it sucks what her dad did. *Both* your dads. I can imagine that brought you two closer," she adds.

I consider her response, but it's wrong.

"Thing is, there wasn't really room for Joss and me to get any closer. Not as friends anyway."

The moment those words leave my mouth, I realize I probably should've kept that last part to myself, knowing how it can be interpreted.

Knowing how I meant it.

When Shawna doesn't answer right away, I'm pretty sure that means the comment didn't go over her head.

"Shit. I'm sorry. I didn't mean to just blurt it like that. I—"

"No, it's fine," she says, dismissively waving her hand. "You only said what was in your heart, and the only person who'd get pissed at someone for *that* is Rose."

Laughing, I have to admit she's got her mother pegged.

There's an awkward silence between us now, as what I've just admitted seems to settle with us both.

"So, you *like her* like her," she says with a slow nod.

If I were going to deny it, now would be the time.

"Since we were twelve," I admit.

Shawna draws in a breath but takes that pretty well. "Wow. Seven years. That's a long time to be into someone."

Fucking tell me about it.

"So, I'm guessing that must make living together kind of awkward."

"Damn, you don't miss much, do you?"

She laughs, not taking my teasing her to heart. "I mean, Pandora makes it kind of hard to miss shit. You'd have to be living under a rock not to know every move the city's '*Golden Crew*' makes."

She isn't wrong. You'd think Pandora didn't have anyone else to talk about but us.

"Well, to answer your question, sharing the loft's been pretty chill."

"So far maybe, but give it time," she adds with a suggestive grin. "I'm curious. What's kept you two from crossing the line all these years? Just fear of screwing up your friendship?"

I don't answer quickly enough, and she draws her own conclusion.

"Ah, I see. *Joss* is the scared one."

She's more perceptive than I realized, leaving me to feel pretty shitty about how my bluntness must be making her feel.

"We don't have to talk about this."

"You kidding?" she asks with a laugh. "I'm getting the inside scoop on the Virgin Vixen from Pretty Boy D himself. People would kill to be having this conversation with you."

Glancing over, I take in her lighthearted expression. "You really are okay with this?"

The sound of shrill screams and laughter surround us as she casually waves me off.

"So, I told you I moved here six months ago, but I didn't tell you why." She pushes her hair behind both ears, then takes a deep breath.

"I thought you came because Rose talked you into it. Were you running from a bad breakup or something?"

"Mmm… probably not the kind you're thinking," she shares with a smile. "There was a guy back home, but we were just friends. His name's Tim."

"Like a *friend*, friend? Or friends-with-benefits?"

"Like the kind who have shared a bed on several occasions, and never laid a finger on each other. Not even once," she answers. "We were tight like you and Joss, but only since high school, so not *quite* as long. Still, we did everything together except date and… touch."

When she laughs, so do I because it all sounds familiar.

"I was basically in love with him since the first time I laid eyes on him, but those feelings only ever ran one way."

I stare down at her again, watching as she gets lost in the memory.

"Long story short, I moved here about three weeks after he announced his engagement to Kipp—a girl who doesn't deserve him and will *never* get him. I just couldn't wrap my head around the idea of watching him start a life with some airhead I can't even stand to be in the same room with."

She's bitter, but I get it. Putting myself in her shoes, it'll be hard not to rip into whatever motherfucker Joss ends up with.

"Have you spoken to him since moving here?"

"A few times, but it's nothing like it used to be. I'd like to think he's hurt about that, but honestly, I think me leaving made his life easier," she says. "Kipp mentioned once or twice that our friendship made her uncomfortable, so now, he doesn't have to choose."

Her comment has me thinking back to the few times girls thought we were close enough for them to give an opinion on my friendship with Joss. They only got a chance to make that mistake once.

"Damn, I brought your mood down," Shawna chuckles after meeting my gaze.

"Not at all. This is shit I think about all the time, but don't really say out loud to anyone."

"Well, from one sad, jilted would-be lover to the next, I get it and you can talk to me about it whenever."

"Same," I say back, glancing down at her again. It isn't lost on me that she's the kind of girl I'd go for if I could even think about that right now.

"Kinda sucks that both our hearts are in limbo, doesn't it? I mean, we've got so much shit in common. Maybe in a different reality this could've been something," she shrugs as we step into line at the Ferris Wheel. "Or, who knows, maybe there's still hope for us. Life's got a funny way of working shit like this out when you least expect it."

I don't respond because I hadn't thought about it that way until now. Maybe the open, honest start to our friendship is good for me.

In more ways than one.

@QweenPandora:

Looks like PrettyBoyD and NotJoss were laughing it up with the king and his queen tonight. Not sure if this was a double-date or a chance meeting, but I can't help but to feel like something's missing.

Or... like someone is missing. Two someones if you count, both, VirginVixen and MrSilver.

Is the Golden Crew splintering? Or is the emergence of NotJoss simply a blip on the radar that'll fade with time? Not sure, but anyone else willing to bet VirginVixen is counting down the days until that happens?

Which one is it, PrettyBoyD? The brainy beauty we all know you've pined over for years, or the newcomer who seems more than willing to take VV's place?

@QweenPandora:

Like always, we'll have to keep our eyes open and a finger to the pulse of the city. We all know our beloved Cypress Pointe will reveal her secrets in due time.

Later, Peeps! 😼

~*P.*

Chapter 15

Joss

The door to the loft opens and then closes, which has me scrambling to turn off my phone. This time, it's not because I'm ogling Dane's half-naked pics. Instead, I'm stalking the ones he posted of him and Shawna tonight. The last of which showcased them smiling big, cuddled up at the apex of a Ferris Wheel. The bright lights of the city provided them a picture-perfect backdrop while he held her beneath his arm. Since there's no point lying to myself about it, I can admit to the pang of jealousy that hit me seeing him touch her like that—like this second date brought them closer. Like, maybe… they're starting to fall.

Not your business, Joss. He's not yours to be possessive over.

Even if it sometimes feels like he is.

I hear Dane's footsteps coming this way and I reach for the book I'd been reading before scrolling my newsfeed. While finding where I left off, an image Pandora posted moments ago flashes in my head. This time, it's of him and Shawna, but they weren't alone. West and Blue stood in the frame, smiling while they all chatted. Honestly, it stung a bit seeing the foursome hang out while I chilled in bed with only my latest book boyfriend keeping me company. I'm not used to being the odd man out with them. Yeah, Dane's screwed around with several girls throughout the course of our friendship, but this feels different.

Shawna feels different.

Now, I find myself not only hoping *Dane* doesn't fall for her, I'm hoping my friends don't fall for her either. Especially now that they're all I have left here in Cypress Pointe.

Listen to yourself. You sound like such a hypocrite—wanting him while also pushing him away. That's not fair. Friendship is safe, it's what you know, so focus on that. And for fuck's sake! Let the guy have a life.

Those words are still ringing inside my head when he knocks on the door.

Composing myself, I clear my throat. "It's open."

He eases in and I pull the blanket to my waist, remembering I only have on a t-shirt and underwear.

"Hey," he says with kind of an odd tone. It's almost like he's preoc-cupied, thinking about so many things at the same time. Or maybe it's just that he's thinking about *her.*

My stomach twists when that possibility comes to mind, but I dismiss it quickly, remembering the conclusion I reached.

You're just his friend. Remember, Joss?

"Have fun?" I don't sound like myself either when I ask. My voice is too chipper, because I'm putting on an act to mask what I'm really thinking and feeling. With any luck, he bought it, thinks I actually *do* hope he had fun.

This just in: I don't. I hope he was miserable with her and thought about me the whole time.

He comes closer, tucking both hands into the pockets of his jeans. "It was cool, I guess. Not sure if you saw, but we ran into West and Blue. Which was interesting," he adds with a quiet laugh.

"I did see, but interesting how?"

He shrugs and drops down onto the edge of my bed and settles close. Goosebumps prickle my skin, getting worse as I study him—perfect features, broad shoulders that strain the fabric of his tee. And he smells good, like always. Lately, he's given me a terrible case of tunnel-vision, making it hard to see anything or anyone but him.

"West was cool, but Blue was kind of weird," he says, reminding me I should be listening and not eye-banging him.

I laugh a bit and pretend I wasn't distracted. "What do you mean by *'weird'*?"

"I mean, she was friendly, but a little standoffish. At least she was with Shawna," he says sort of under his breath.

I rejoice inwardly, hearing that Blue didn't welcome this girl with open arms. Yes, it's petty AF, but it's honest.

"Hmm, wonder what that was about." He doesn't seem to catch that I'm gloating a bit, so I cool it before I give myself away.

"No clue, but Blue asked about you, so…" His voice trails off with a shrug and I hold in a smile.

"Cool. I'll text her later."

He stretches, yawns, and then reclines onto my mattress, folding his arms behind his head to rest on them. With his body being impressively long, both feet are still planted firmly on the floor. I swallow hard, knowing I'm staring again, but shit. He's laid out in front of me like a damn dessert cart. My eyes do a slow scan of every inch of him. From where his pecs protrude through his shirt, to where a couple inches of his tight waist are visible above the band of his boxers. There, a perfectly carved V leads my gaze lower, right to the thick bulge at the front of his jeans.

Fucking. Huge.

Breathe, girl.

"So, what'd you do all night?"

The question snaps me out of it, and I meet his green stare.

"Uh… nothing too exciting. Just got in a bit of reading," I say, forcing an awkward smile with hopes that he somehow missed me gawking at his dick.

"Sounds fun," he replies with heavy sarcasm. Then, the dim smile on his mouth fades into a slow, sexy lip bite.

Damn you Dane. Damn you.

"It *was* fun, actually. I got through a few chapters before I got an interesting phone call."

He glances over. "From who?"

"My dad."

His head pops up a little now, and I don't miss the concern in his expression. "Everything go okay?"

I shrug because I'm honestly not sure. "Guess so. He just said he's got some business to handle, so he'll be back in town eventually and hopes we can talk."

When I don't add to that, Dane's brow arches. "Could've gone worse."

I nod, agreeing. "It definitely could have."

He turns his head and faces the ceiling again, and when he sighs, I focus on how his torso tenses, and then relaxes again.

"It's been a long damn time since I've been in a bed. Kind of forgot what one feels like," he says. I know he's joking, but I still feel sorry for him. For the past few weeks, the couch is where he's laid his head every night.

"If I doze, just throw a blanket over me and pretend I'm not here," he adds with a laugh.

My lips twitch, thinking of proposing something that could *seem* innocent, but deep down, I know it would be far from it. I do have an *alternate* suggestion, though. One I think could be fun. One that *doesn't* involve inviting him to stay—which was my first idea. Instead, I'll extend a much safer invitation.

"We should watch a movie. I can pull one up on my laptop."

Dane glances over, arching that brow again, maybe surprised I just suggested an activity that would require us to be close for more than five minutes.

In a way, I guess I'm kind of surprised myself.

"I'll change and be right back," he says, groaning when he sits upright, then stands.

"Cool. I'll grab snacks."

Half a second after he leaves, I hop up to close the door behind him, then quickly slip into a pair of shorts. So, I guess we're doing this —our first one-on-one movie night as roomies.

My mind cycles through a hundred different ways this could go from good clean fun to good *dirty* fun in zero seconds flat, but we're adults. We can handle this.

Nothing at all to worry about.

I head to the kitchen next and grab a big bowl, filling it with chips and manage to beat Dane back to my room. I intentionally settle on the side of my bed closest to the window. Chances are, we'll choose something scary to watch, so it only seems right that he'd be the one to sit near the door.

Pretty sure that's an unwritten code or something.

I hear his steps first, then he enters my room. Basketball shorts hang low on his waist and a black, ribbed tank hugs his torso. Boy has a body like nothing I've ever seen, and I'm admittedly a fan.

A *big* fan.

He drops down onto my bed like it's nothing, letting his arm settle against mine. When he joins me beneath my comforter next, I'm reminded that he's always been so at ease with the closeness. It's *me* who clams up just at the thought of it.

He takes the bowl while I search for a movie, finding something creepy right off the bat. Horror is kind of our go-to genre, so I don't have to ask if he's interested.

I follow the movement of his body as he stretches to the nightstand to turn off the lamp. When his back settles against the headboard again, a faint hint of cologne floats in my direction and I breathe it out, trying to rid my head of the scent. But we're hip-to-hip and there's no escaping it. No escaping *him* as his heat becomes *my* heat beneath the blanket.

I'm doing my best to focus on the screen, but I can't. Not with him so close. It doesn't help that the pages I read before he came home concluded with a sex scene. One so steamy I considered popping a couple new batteries into Victor and letting him buzz me into a coma. Honestly, had I not gotten distracted by Pandora's posts, I would've probably done exactly that and been asleep long before Dane even made it home.

But alas, here I am, nestled in bed beside my hot best friend, wondering if the real thing is better than a toy.

Sorry, Victor. Nothing personal.

The movie starts and I finally get comfortable. Well, sort of, considering how Dane's proving to be an endless distraction. As soon as I think I've escaped the dirty thoughts he has running amuck in my head, he moves and some part of him brushes against some part of me, and it starts all over again. Even the sensation of the fine hairs on his leg moving over the smoothness of mine sends a flash of heat through me.

It's becoming clear that this was a horrible idea.

He sets the bowl aside and crosses both arms over his chest. My eyes are drawn to the definition in his dense pecs and I... I can't believe I'm thinking about this.

Forcing myself to face forward, I try following the movie despite having no clue what's happened up to this point. It's something about a couple finding a cursed mirror in the basement of their new home, I think. Other than that? I'm lost.

As if the universe is conspiring against me, the guy's bare ass passes in front of the camera as he makes his way to the bed. His wife is lying there, ready and waiting.

"Well, shit. Not sure it's smart to take a fuck-break while there's a demon out to kill you, but you know, everyone's priorities are different," Dane jokes, reaching to pop a chip into his mouth.

On the other hand, there's me, scrambling to fast forward past the scene before things go too far. It's got nothing to do with me being a prude. Being a virgin doesn't mean I'm anti-sex, it just means I haven't gotten any yet. But what this *is* about, is how even the brief flashes of skin on the screen have me breathing deeper, getting worked up.

"Hold up! What're you doing?" Laughing, Dane blocks me from touching the keyboard. "This is the best part."

Of course, he'd think that.

"Actually, it has absolutely nothing to do with the plot. It's pointless," I argue back. However, when he flashes a grin at me, I realize I should've just let this shit play out.

"Damn, Joss. You look a little uncomfortable. You okay?" he teases, probably noticing how flustered I am all of a sudden.

Usually, I can play these things off, but it's hard considering the fact that I was already lowkey horny tonight. Also doesn't help that I'm sitting next to *him*.

"I'm fine," I answer, flashing a dismissive smile, hoping he thinks he imagined my weirdness. Right away, I can tell he isn't buying it, though.

I'm already rolling my eyes when his smile grows. He's about to say something super awkward. I can feel it.

"Dane, no—"

"I'm just saying. We're friends, right?" he croons. "We talk about everything, but you're telling me two friends can't have a mature conversation about sex?"

Not when one of those friends looks like you. Not when you make me feel the way you do.

I take a second to respond after that thought leaves me. "No, we can't. Not now. Not ever."

"Well, we should at least be able to have a discussion about why this scene, in particular, upset you so bad."

"I'm not upset," I sigh, trying not to smile.

"Then, that brings me to my next point," he says with a smirk. "Admit that watching shit like this turns you on."

I look him straight in the eyes and speak without wavering. "I, Josslyn Grace Francois, am not turned on."

"You're lying. Right to my fucking face at that," he accuses with a laugh.

A deep breath fills my lungs and I feel the temperature in the room climbing.

"Admit it," he presses. "You know I'm not here to judge."

I laugh when my nerves get the best of me. "There's nothing to admit, Dane! What about you? Does watching Lois and Bob get it on get you hard?" I ask sarcastically, making up character names when the real ones slip my mind.

"Honestly?" he says, one corner of his lips tugging up with a grin. That's all it takes to send my temperature soaring even higher.

"Just forget I asked," I mutter.

I can't help myself. At the thought of him having an erection beneath the blanket, my eyes are definitely tempted to drift lower just to peek. I resist, though.

Somehow.

"I'll tell you if you really want to know," he says with a shrug, showing zero sign of embarrassment.

Without a doubt, he *would* admit to such a thing, and now my mind's gone to places it shouldn't. My body begins to overheat, even more than it already was.

"Ready to give me a real answer?" he asks, slow and even, his tone marked with confidence.

"I already told you, it didn't affect me."

Contrary to the tenacious answer I've just given, Dane's silent stare has me breathing erratically. Like I've been running laps around our building.

"So, you're telling me you're not curious how it'd feel to be her right now?" he rasps, pointing at the screen just as the lead actress gives us her best orgasm-face.

"Yes, Dane. I can tell you, beyond the shadow of a doubt, that's not something I'm thinking about," I lie. In truth, I'd give anything to feel what she's feeling.

He scans me with that deep, penetrating stare of his again, then a wicked grin touches his lips.

"So, you're in total control of yourself?"

I nod. "Completely."

"And you could keep your cool if someone touched you like he's touching her?"

I shoot him a skeptical glance, as if what he's just said is a no-brainer, proceeding to taunt him with a falsely confident smirk. Then, my dumb ass goes as far as to give the snidest answer I can muster.

"Easy."

He scans me with a smoldering look, one that screams *'danger'*, like I've just awakened the devil himself. I swear the mounting heat between us burns away the air in this room, and it only gets worse when the challenge I didn't mean to put into the atmosphere is answered. When he speaks, he does so with such confidence that I am more than aware of having lost this game before I've even gotten the chance to play.

"Ok, then," he says with a slow nod. "Fucking prove it."

Chapter 16

Joss

In a state of complete and utter shock, I frown at him. "How the hell would I prove a thing like that?"

He shrugs and the couple are now basking in the afterglow, still not thinking about the evil presence that lurks in their basement.

So realistic.

I glance over at Dane as he thinks quietly. Meanwhile, my heart's racing like crazy.

"The fact that it's taking you so long to respond only confirms my point—that there's no way to prove a thing like that," I gloat.

"Hang on."

When he speaks, I pause the movie with a smile ghosting on my lips. It feels like I might've just regained the upper hand, so I'm confident.

"What could you possibly have to say now?" I'm smirking right up until my gaze locks with his. It leaves because there's something about the sudden intensity and focus of his expression that has me shaken.

"You claim you're in complete control, so… I'd like to put that to the test."

"How?" I ask, hearing the sound of my own quivering breath.

Dane, on the other hand, is confident, focused.

"We'll play a game," he answers. "Let me push your limits, see how much you can take before you ask me to stop."

I don't move. Yeah, we've flirted here and there, but in all the years we've been friends, he's never been so bold.

My heart damn-near leaps from my chest and, for several seconds, I question whether I misheard. But the longer we remain focused on one another, I'm positive that's not the case.

"We can't just—"

"Joss… you know you can trust me."

The way he says my name has the excuse I was prepared to give locked inside my brain, proving that my mind and body have differing opinions as to how this should play out. His stare moves down to my mouth and I swear I can taste him.

"What's your goal? What are you hoping to prove?"

His brow arches and he doesn't make me wait for an answer. "Guess I'm just curious what'll happen. You said watching those two fuck didn't make you feel anything. I'm wondering if, maybe… you'll feel something with *me*."

I don't think he meant for those words to hold a double meaning, but I pick up on it either way.

The laundry list of excuses I've made over the years—to myself, to others—it flies through my thoughts at warp-speed now, and as badly as I want to hurl each one of them his way, I don't. Instead, I'm thinking about that game of Truth-or-Dare we played months ago, thinking about how badly I wanted to kiss him then, while I had an excuse to do so.

And… it feels like that chance is circling back again.

Dane doesn't blink and I can't believe I'm about to say this, but…

"Okay."

This is completely reckless, and I know he feels it, too. He must. I also know there's more to this experiment than him wanting to test my limits, which should've been all the more reason for me to say no.

There's a fleeting thought that comes at me hard and fast. It's the reminder that he's *just* come home from a date. With another girl. But then *that* thought is followed by two others. The first being that our history runs deep, and he'll *always* be more to me than he is to any other girl. No matter what title she's given, no matter the role she fills. I'm possessive of my place in his life and won't be moved easily.

The second thought is a simple one. Two words.

Fuck Shawna.

As far as I'm concerned, she's a nonfactor and means nothing in the big scheme of things. Now that I've gotten that out of the way, all I can think about is the fact that I've just given Dane carte blanche to take things as far as he wants to until I tell him to stop.

His emerald-green eyes are trained on me and I can't move. I know I agreed to this, but I'm admittedly not sure how two friends who've never shared more than a hug go about venturing into these uncharted waters.

But apparently, Dane's not so confused.

My eyes stay trained on him when he sets the laptop on the night-stand and closes it, plunging us into darkness. I stare as his back settles against my headboard, and the only light that touches us is the silver glow of the moon where it filters in through my window. He pushes the comforter off his lap, and I don't move a muscle until I'm coaxed by the warm hand that reaches for me, then smooths across my waist. He grips just tight enough to draw me closer, bringing me to straddle him. My knees settle deep into the mattress and, perched on top of his solid body, I feel weightless, safe. His cock's hard as a brick beneath me, the bulge straining against his shorts, aligning perfectly between my legs.

Ho-ly shit.

The contact draws a deep breath out of me, leaving me to wonder if I've ever wanted to give in to someone more than I do in this exact moment. We're best friends, sometimes more like each other's family, but... I'm imagining him naked right now, and there's nothing friendly or familial about it.

"Before we move forward, I only have one rule," he breathes close to my ear.

"What's that?'

I feel him exhale against my skin and the sensation has me leaning into him, letting my breasts push against his chest.

"From now until we're done, no lying," he warns. "Every word that leaves your mouth has to be true."

I'm shaking a bit when I nod. "Okay."

Dane breathes warm air over my mouth, and I swear we're right back in Louisiana. Right back in his grandfather's living room playing Truth-or-Dare. Only, this time, we're not surrounded by spectators waiting to see what will happen next, spectators whose presence would've stopped us before things went too far.

Here and now, it's only us and what little willpower we have that might pull us back before things go too far.

There's a subtle roughness to his palms that's got me addicted, wanting to feel them everywhere. They push up from my knees, slowly moving over my thighs where I think he intends to stop, but… he doesn't. Instead, he reaches back and grabs my ass. Tight, squeezing just enough that I release a sigh inches from his lips.

"I have a confession," he says with a labored breath.

My breasts heave when I gather air to whisper, "What's that?"

"I know we're supposed to respect each other's boundaries and shit, but… you have *the* most incredible ass I've ever seen in my fucking life," he rasps.

On cue, he squeezes tighter and at the feel of it, I bite my lip.

"Still don't feel anything?" he asks in a low, gravelly voice.

Lifting his hips, his erection pushes into me, pressing against my clit. In a completely involuntary motion, I grind into him and wish I could get so, *so* much closer. Needless to say, I can't think to answer, which fills my room with dead air. Mostly, I'm wondering how my lonely night with a book, and Dane's night out with another girl, turned into this—me riding him slow while we both secretly wish all these damn clothes weren't in the way.

"I don't… know what to say," I eventually respond.

"There's no wrong answer," he points out with a deep laugh. "Just tell me what you're thinking."

Then, the next sensation that overwhelms me is the feel of his lips pressing against my neck, followed by moist heat where he gently sucks the hollow of my throat.

My eyes fall closed, and my hands move from his shoulders to the back of his hair.

"I feel confused," I admit, which has him chuckling against my skin.

"And?"

After asking, he gently lifts his hips again, wedging his dick deeper between the lips of my sex, taunting me because it's still not enough.

"And... weak."

This time, my confession doesn't draw a response from him. Which could mean that's the answer he hoped to hear.

I'm so wet for him. Like, soaking-through-my-underwear wet. All from barely having been touched tonight. But the longer he holds me like this, the longer his tongue and lips move over my throbbing pulse, the more possessive I feel. So much that, when a thought of him touching someone else this way enters my head, it makes me furious.

I'm sorting through my feelings, trying to understand why he has so much control over my emotions when his mouth moves up my throat, to my chin, and finally to my lips. It's just one gentle peck, but I'm not sure what to do. It's not that I've never kissed a guy before, but I've never kissed *him* before.

Although, I've imagined it many, *many* times.

He comes closer and, slowly, his mouth touches mine again. My lips come to life as fear falls away. We've been careful for so long—denying ourselves the pleasure of touching one another—that this feels foreign. But when his tongue passes my lips, I welcome him in, gripping his hair in my fingers when I do.

It's not every day that a girl can end the mystery surrounding what her best friend might taste like. Mine leaves a hint of mint and something sweet in my mouth.

His dick swells more, and I'm not sure how much longer either of us can stand this teasing.

"How about now? What do you feel?" he asks during the brief second that we tear ourselves apart.

I don't bother with an answer because he already knows—I feel everything.

It'd be so easy to just… lower his shorts a few inches, pull my panties over just enough for him to slip inside me. At the thought of it, I move one hand over the smoothness of his shoulder and down his chest, until I feel the ridges of his abs against my fingertips.

And then… his waistband.

Realizing how desperate I am to touch every inch of him, I feel oddly vulnerable, lacking the control I bragged about before this all began.

"We should take this a step further," Dane breathes into my ear.

I'm only half-coherent as my face turns into his hair, breathing him in. It's on the tip of my tongue to answer, *'You can take whatever the hell you want,'* but I catch myself just short of letting those words slip out.

"You plan to lose your virginity this summer," he says. "So, I'm thinking… maybe I can get you ready for that."

The suggestion has my eyes opening slowly, processing what he's just offered.

"There are things you might want to learn first or… *try* first," he adds.

While I think, he slowly moves both hands beneath my shorts and inside the elastic of my panties, gripping my bare ass this time, clouding my judgment.

"Does that sound good to you?"

Honestly, there isn't much I wouldn't agree to right now, but I manage not to blurt the first thing that comes to mind.

"Before you answer, I need you to know something," he adds. "We've been friends since we were kids, Joss. You're not just some girl to me. You do know that, right?"

My heart races, staring at his outlined silhouette through the darkness as I nod.

"I know, but… there are things I haven't told you, Dane, reasons I hold back."

His eyes stay trained on me. "What is it?"

My head's spinning and I feel the moment slipping away, the heat of it dissipating as we wander into more serious conversation. One we probably should've had a long time ago, instead of me letting him think I was fighting the pull toward him for other reasons.

It's hard to think while we're close like this, so I slide off to the side of him where I can hopefully gather my thoughts more easily. His hand settles on my thigh, though, and the feel of it makes me want to pick up right where we left off, but we can't.

"This is how things started for my parents," I begin. "They met as friends their first year of college when they both moved to the States. I think it was that common thread—that notion of not quite feeling at home—that drew them together. They were tight like us, told each other everything, double-dated with whoever they were seeing at the time. But then, their junior year of college, they crossed the line. Mom says they were able to keep things in perspective for a while and were just having fun at first, but then things turned serious. That lasted a while, until they started bickering more and drifting apart."

Dane's focused on me, listening as I share details my mother shared with me years ago.

"They eventually broke up and stopped speaking altogether. It didn't matter that they'd been friends before, didn't matter that they were once each other's everything, because once things started going bad, it consumed them."

Dane squeezes my thigh, drawing my attention to his gaze despite how difficult it is to look at him right now.

"You know they're not us, though, right?" he asks. "I mean, you know I'd never hurt you or let *anything* ruin what we have, don't you?"

I sigh, feeling like he's missed the point.

"I'm sure they didn't think that either, Dane, but it happened," I say.

There's so much more to the story, but I'm not in the mood to go there right now. I already feel raw just having said *that* much, which forces me to realize how deep *their* wounds have cut *me*. I guess growing up in a home where the love was professed out loud but never shown stuck with me, damaged me.

When Dane's finger touches my chin and I'm made to look into his eyes, a tear slips down my cheek. I think he takes it for what it is—a sign of how seriously I'm taking this, how important our friendship is to me.

"Joss, you have my word that we'll never turn into them. Whatever course we take, we won't end up like that."

It's dark, but I can still see his sincerity. And when he kisses me, I feel it.

This is new—impromptu displays of affection.

Is this the door we've opened? Who we've become—friends who kiss and touch?

He pulls away and I inhale slowly to steady my breaths.

"If you don't want to do this, I'm cool with that," he adds, "but my offer stands."

My body's still overheating from our make-out session, but I know that has nothing to do with the answer I'm about to give. But first, like with anything else, there have to be rules, boundaries that will hopefully prevent disaster.

"If I say yes, we have to promise each other a few things."

His brow quirks when he smiles. "Ok, shoot."

"We have to swear to keep our emotions out of it."

Right after I speak, there's this weird twisting in my gut. Like my body's trying to tell me that I've already broken this rule. Hell, maybe he has, too, but it needs to be said anyway. The point of this isn't to fall for each other, but rather for me to experiment with someone I trust.

And... maybe get some things out of our systems before curiosity burns us alive.

I don't miss how he seems to sober up a bit more before answering. "Sounds fair, I guess."

"And you have to promise there won't be other girls. I don't mean you can't go out or anything, just no... physical stuff," I say shakily, feeling like I have no right whatsoever to make these kinds of demands. Mostly, because I'm not his girlfriend and this is clearly just a friends-with-benefits situation, but these are my terms, what I'm comfortable with if we're to move forward.

He can absolutely turn them down and I'd understand.

However, he doesn't even hesitate.

"You have my word."

I search his eyes and see that he means it. I've known him long enough to spot a lie.

"Then... okay," I say, agreeing to something I never thought I'd agree to, but by it being Dane, it feels different.

It feels *right*.

He leans in and kisses me again, and it's soft this time, not meant to lead to anything more. A girl could get used to this feeling, get addicted to it even. And now that we've reached an agreement, I imagine this summer will be filled with many more just like it.

Chapter 17

Dane

Sterling slams his locker shut, then drops down onto the bench beside West. Wiping sweat from his brow, he gazes up to where I'm leaning against the painted brick wall just beneath the university's logo.

"And it ended just like that?" he asks, finally responding to the news I shared about me and Joss. News I thought about all night, and again all through today's practice.

I shrug at his question. "Yep. She set out a couple rules—which didn't surprise me, we made out a little more, then I left and went to bed."

Well, I beat off in the shower, *then* went to bed, but they probably don't want to hear that.

West has this I-told-you-so grin set on his face that I don't miss.

"Got something to say?" I ask with a laugh.

"Only that I called this shit way back in eighth grade. I should've put money on it."

He isn't lying. He and Sterling have *both* been predicting that Joss and I would eventually hookup, but I don't think any of us imagined it would go quite like this. She's always been kind of reserved, which is why I thought she'd shoot down my idea last night, but she didn't. Proves she's more ready than I realized. Clearly, number eleven on the list wasn't just an afterthought.

"Guess we know what distracted you from catching that easy-ass pass I threw you," West adds. "And here I was thinking it was *Shawna* who had your mind gone."

I don't say it out loud, but, honestly, I haven't thought about her since we parted ways after the *'date'.*

"So, what now?" Sterling cuts in. "You two just planning to dry hump all summer."

Laughing, I shake my head at him. "Shut the fuck up. What's next is we take things slow, so she doesn't retreat into her shell. But not so slow that she starts thinking too much, convincing herself this was all a mistake."

That *sounds* good, but I have no idea how this plan should actually go. I mean, do I wait a week to approach her? Wait until she approaches me? Hell if I know.

I glance toward West when he stands and starts gathering things from his locker to shower.

"Well, I don't have any answers, but I think this arrangement is just a means to an end. Everyone knows you and Joss are gonna get married, have a bunch of kids we're all gonna spoil, then grow old together."

With that, he leaves me and Sterling on our own.

Sterling pushes off the bench, but I stop him before he can bail. "Hang on a sec. Where the hell have you been?"

He meets my gaze and quirks a brow. I hold off on speaking when a few teammates pass, wanting to make sure no one overhears us.

"Feels like you've been avoiding my calls. If it weren't for practice kicking off today, I would've thought you skipped town or something. What's up with you?"

Our father's face has been all over the news, which is why I've given up on TV, but we're all still affected. My first guess for why Sterling's been M.I.A. is that it's getting to him a bit more than the rest of us. Maybe because he's still living in the penthouse for now, ground zero, the place that holds all the memories, most of which are too fucked up to talk about.

He pushes a hand behind his neck and something about that look on his face tells me I've gotten it all wrong. So, I rack my brain for a different explanation as to why he's been ghosting.

Then, that's when I remember Pandora's post. The one where it *looked* like he might be entertaining our former headmaster's wife. She's had her eye on him since we were at least fifteen and it was always a running joke that he'd eventually give in. Only, I never thought it'd actually happen.

Not to mention, the woman is the dean here at the university.

When he looks off instead of answering, I know.

"You fucked her, didn't you?"

His gaze lowers to the tile. "No, it's not like that."

"Bullshit."

She's been on his ass since graduation and must've caught him in a moment of weakness. Even if he doesn't want to admit it right now.

"All I know is, you'd better find some way to cover that shit, or… *whatever* went down. Pretty sure fucking the dean is frowned upon."

"I didn't fu—" his voice trails off when he pauses to breathe deep. "I'm handling it."

My hand slams down on his shoulder. "Let me know if I can help, but in the meantime, keep your dick in your pants," I tease. "Or, at the very least, keep it out of Mrs. Harrison."

Chapter 18

Joss

Sitting poolside with a fruity drink in hand feels like the perfect time to spill the beans.

Blue and I have spent a better part of the day together, hanging out at her place, and I still haven't shared the latest development between me and Dane. Not that she hasn't asked how things are going, I just didn't know what to say, didn't know how to tell her.

So, I'm just gonna blurt it. Why the hell not?

I glance to my right and stare at her from beneath the brim of the plaid bucket hat Dane bought me as a joke. It was a souvenir from when his family vacationed in Fiji a few years ago, but I pop it on every now and then when I'll be out in the sun.

Blue's completely relaxed in her lounger, and possibly asleep. It's hard to tell with the dark, oversized sunglasses covering her eyes, looking all glamourous and shit. She won't mind if I wake her for this, though.

"So, Dane and I kissed," I say casually, to which Blue responds by nearly leaping out of her skin. Those sunglasses are ripped off and she's staring right at me.

"No. Way."

I nod, holding in my smile.

"Joss! You've been keeping this to yourself all day? I can't believe you! Tell me all the things," she gushes, turning to sit on the edge of her seat.

I breathe deep and imagine everything I felt last night.

"Well, he came in from his date and the plan *was* to just hang out and watch a movie, but… it didn't end that way."

"OMG! Did *he* initiate? Or was it you? I'm dying!" she squeals.

"It was him, I guess you could say? But I definitely wanted it to happen. And by the end of it, we… kind of made a deal."

She doesn't miss how I trail off there. In fact, her eyes narrow with suspicion.

"A deal?"

I nod first, gathering the courage to say more. "We've… officially shifted to a friends-with-benefits situation. The only two rules are that neither of us will fool around with other people while we're involved in said situation, and we swore to keep emotion out of it."

She was with me right up until then. I know as much because her expression just went from elated to deflated.

I'm almost afraid to ask why that is, but when she cocks her head to the side and raises a brow, I may as well.

"Ok, what's the look mean?"

"Do you even have to ask? No emotion?" she scoffs. "Are you two seriously denying that that ship has already sailed? I mean, it's already gonna be a push to compartmentalize this whole thing, but now you've closed the door to honesty, put both of you in a box where you're allowed to fool around but not express how it makes you feel," she reasons. "Just my two cents, but I think you *might* want to reconsider that rule."

I hear her, but I also know my limits. I've already crossed the line that I, myself, drew in the sand when it comes to him. If we're going to keep things in perspective, if we're going to avoid the drama that befell my parents and preserve our friendship, we have to stick to the plan.

She must see me overthinking things, because she places her hand on mine and her expression has softened.

"Listen, I'm all for this deal between the two of you," she assures me. "I just want you both to be openminded about where it could lead. That's all."

I exhale my anxiety and nod. "I get it."

She smiles, then sweeps both feet back onto her lounger. To keep things from getting awkward, I change the subject.

"You guys are really settling in here. Does it feel like home yet?"

She glances over and there's so much contentment on her face it's overwhelming. If happiness were a drug, she's high as hell right now.

"Pretty sure I could be *anywhere* with West and it'd feel like home," she answers.

Their love was hard won, so to see them stable and head-over-heels for one another is incredible. Not so long ago, the pair shared a hatred for one another that ran bone-deep. It was ugly to witness from the front-row seat being West's friend provided me, but I can imagine it was even uglier to live through. So, if *they* were able to sort things out, there's hope I could be as happy as she is one day.

Maybe.

She reaches for her phone when it vibrates on the table between us. Lifting her sunglasses again, she glances at the screen for half a second before returning a text.

"Speaking of West," I tease.

"Actually, it's not him," she says with a laugh, pausing to finish her message. "It's Detective Roby's daughter, Dez. We used to be tight a long time ago, back when our dads were partners on the force. Roby filled her in on everything that's happened this year, and after she reached out to see if I was okay, we just kind of kept in touch. She's even planning to join in on our girls' night in a couple weeks, so you, Jules, and Lexi can all get to know her, too."

"Well, I'm open to meeting new friends, so it should be fun."

"I get the feeling she's had some personal shit going on, but she doesn't talk about it much. She's back home for a bit, though, so more friends is probably a good thing," Blue reasons.

There's a story there to unpack, but I'll mind my business. "Well, if she's got drama she's trying to outrun, she's found herself the right crew."

The comment makes Blue laugh, but she doesn't deny that it's true.

"Speaking of outrunning trouble, how's Ricky?" I face her again after asking.

"You'd have to ask West," she answers with a laugh. "For every one time I hear from him, West has heard from him three times that. Never thought I'd have to compete with Ricky for my boyfriend's attention."

My, how things have changed. There was once a time when Blue's ex, Ricky Ruiz, was the thorn in West's side. But due in part to it coming to light that the duo's fathers are actually half-brothers, they've managed to work things out.

"Any idea when it'll be safe for him to come back?"

There's a hint of sadness in Blue's eyes when she shakes her head, because before Ricky was ever her ex, he was a friend.

"Not any time soon, I don't guess. The Ruizes and Navarros have had more drama between them than usual—beef over turf or some shit like that—so I think Ricky's planning to stay where he is for a while. Can't blame him," she adds.

Apparently, everyone in our circle is running from *something*—the law, a bad reputation, feelings.

"Ok, not to keep jumping subjects, but I have to ask. What's the deal with this Shawna chick?" Blue snatches off her sunglasses again and I shrug, smiling an uncertain smile.

"What about her? I mean, Dane hanging out with her is work, so… I guess that'll continue."

Blue keeps staring and I'm almost as good at reading her as she is at reading me. She doesn't like that whole situation between the two of them, but it is what it is. He only agreed not to be *physical* with a girl, not that he wouldn't date.

When she takes a deep breath and settles into her seat again, she keeps her eyes trained on me.

"If you need me to take my baseball bat out of retirement, I'm willing to do that for you. And I know for a fact that Lexi would be down."

I laugh, knowing from experience that those two aren't shy about swinging bats.

"Noted. If Shawna becomes a problem, you'll be the first one I call."

She smiles and puts her sunglasses in place on the bridge of her nose. Her question has me thinking, though. Not that this is the first time Dane's obligation to continue things with Shawna has come to mind, but I guess I'm trying to keep my word about checking my emotions at the door.

Despite the potential for complication, I have to believe that if any two people can navigate these uncharted waters, it's me and Dane.

Hopefully.

Maybe?

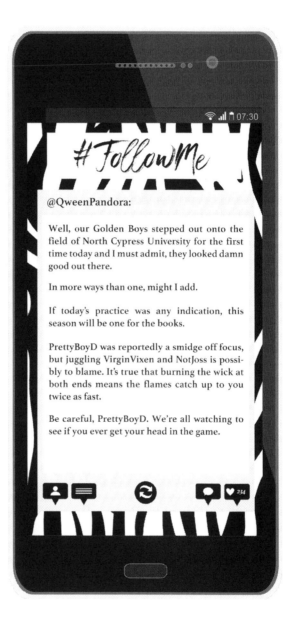

@QweenPandora:

Well, our Golden Boys stepped out onto the field of North Cypress University for the first time today and I must admit, they looked damn good out there.

In more ways than one, might I add.

If today's practice was any indication, this season will be one for the books.

PrettyBoyD was reportedly a smidge off focus, but juggling VirginVixen and NotJoss is possibly to blame. It's true that burning the wick at both ends means the flames catch up to you twice as fast.

Be careful, PrettyBoyD. We're all watching to see if you ever get your head in the game.

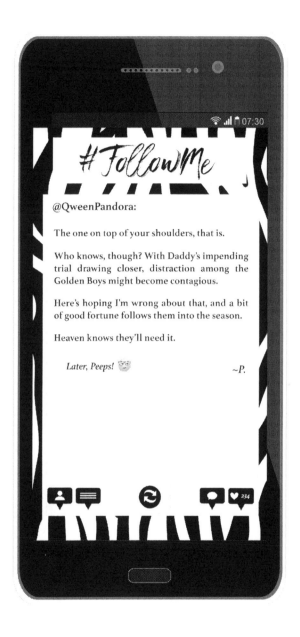

@QweenPandora:

The one on top of your shoulders, that is.

Who knows, though? With Daddy's impending trial drawing closer, distraction among the Golden Boys might become contagious.

Here's hoping I'm wrong about that, and a bit of good fortune follows them into the season.

Heaven knows they'll need it.

Later, Peeps! 😼   ~P.

Chapter 19

Joss

"Shit!"

The basket slips from my hands and hits the floor with a thud. Snatching out my earbuds, I stumble back a few feet. I didn't expect to see Dane standing on the other side of the threshold when I opened the door to the loft, so now my heart's racing a mile a minute.

"Didn't mean to scare you," he says, but that smile on his lips tells me he's not all that sorry.

I look him over, forgetting what I was even doing before this. He's so hot it's literally killing me.

"I was… just heading down to do laundry," I explain, stooping to retrieve the fallen basket. When I stand straight again, he's staring at the book resting on top of my clothes.

"Planning to be gone a while?"

Geez, I can't even look him in the eyes to answer a simple question.

"Figured I may as well wait down there until they're done. I've only got one load."

He's quiet and I wonder what he's thinking.

"Give me a sec. I'll join you," he offers.

Clearly, I'm the only one trying to find my footing after last night. He's not even rattled a little.

My eyes are on him when he leaves me at the door, makes his way down the hall, then disappears in his room. We've been apart all day.

After practice, he hung with his brothers a while. I only know as much because Pandora's posted about them at least three times between this afternoon and evening, making sure no one missed it.

Bitch also made sure no one missed that little bit about the perceived love triangle between him, me, and Shawna. Or NotJoss, as she prefers to call her.

My chat with Blue a few hours ago is mostly all that's on my mind, though. More specifically, her belief that Dane and I are kidding ourselves, thinking we can keep our feelings out of the deal we struck.

"Ready," he announces, coming toward me with that cocky walk of his. It's unintentional, of course, but it just adds to his ability to own whatever space he graces with his presence. I've always enjoyed watching him enter a room—the audacious roll of his shoulders, the confidence in his stride.

I don't speak while waiting outside our door for him to lock up. Then, when he's done, he relieves my hands of the basket without asking. We walk to the elevator in silence, and still don't speak as we descend four floors. When we step off and venture into the darkness of the building's basement, I'm admittedly grateful he's with me this time. I'd only ever been down here alone, so having his company is nice.

Maybe I won't get creeped out like the times before.

He holds the door and lets me pass to step into the laundry room ahead of him. It's just us, and the round windows on the doors of all six machines show they're empty. So, I pick a washer and load my things while Dane leans against the adjacent wall. Grabbing the bottle of detergent buried beneath my clothes, I glance up to find his eyes are already trained on me.

Breathing deeper, I pretend not to notice and finish getting the load started. When I'm done, I set the basket aside and stand near him.

"So, Sterling made a good suggestion at lunch," he says, breaking the silence.

"What's that?"

"Puerto Rico for Spring Break. I mean, now that we know we have family there, the trip would serve a dual purpose. We could hit the beach, plus maybe meet some of the Ruizes who haven't relocated to the States."

I smile a bit. "You had me at the word 'beach.'"

He smiles, too. "We'll probably reach out to a travel agent this fall so we'll have around eight months to plan. It's gonna be epic."

I nod, agreeing. "No doubt in my mind that it will be."

"I don't want to do a hotel. Maybe a villa or something," he adds, slipping his hands into the pockets of his jeans.

The motion draws my eyes below his waist and, just like that, I'm remembering straddling him last night, *feeling* him.

"You hung with Blue today?"

My eyes snap to his. "I did. We swam a bit, but mostly just laid out in the sun."

And talked about you.

I keep that part to myself, but it does make me wonder if he mentioned anything to his brothers. It's hard to tell with most guys. Sometimes they share things with each other, sometimes they don't, but the triplets rarely hold secrets from one another.

"I think I finally got to the bottom of what's been up with Sterling," he says, piquing my interest.

"Is it this shit with your dad?"

He shakes his head. "Surprisingly, no. It's… the *other* thing."

I only have to think about that a few seconds before I get it.

"Gina Harrison? As in, dean of the university? He didn't!"

"Well, he *says* he didn't, but…" Dane grins a bit when his voice trails off and, in contrast, I feel myself frowning.

"I really hope he's smarter than that. Do you know what deep shit he'll be in if they get caught?"

Dane shrugs. "Again, his story is that it's not what it looks like, but whatever the case, I know my brother. He'll figure something out. Always does."

These Golden boys are trouble incarnate. If there's one thing I can attest to, it's the truth in this statement.

We chat some more about how we spent the afternoon, and about my first day of cheer practice tomorrow morning, slipping into an easy conversation. Before I know it, the awkwardness is gone and my load's done. While I shift my things to the dryer, I have that sense of knowing Dane's staring again, but don't look to confirm.

I hit *'start'* on the machine, then move toward the wall to rejoin him. Only, he's pushing off from it.

"Dropped something," he says, leaning down to grab a piece of lavender-colored silk from the ground—a pair of damp panties I hadn't realized missed the dryer.

Laughing, I attempt to snatch them from where they're dangling on his finger, but he lifts them high into the air before I have the chance. My body slams his when I reach, my breasts meeting the unyielding firmness of his chest as I stretch upward. On contact, my nipples harden beneath the lace of my bra.

"Are we really gonna play this game?" I ask, still smiling.

He shrugs and I breathe in traces of his cologne. I reach behind him this time, and our game of keep-away erases the space we maintained until now.

"If you really want them back... I can probably be persuaded."

I'm intrigued, curious to hear what he'll say next. So, I take the bait. "How?"

He turns his lips toward my ear when I ask, breathing hot air against my skin. Then, his free arm slips around my waist and draws me dangerously close.

"Kiss me."

We're both completely silent now. The only sound being the rhythmic hum of the dryer where it thumps and groans behind me. I lean away, just enough to meet his green stare. His lids are half mast, smoldering. I've seen that look before, but it's far more intense now.

Still having the taste of him in my mouth, I recall our deal and... let it happen, let my lips touch his.

He breathes me in, and I push both hands over the muscular curves of his shoulders. Working my fingers into his hair, I bring him closer. I'm not sure where the panties have gone, but he grips both my hips, erasing the small space that existed between us, until his body's flush against mine.

The dryer's heat and vibration at my back match Dane's warmth that covers the front of me. He leans in and I'm trapped. Tension builds in my core and I'm reminded how it felt having him locked between my legs last night, feeling him rock-hard against me.

His hand slips between us and I lose my breath when he grips the mound at the meeting of my thighs. There's this feeling of ownership that exudes from his touch, and it's so powerful that I all but believe it myself. That he owns any and every part of my body he dares to touch. His hand creeps higher until he's able to undo the button to my shorts, but what surprises me more than this unexpected contact, is the fact that I never even consider stopping him.

My lips are damp, hot, and swollen when he tears his away. He's in my ear again and I melt against him.

"Can I touch you?"

Those words swarm around me like a thick cloud of smoke, slinking over my skin. When I finally answer, offering nothing more than a semi-lucid nod, his lips are back, and the kiss deepens.

His hand moves low again, but this time, he's inside my under-wear. I gasp against his mouth as the tip of his middle finger feathers over my clit, then makes that slow, soothing push inside, discovering the truth.

That I'm completely wet for him, despite how well I hide what he does to me.

He breathes into our kiss and brings his finger back to that deliciously sensitive spot that has my heartrate spiking. No one's ever touched me like this but me, late at night, while I lie in bed, thinking only of him.

His teasing is unending, rubbing the now-slippery bud in small, soft circles, pinching it lightly between his fingers to drive me insane. With every stroke, it only becomes harder and harder to breathe. So much that I'm forced to abandon our kiss, instead pressing my cheek to his while I cling to his neck.

Both knees want to give out as I puff air against his skin, feeling the familiar tingle that creeps in from my core, spreading like a slow-burning fire. Even when the elevator bell sounds, I don't want to stop, and Dane doesn't show signs of caring that we might be seconds from being caught.

His fingers stir faster, stealing even more of my focus. It feels like a million butterflies were just set free in the pit of my stomach and I shudder against him. When I clench him tight in my arms and whimper quietly into the crook of his neck, he knows I'm coming.

The door creeps open and an elderly woman gasps a shocked, "Oh my!" that hardly even registers. She's gone before Dane's fingers finally go still, and he pulls his hand free to grip my waist, warming the skin there with my own wetness. His eyelids are lower now, staring at my lips while we both pant, breathing one another's air. He kisses me again, but this feels different. It feels like we're breaking our 'no emotion' rule, but I'm weak for him, so I don't stop it.

It feels too good.

Too right.

I'm still lost in the surrealness of the moment when he backs off a few inches, and then refastens the button on my shorts. I flash a look toward him through my lashes, finding his gaze already trained on me. Without a word, he removes the panties that started all this from the top of the dryer, then places them in my hand. Afterward, he does that fucking cocky strut right back over to the wall where he stands posted, just like before.

I had no idea what I signed up for when we agreed to this arrangement, but more than ever, I'm eager to see where it will lead.

If he's made me want to throw caution to the wind with just his touch, I can only imagine what he'd do to me if we removed *all* the boundaries.

Last night, I'd been content to simply experiment with each other, but... it's entirely possible I may give Dane what I swore I never would.

I might just give him everything.

Chapter 20

Joss

My fingers have barely curled around the brush handle when I'm startled by a knock. Placing it down on the bathroom counter, I open the door and lay eyes on Dane wearing only his towel, flashing a half-grin that brings a surge of heat to my face.

"Sorry to bug you, but I overslept and just need to hop in the shower," he says.

I don't miss how his eyes sweep over me like I'm prey, like he'd consume me if I'd only give him permission. His gaze drifts lower, from where only a black sports bra covers my breasts, to my exposed torso, to the tight cheer shorts that leave little to the imagination. He made it clear that my ass is one of his favorite things about me physically, so it doesn't surprise me when his head tilts ever so slightly and he focuses there.

"I'll be done with my hair in just a few, or will it make you late to wait?"

The dense muscles in his chest jump when he laughs—soft, deep.

"Actually, I can just slip in while you finish up," he suggests. "I mean, if you're okay with that."

I breathe deep again and want to play it cool, calm, and collected, so I force a smile that feels awkward, and probably looks it, too.

"Uh… sure," I answer, forcing my eyes toward the mirror and away from him.

"Cool. Thanks."

He steps in then, and I try to ignore the sound of water pelting the tile when he turns it on. But what's not so easy to ignore is when he drops his towel, giving me an eyeful as I stare at the chiseled perfection of his muscular back and perfectly toned ass. My vision of him in the reflection is cut off when he disappears behind the shower curtain.

"What time's cheer practice start?" he asks, prompting me to blink for the first time since he entered.

"Eight," I answer. "What time do you have to report in?"

"Eight thirty. I'm usually early, but I'll be cutting it close today."

I knew he'd gone to bed late. At least, I saw light coming from the living room TV well past midnight, but I wasn't sure he was still awake. Guess I could've gone to check but, honestly? After I finished with laundry and we returned to the loft, I stayed to myself.

Call me crazy, but coming on your best friend's fingers makes things a tad bit awkward. Although, I must say, Dane rebounds from these encounters with impressive ease. It's like getting so close to one another doesn't even faze him, like it feels completely natural.

"You're quiet this morning," he notes, just as steam and the scent of his body wash are starting to fill the small space of our shared bathroom.

"Am I? I didn't realize."

He goes silent then, which makes me even more aware of my weirdness. Geez, I really have to stop doing this shit to myself—overthinking, letting anxiety get the best of me. It's Dane, the person I'm closest to, out of everyone. I've got to relax.

"Mind if I ask you something?" His voice trails off and more of that tempting aroma wafts my way.

"Sure," I say, smoothing my hair to where I intend to secure my ponytail.

"Last night was the first time someone's touched you like that?"

He asks this question already knowing the answer, seeing as how we hide very little from each other. But I'll be damned if my pep talk didn't just go right out the window, knowing he expects an answer. Just like that, I'm all nerves again.

"It… I… yeah," I finally admit, uncertain why I had such a hard time getting those words out.

"Hm," is all he says at first, which has my mind going in a thousand different directions.

"I know. I've lived my life like a nun, right?" I say with a laugh, hoping it'll help me loosen up.

"I wasn't thinking that."

When his words cut off there, I'm left hanging on the end of his sentence.

"Then, what is it?"

"Just that… something else came to mind. Something you might enjoy more than me fingering you."

He stops there and doesn't elaborate. The possibilities that race through my thoughts have my heart beating double time.

"Like what?" My voice quivers when I finally manage to get the words out.

I'm finished with my hair, but still lingering, desperate to see where this conversation goes.

"Has a guy ever gone down on you?" he rasps, making my eyes flutter with the question. He's so straight-forward, so confident, sometimes it's staggering to be on the receiving end of whatever he has to say.

"N—no. Never," I practically choke out.

"Hm."

He makes that vague noise again and I'm no more certain what it means *now* than I was the time before. Thinking the conversation is over, I push off from where I've leaned against the counter's edge and take one step before Dane's voice rings in my ears again. It sounds different, though.

It's contemplative, deep, smoky.

"If you're ready, we can try that next. Just say when."

I process that, his offer. Then, I imagine it. That's enough to make the sensitive areas he touched and probed last night awaken with need.

A quivering breath puffs from my lips and I leave him without a response. Not because he doesn't deserve one, but rather because... he terrifies me. Like, legit scares the shit out of me. I didn't know this side of him, the side that's sexual and ravenous and so, so tempting. He leaves me raw, feeling like there's not much I wouldn't agree to when it comes to him.

All because I've never wanted to be so close to anyone in my entire life.

We have a rule—that we won't let our emotions come into play. Only, the more we touch, the more I let him in, I feel that barrier I've built up beginning to crumble. Piece by piece.

It's enough that, I'm wondering if we should stop before we've really even gotten started.

But there's a large part of me that's telling me something I don't think I'm ready to hear.

That if the plan was to *not* fall for Dane... I'm already years too late.

My concentration's been shit all practice.

I've missed half my cues, got slapped in the face by a blonde pony-tail when I wasn't paying attention, and I think one of my coaches already hates me.

Why?

Because my squad's working out on the track instead of inside the gym. Which means I've had my eyes glued to the practice football field where Dane and his teammates run plays.

All I can think about are his words. The ones that have had me living in a fantasy ever since he spoke them.

Football practice is almost over, so the guys are mostly just throwing passes and hanging out while the coaches talk on the side-lines. I spot all three Goldens—because being so close, they flock to each other like magnets. Dane stands out, though. More than *anyone*, actually. The sun's beating down on his broad shoulders as he sweats in this insane heat, free from the pads and jersey that once blocked my view. He tosses his head back with a laugh and, with the distance between us, and over the music streaming through Coach Melissa's speakers, I can only hear its sound because I've memorized it.

"Francois!"

My head snaps toward the sound of my name being called. The voice is sharp and filled with frustration. And it isn't until now that I realize the reason I heard music is because our next set of squats was supposed to start.

And I missed the signal.

"I'm so sorry. I—"

"Save it," Coach Melissa snaps. "Step off the track until you fix whatever the hell has you so distracted."

Embarrassed hearing a few members of the squad laugh behind their hands, I do as I'm told, knowing I have to get my shit together. But another glance in Dane's direction has me thinking about Coach's words.

Fix whatever has me distracted.

Before I can talk myself out of it, I reach for my duffle and pull out my phone just as Dane drops down onto the bench beside Sterling. I type out a message and hit send quickly, knowing I'll change my mind if I don't.

My heart races as he pauses mid conversation to reach for his bag, retrieving his phone I'm guessing at the sound of the notification my text generated. The slow smile that spreads across his lips tells me I'm not the only one looking forward to what comes next.

And all it took was sending him one word.

Joss: Tonight.

#FollowMe

@QweenPandora:

Holy back-tatts, Batman. No clue how well football practice did or didn't go, but these pics are about to break the internet! Our boys have certainly been eating their Wheaties!

With reports of VirginVixen blatantly screwing up cheer practice, is it safe to say she was blinded by the sunlight glinting off her bestie's chest?

I'm going to go out on a limb and say I've nailed it.

Also, it bears mentioning that my fave messy trio—PrettyBoyD, VV, and NotJoss—have been blowing up, haven't they? I checked their followers this morning and WTF! Pretty soon, they'll have more people tuning in than me!

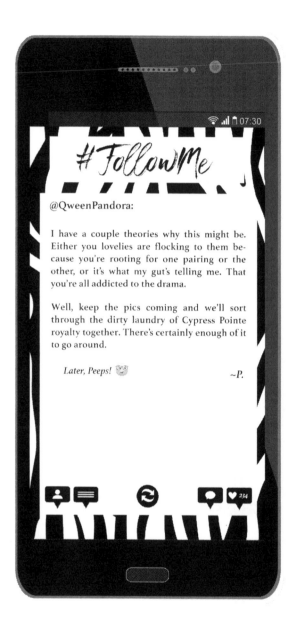

#FollowMe

@QweenPandora:

I have a couple theories why this might be. Either you lovelies are flocking to them because you're rooting for one pairing or the other, or it's what my gut's telling me. That you're all addicted to the drama.

Well, keep the pics coming and we'll sort through the dirty laundry of Cypress Pointe royalty together. There's certainly enough of it to go around.

Later, Peeps! 😼

~*P.*

Chapter 21

Joss

Dane: Be there in five.

That text has a quivering breath puffing from my lips.

Nervous wreck?

Jittery mess?

Yep, that's me.

He had plans after practice. He and his brothers had a date to sort through some of their father's things to ready them for a charity pick-up, per their mother's request. So, I used the time alone to try to relax, ending the task with a piping hot bath that helped some. Now, I'm standing naked in the mirror, asking if I'm ready for this. Ready to be seen.

And I mean *completely* seen.

I moisturize from head to toe, then spray a little perfume, but *still* don't feel settled. I'm obsessed with being perfect, so despite having shaved yesterday, I did it again tonight. Simply because the idea of being so exposed has me self-conscious.

I ignore the thought that comes next—that I'm not concerned with perfection in general, but rather that… I want to be perfect for *him*.

Shit. I can't believe I agreed to this.

The thought hits me that it's not too late to back out, tell him I spoke too soon. But then I think about last night and, if I'm being honest, I kind of love it when he touches me.

Removing matches from the top drawer of my dresser, I light both lavender candles placed on the edge. Then, right away, I consider blowing them out because it feels like I'm trying to set a mood. But maybe I am, so I leave them lit.

The door to the loft opens then closes, and I panic a little. He's here and I'm not even dressed. What the hell am I supposed to wear anyway? I don't own any *real* lingerie. So, should I go with a night shirt?

I decide on a pair of black panties with matching bra, then take the fluffy robe off the hook behind my door. Dane's steps bring him closer, and I stare at the knob, expecting it to turn. So, when it doesn't, the anticipation builds.

From what I can hear, he makes a stop in his bedroom, then back-tracks to the bathroom where the shower turns on. While I wait, I kill the light and find a quiet playlist to fill the silence. Then, I get situated on the bed, changing positions at least thirty times before deciding to just scoot to the top and rest my back against the headboard.

Relax. It's just Dane. You know him. You trust *him.*

The shower turns off and I expect his steps to head in the direction of his bedroom, but they're headed toward mine. They stop at my door and a quiet knock follows.

"Come in," I call out, my voice quivering.

He doesn't hesitate, which proves I'm the only one who's nervous. He steps in and my breaths come hard and fast, rushing over my lips as I drink in the sight of him—smooth, damp skin, rigid muscle every-where my eyes land, smoldering green eyes. He stares back and I try to ignore that he's only wearing a towel.

"Hey," I say breathily, not knowing how else to address a living, breathing wet-dream.

A smile tugs at one side of his lips, but he doesn't return the greet-ing. A command leaves him, sending a chill racing down my spine.

"Stand up."

The gentle yet forceful words have another breath hitching in my throat, but I do as I'm told. He's maybe a foot away, but not for long because he takes my wrist and draws me closer. His eyes don't leave mine. Instead, they stay trained on me as he undoes my robe, slowly tugging the belt free. It's only as his eyes dip to my chest that I see how heavily he's breathing.

He focuses on the dark, lace bra that covers my breasts—the silver clasp at the front in particular. Then, his eyes lower to the black panties that leave little to the imagination. There's something feral in his eyes and I try to swallow my nerves, imagining he'll want them off next. He slips his hands inside my open robe and the subtle roughness of his palms moving down my back has me leaning into him. His warm breath moves down the side of my neck and I close my eyes when he places a kiss there. He makes a trail back up to my ear.

"I want you naked."

When he steps back, I open my eyes, seeing his are hooded, full of lust and need. I don't move right away, though, and he senses my hesitation. I know as much when his brow quirks.

"Would it make things easier if I go first?" he asks.

That hammering inside my chest triples at the mere thought of him revealing himself. But when I nod, I swear I haven't even given my body permission to respond. So, as his hands lower to the towel secured around his waist, and my eyes follow, I'm aware of my curiosity.

He loosens it slowly, maybe just to toy with my fragile heart. Then... he drops it to the floor.

My shoulders rise and fall as I stare. The length and thickness of him leaves me absolutely speechless. I'm fighting myself—knowing I shouldn't gawk but can't look away. I've envisioned him like this many times over the years, but not even my imagination did him justice.

He's fully erect, the smooth head of his cock pointing skyward. A network of veins shows faintly just beneath the skin, and I'm still stunned by the magnificence of it all. My first thought is of how badly I want him. Then, second, I'm reminded of the throbbing pain that would likely follow.

Still, might just be worth it.

"Now you," he says in a low voice as his gaze fills with expectation.

Slipping the robe off my shoulders is the easy part, but my fingers linger on the clasp of my bra, knowing this is the point of no return. Yes, I've officially seen my best friend naked, but showing myself to *him* is a whole other ballgame.

Just do it.

I twist my fingers quickly, feeling the slight click of the hook coming undone, and then I release it. The weight of my breasts forces the fabric apart quickly, and my nipples harden in the slightly chilled air.

Dane's eyes are on me—impatient, hungry.

He raises his hands to touch me, and I hold my breath, only exhaling when his palms settle high on my ribs, brushing his thumbs across the firmness of my nipples.

Our gazes lock and the tension between us is through the roof. His hands make an unhurried descent down my torso, stopping when he reaches the elastic of my underwear, and I'm breathing his air as the thin satin is lowered to my thighs, and then falls to my feet.

I step out of them, still unable to look away from the deep green irises that have me feeling emotions I'm not supposed to feel.

Emotions I'm not *allowed* to feel.

But the rational part of my being isn't really in control right now.

My heart is.

"Fucking beautiful," he says in a low voice.

"Thanks." That word leaves me as I let Dane's eyes roam parts of my body no one else has ever seen.

"Climb up on the bed."

I obey just like I've obeyed every other gentle order I've been given tonight.

My eyes are glued to his masculine perfection as he joins me, kneeling where my feet are stretched toward the footboard. He lifts my right leg, and I didn't expect to feel heat from his lips covering my tattoo. I'm fixated on him, watching as he kisses a painstakingly slow trail over the top of my foot, up my ankle, to my calf. I swear I'm hyperventilating as his path continues to my knee, then my inner thigh, and he settles there, lying flat on my bed.

Slowly, adding to the tension that has my entire body vibrating with need, he inserts a finger into me. If I had to guess, he's just realized how ready I am, how much I want this even if my nervousness implies otherwise. Then, gentle licks that trace my slit come only seconds before his beautiful face disappears between my legs.

"Shit!" I gasp as my back arches off the mattress. Dane's tongue probes and seeks, and there's already so much unshed tension building within me.

He cups my ass in his large hands, squeezing, conveying that sense of possession I've felt before. The sheet gathers in my fists when I claw at them, having nowhere else to direct the pressure mounting inside me, screaming to be set free.

I will myself to glance down my body at him, watching as he shamelessly and skillfully feasts. Somehow, he senses that he has my attention, and that wickedly sexy stare of his locks with mine. He doesn't break our gaze as he lifts his head, teasing me with a slow swipe of his tongue over my clit. The action inspires another of my sharp gasps, but nothing like the sound that leaves me when licking turns into feverish sucking, drawing the tender bud between his lips.

My head crashes back to the mattress, panting in uneven rhythm as my body contorts in strange ways. Both legs quake where they're positioned over his shoulders, losing my grip on the last ounce of control I've clung to for dear life.

His talent has me at my peak faster than I ever thought possible, but there's no fighting it. I'm coming, soaking the sheet beneath me, and it's the single most powerful thing I've ever felt.

It takes several seconds for the wave to retreat, and when it does, Dane's pleasant assault on my clit slows, then finally stops.

I don't open my eyes, concentrating on my own wild breathing as feather-light kisses move over my thighs, then to my stomach as my heart begins to settle to a normal pace.

"You okay?" he asks, the sound of his need hanging on every syllable.

I can't form words yet, so I only nod, gripping my hair in both hands.

The response draws a throaty laugh out of him, and it's got to be the sexiest sound I've ever heard.

"Good," he says. "I thought this might be something you'd enjoy."

The bed shifts beneath his weight, and then he stands. It isn't until my skin goes cold where he once warmed it that I open my eyes to finally look at him. He pushes his hand down his chin, removing traces of my wetness that were left behind.

"You're leaving?"

Shit. That sounded desperate. Needy.

When his brow quirks with surprise, I realize he wasn't expecting it either. Right away, insecurity sets in and I know I'm breaking the rules. Granted, they're rules *I* put in place, but he agreed to them.

"I'm gonna hit the shower, but... I can come back after," he says.

At first, I'm confused. He's already clean. The hints of his body wash and shampoo mingling with the scent of my lavender candle are proof of that. But then, when I glance down to where he's just re-secured his towel, to his still-hard cock, I understand.

He needs to finish.

Not that he's complained, but this agreement of ours shouldn't just be for *my* benefit. Knowing I've left him hanging twice now—*three* times if you count the night we made out—I feel guilty. Maybe even a little selfish.

The words I'm thinking get caught in my throat, but I force them when Dane turns to leave.

"Or... I can do something."

My heart's racing and I'm not even sure he knows what I'm trying to say—that I'm willing to step outside my comfort zone for him. That I'm curious what it'd be like to touch him like he touches me.

One dark brow shoots up when he smirks. "You know you don't have to do that, right? I'm fine just—"

"No, I *want* to," I cut in, hearing the shakiness in my voice.

He hesitates, standing beside my bed with a massive hard-on that neither of us can ignore, then he agrees to this, nodding before he drops down onto the mattress. He's close. So close that his right side is pressed against me, his bicep brushing against my breast.

I'm still completely naked, but when I smooth my quivering hand down his abdomen and undo his towel again, so is he.

He is... fucking splendid in the nude—not a single thing lacking, completely devoid of flaws. There's only total perfection from every angle.

I've never done this before, touched a guy like I'm about to touch him, but I've watched enough porn to know the basics of giving a hand job. Still, it's different when you're the one giving it, and the one receiving is someone you've friend-zoned for the past seven years.

"Can you pass me that?" When I ask, his gaze follows mine to the bottle of lightly scented oil I left on the nightstand after my shower.

The thick muscle that pads his ribs flexes when he reaches for it and then hands it over. I'm trying not to be so deep in my head as I drizzle a little into my palm.

You can do this.

You want *to do this.*

I breathe in, then exhale as I take him into my hand, surprised by the density of his cock. And it's warm, like wrapping my fingers around a steaming-hot pipe.

A surge of air fills his lungs, and his head falls back against the headboard. I begin to stroke his length, slowly lowering my fist to the base, and then sliding up until the edge of my finger caresses the crown.

He hisses a breath between clenched teeth, which I take to mean he liked that. So, I do it again, only a little faster, matching how quickly he draws in air and releases it again. I watch him, not wanting to miss a single reaction as his pulse throbs at the base of his throat. In this moment, I'm obsessed with the thought of being the one pleasuring him, the reason his teeth just sank into his bottom lip. Completely turned on, my nipples harden, and I squeeze him tighter.

My gaze flits to where I have him locked in my grip, his length glistening with oil in the faint glow of candlelight. I smooth my thumb over the small slit on the tip and it draws a groan from him that excites me even more.

I squeeze a little tighter, stroke him faster.

My attention's averted from his cock to his sex-drunk gaze when he takes me by my chin, half a second before I'm kissed so hard and deep it draws a gasp from me. His tongue glides over mine and I taste lingering hints of my own arousal. He breathes into our kiss and I pump my fist faster, until his mouth goes still, and he's been reduced to breathing erratically against my lips. Long fingers slip to the back of my neck and his forehead presses to mine.

"Fuck."

The word leaves his mouth in a strained grunt, cascading off his lips when he breathes. He tenses all over, then with a deep groan that is now, hands down, my new favorite sound, he finishes, releasing his load in one powerful burst. Something about having his warm cum spilling over the back of my hand, down my fingers, has that feeling of possessiveness transferring to *me*. Like, no one on the entire planet should be allowed to experience him like this.

He's panting against my cheek and I don't stop until I'm positive he's just as satisfied as he left me. Then, I let go.

His back falls to the headboard again. I'm still transfixed on him, shocked by the overwhelming pleasure I got from tending to *his* needs. And… maybe a little terrified by it.

An exhausted grin brings life to his expression. Then, the next second, he takes my hand and wipes it clean with his towel before cleaning himself off, too.

My eyes are glued to his perfect ass when he stands and leaves without a word. I can only guess the confusion that crosses my face because… *what the actual fuck?*

Isn't there some kind of handbook that makes it clear how a guy shouldn't just walk out on a girl after what we just did? Only, I barely have time to get worked up, and I also barely have time to slip into my underwear, when his tall frame darkens my doorway again.

I smile, but hold back a little, taking in the sight of him standing there with his pillow tucked beneath his arm, wearing a pair of boxer-briefs that hug his muscular thighs.

I grab a t-shirt from the laundry basket beside my bed and slip it over my head while he stares. He steps into the room, not bothering to tear his eyes away from my breasts.

"I... thought you were leaving me for the night," I admit, knowing he hears the relief in my voice now that he's returned.

His brow quirks with a look that screams *I'd never leave you* and it has my stomach twisting in knots.

"Sorry," he says. "I didn't think to tell you I was just grabbing my things. Figured I'd hang out in here for the night. That is, if you're cool with it."

Hang out in here for the night? As in... sleep in my bed?

My expression must give everything away, because he backtracks the next second.

"I know we have rules, so if you want me to drag the armchair in and sleep *there*, I can," he offers. "I just don't think you should be alone tonight."

There's a level of innocence and sincerity in his eyes that hits me square in the chest.

He didn't want me to be alone after everything.

Because it's like he once said, I'm not just some girl to him. I mean something.

I exhale and take in the sight of him, knowing what my answer *should* be, but instead of saying those words, I pull back the cover, inviting him in.

He stops at the dresser to blow out the candles, then his heat warms my back when he fits against me like the missing piece of a puzzle. His arm falls over my waist easy, like we've done this a thousand times before. And in similar fashion, my hand goes to where his now rests against my stomach and our fingers lace together.

I'm not sure if best friends spoon and fall asleep in one another's arms, but apparently *these* best friends do. As my lids fall closed and a slow, steady rain begins to pelt the steel frame of my window, I can't find any reason to fight what I feel happening between us. And while I should be reveling in what I know to be the beginning of something I swore would never happen, instead, it scares the hell out of me.

History often repeats itself. So, here's hoping Dane and I somehow manage to avoid the pitfalls that ruined my parents.

Because as much as I sometimes wish it weren't true… I need him.

Chapter 22

Joss

A smile touches my lips as the little girl in the next car holds her doll up to the window for me to see. I wave, then the light turns green, and we take off. For some reason, her sweet, cheerful face reminds me what a good day it's been.

An oddly smooth day.

At random, I've drifted in and out of memory lapses from last night—feeling Dane's touch, feeling his skin against my own hands. Being involved with him in this way, it isn't for the faint of heart, that's for sure. He has this way of getting to you, getting so deep inside your head, under your skin, it makes me wonder if there will be any turning back after this, any going back to who we were once this experiment is all over.

Waking up with my cheek pressed to his chest, his hand against my back, I also wondered if it had been wise to let him spend the night in my bed. But the gesture hit me right in the heart. Any girl in her right mind would've told him yes.

Surprisingly enough, there was very little awkwardness once we got out of bed and made our way to the kitchen for breakfast—eggs and toast that *he* cooked. Well, maybe it started off awkward, but Dane burned all that away. Seeing that nothing had changed with him, seeing he's still the same chill person he was even before all this started, I relaxed, and we fell into just being us.

Easy.

Normal.

The breeze wafting in through the open window snaps me out of the daze, as does the biting sting at the top of my ear. The piercing wasn't nearly as painful as it was half an hour ago, though. Dane was right—getting high first helped. Plus, we killed two birds with one stone—getting my cartilage pierced and me smoking my first joint—which is why neither of us was in any shape to drive. Instead, we opted for the Uber currently maneuvering us through traffic.

In my head, I visualize the lined notebook paper with my list written in purple marker, then I cross off the three items Dane selected. I got my tattoo, I got high, and I got pierced. Now, the only thing left is number eleven. I've admittedly thought about losing my virginity more in the past few days than I've thought about it my entire life.

Why?

Asking myself that question, my head swivels left, toward the green-eyed tempter sharing the backseat with me. He's slouched toward me with his shoulder pressed to mine, scrolling through his phone. Even when he isn't trying, he's sexy. From the way his free hand aimlessly rakes through his dark, glossy hair after the wind tousles it. To the way his teeth drag across his lip while he concentrates. Then, sunlight filters in, outlining his perfect features in shimmering, gold light and, best friend or not, I kind of want to kiss him right now.

"Our video's blowing up."

I force my eyes away from him when he speaks, pretending my thoughts hadn't been on him a second ago.

"You mean the video you shared without my permission?" I ask, arching a brow before a smile breaks free.

"Come on. You know my followers love when I post shit about us," he reasons with a smirk.

"Maybe, but will *Rose* love it?"

Right away, I regret letting that slip. I haven't so much as hinted that there's any kind of tension between she and I. But with Dane's silence, I know the comment didn't go over his head.

"Did she say something to you?"

He's on the defense. The sharp edges of his words make that abundantly clear. I'm reminded of that day in Mrs. Kent's homeroom when he taught Alex a lesson. One I'm certain the guy has never forgotten.

"Not really. It was more or less… a vibe."

That word fits best, so I leave it at that.

I glance his way, finding him deep in thought, and maybe even a little angry, which wasn't my intention at all.

"Honestly, I probably read too much into things," I say. "At the most, she might've made me feel a little uncomfortable."

When his eyes flicker toward mine, I believe he sees right through the lie. Even though I only told it to protect him. He shouldn't feel obligated to defend me, obligated to choose.

"Why am I just now hearing about this?" His voice is quiet and reflective, but still holds a flare of anger.

"Because it really wasn't that big a deal to me."

"Well, you being disrespected is a big fucking deal to *me*," he snaps.

The venom in his tone is only meant for Rose.

He seems to become aware of the spike in anger, then relaxes into his seat a bit, averting his eyes out the window.

"She called the night of the shoot," he reveals. "Your name came up and I checked that shit right away, so she shouldn't be a problem anymore."

My brow ticks a bit. I guess his response to Rose prying into his personal life is a little surprising. I mean, I know Dane cares for me, but I also know how hard he's worked to lay the foundation for the empire he hopes to build. Rose is a key part of that right now. From what I'm hearing, though, he risked there being bad blood between them to speak up on my behalf.

"I didn't know she mentioned me to you," I say quietly, wondering about the specifics of what was said, but not having the courage to ask.

"Just know it was a very short, very cut-and-dry conversation," he says. "I'd never let anyone trash you. I don't give a fuck *who* they are."

All these years later, he still hasn't changed. Of all the people who've ever had my back, most have also failed me at some point, but not Dane. He's been my one constant.

When his gaze flickers toward me, I'm caught staring this time. The tip of his tongue separates his lips when he wets them, and I draw in a breath, remembering all too clearly how they taste.

"But Rose's bullshit aside, I have an idea," he rasps, grinning a little. "We should do another movie night tonight, and you have my word that I'll keep my hands to myself this time."

The quiet laugh he lets out after speaking makes this promise very hard to believe.

His hand settles on my thigh then, and my gaze lowers, focusing on the black, beaded bracelet around his wrist.

"You'll keep your hands to yourself?"

I peer up and he's still smirking. "Well, maybe I should've said I'll try."

With us both sort of leaning into each other, he's already close. Close enough that, if I were brave, I could kiss him. My eyes lower to his mouth and a breath leaves me. I'm aware of how the space between us has narrowed but I don't fight it. Actually, I lean in, meeting him halfway.

His hand slips up my thigh another inch and my heart's racing so fast my pulse vibrates in my throat. The noise of the city fades until I can't hear it at all, until it's swallowed up by the haze of need thickening around us.

We've kissed before, a few times now, but none felt like this. Our lips have become so familiar with one another's—mine anticipating how his will move, knowing when to part for his tongue. There's a rhythmic ebb and flow that draws me right into him.

His hand slips free when he shifts in the seat, facing me as the kiss deepens. I breathe him in and welcome his taste inside my mouth. He grips my waist, burning my skin with his heat where he holds me tight.

My soul chases after his when he pulls back, but I'm too proud to ask for more. I will my eyes to open and only then does Dane's hand fall away from my skin.

"Had to get that out of my system before tonight. Otherwise, I can't say for sure I wouldn't go back on my word."

I hardly hear what he's said despite my eyes being glued to his mouth. With the energy that surges between us, there's no doubt that a traditional movie night would be difficult, if not impossible, for us to pull off.

This wasn't the plan. I wasn't supposed to get to the point that I swoon after kissing him. Our arrangement was supposed to be physical only. Not... this. Not my heart fluttering because he's tracing a figure-eight on my knee with the tip of his finger. Not me thinking I want him in my bed again.

I'm breaking the rules, getting too comfortable.

Shit.

A sharp rush of air fills my lungs when he gets a notification and I'm jarred back to reality. I'm not *trying* to read the message, but it's kind of hard not to with how close we're sitting.

It's Rose and my stomach turns a bit.

Rose: I lucked up on tickets to the Arland-Danston Modeling Agency's meet-up. They're hosting it downtown at the art gallery! This is huge!

Dane: Sweet. When?

Rose: Tonight. I've been trying to get these since last month, when I first heard they'd be in Cypress Pointe. A friend with tickets fell ill and offered me hers. My assistant will be bringing a tux to your door in thirty minutes, after she checks on Shawna at the salon. Then, I have cars picking you both up at 6.

Dane: Tonight's kind of short notice, isn't it?

Rose: Short notice, yes, but this isn't just any event, Dane. Whatever you have going on can be postponed, I'm sure. Don't let me down.

The rims of my nostrils flare with frustration. It's not one particular thing that rubs me the wrong way, but the whole exchange. Rose herself, how pushy she is with Dane, and her mentioning Shawna.

Mostly her mentioning Shawna.

Dane's fingers move across the screen and, again, I glance down at the message. He's halfway into a response, turning down Rose's offer when words fly from my mouth.

"You should go."

Not only do I *hear* the silence, I feel it. All around me as Dane's confusion mounts.

"But we just made plans," he says flatly. "Rose doesn't get to alter my life with a last-minute text."

I understand and appreciate what he's doing, honoring our movie date, but I can't help but to see this as a sign. We've been moving so fast—maybe even *too* fast—and some time apart might be good for us, might lessen the pull, might extinguish some of the heat.

Hopefully.

But I don't miss the frustration that marks Dane's expression as he keeps his eyes trained on me.

"You really want me to say yes to this? A night out with Shawna?" he asks.

My heart thunders against my ribs, the two responses inside my brain struggling against each other. That is, until one wins and I rush to speak.

"It sounds like this could be a good networking opportunity," I reason. "These meet-ups draw some pretty important people out of the woodwork. And... that's kind of huge for you right now. No telling what you'll miss if you don't go."

Something flickers in his eyes and I try not to let it affect me, bracing myself.

"There's no telling what I'll miss if I *do*," he says, his stare darkening with the words.

Heat creeps up my spine, and that feeling is precisely the reason we need a break.

"Joss." His voice is distant when he speaks my name. Like he's holding back, fighting himself on saying more.

My chest rises with the deep breaths that follow. I'm not strong enough to keep up this façade for long, so I pray he doesn't push.

"Just say the word and I'll turn this down. In a heartbeat," he says softly, pinning me to my seat with that deep gaze he's kept set on me this whole time.

I want to cave. Everything *in* me wants me to cave, but… I can't.

Memories of my parents' loveless marriage flash in my thoughts—empty glances, broken promises, betrayal—and they sober me quickly.

We cannot become them.

Ever.

"You have to say yes," I answer. "Besides, I've got work to catch up on, too. I haven't replied to any of your email messages in a few days and I need to get started building your website. So, yeah. I think you should go."

On the outside, I try to make it look like I don't care, but on the inside, I feel everything—instant regret, jealousy at the thought of another night spent with Shawna, anger toward myself that I can't seem to just let this happen.

With a sharp tick of his jaw, Dane's brows gather in the center and, damn, his frustration is palpable. My eyes stay glued to him as he lifts his phone again, watching as he erases the first message, replacing it with another. One that's more sensible, one that's safe, one that's better for us both.

Dane: I'm in.

With that, he shoves the phone into his pocket, then shifts his weight in the opposite direction, leaning away to settle against the door instead.

He watches the city pass outside his window and I watch *him*—the only boy I've ever really trusted, the only one who makes me feel like, saying yes to him, could be the difference between having it all and losing it all. And, if I'm honest, that scares the shit out of me.

He hates this, being kept at arm's length, but only because he doesn't know what I know, hasn't seen what I saw growing up with two people who started out very much like we have. I'm protecting our friendship, protecting our hearts.

Protecting him.

As bad as this hurts, it's what's best.

Chapter 23

Dane

A pocketful of business cards, a dozen calls scheduled to discuss photoshoots, a girl on my arm most guys would chew their own hand off to be with. But me?

I'd rather be home, chilling with the girl who's made an art of pushing me a way.

That shit sucks.

Big time.

Shawna reaches across my shoulder to adjust my collar, then smiles up at me. I try to flash one back, but it feels awkward as hell, which means it looks at least that. I've never been good at hiding my feelings, and tonight, the pervasive thought preventing me from having a good time is of how much it pisses me off that Joss is still in denial.

She thinks *her* parents were screwed up? Well growing up under the same roof as Pam and Vin Golden was no fucking picnic. And, yes, being an eyewitness at ground-zero of our parents' trash relationships messes us up, but she fucking knows me. Knows I'm nothing like her piece-of-shit father.

"You okay?" Shawna's question has me glancing down to her.

"Fine. Why?"

Her brow shoots up curiously. "Well, for one, you're super distracted. But there's also the fact that you're squeezing my fingers like a tube of empty toothpaste," she answers with a laugh, slipping her hand from mine to shake it a bit.

Guess I'm not hiding my frustration as well as I hoped.

"Sorry. Just got a lot of shit on my mind."

"Wanna talk about it?"

We push past a group near the balcony door, then step out into the open air before I answer.

"It's nothing you'd want to hear."

When I sigh, leaning over the railing, Shawna's stare deepens.

"Trouble on the home front?" She lets out a humorless chuckle when she turns, facing out over the courtyard below us.

"You could say that."

There's unacknowledged tension lingering between us. Like there are things we both want to say but can't for about a million reasons. Mine mostly involve me knowing she won't want to hear me gripe about the Joss situation. Because she'd know the frustration is rooted in something else, a much deeper emotion I'm starting to think I'm an idiot for even feeling.

"Saw your video today," she shares. "Looked like you and the roomie had a good time. Well, it *always* looks like that, I guess."

I shrug, not really wanting to discuss it.

"So, since you seemed fine in the video, did something happen after that? Did it have something to do with having to be here tonight?"

Glancing down at her, I realize she thinks she's the problem, thinks I hate having to be here with *her*, and it makes me feel like shit.

"It's not about attending the event," I explain. "Well… not in the way you're thinking."

I hear her wheels turning as she pushes the length of her hair behind both ears.

"Hmm… Is she upset that—"

"Before you finish, no, she's not mad I'm here with you," I say with a sigh, not ignoring the fact that I *wish* that were the problem.

"Well, I give," Shawna huffs. "And I'm also starting to think I was right; coming tonight was a bad idea."

167

My gaze slips toward her just in time to see she's starting to sulk a little. Exhaling, I pull my head out of my ass and realize I've been terrible company tonight. I haven't had much to say and when I *have* spoken, I've been short with her.

"I'm sorry. I've been so preoccupied with my own shit that I've been a complete ass."

She slips me a look, holding in a faint smile now. "You didn't even compliment my dress."

Turning toward the courtyard again, and away from her, I laugh a little. "You look beautiful. My failure to say it out loud doesn't mean I didn't notice."

She steps closer and leans on the rail beside me. I guess she just now realized I won't bite.

"You look good, too. I've wanted to tell you since you first stepped out of the car." There's a shyness about her I'm not used to. Seems like she's always so confident. So sure of herself.

"Thanks."

"Welcome."

The conversation lulls and, without fail, my thoughts lead me right back to Joss. Wondering what she's doing. Wondering if she's talking to Carlos just to avoid thinking about me, about last night.

And just like that, I taste her on my tongue, then feel the softness of her hand encircling my cock. I know I'm not crazy. We were electric together. I can't be the only one who felt that shit.

But since she doesn't want to admit it's a thing, I'll do my best to forget.

"You really started not to show?"

"Didn't see the point," Shawna sighs.

That wasn't quite the response I expected, so I'm admittedly curious. "What does that even mean?"

She smirks when I do.

"It just means that PTSD from one rejection is enough for me. The whole *'Tim thing'* has me gun shy to fall for someone new and, if I'm honest, you kind of scare me. Because I could see that happening with you," she admits. "Guess the video today just seemed... different."

I face her fully now, resting my elbow on the rail to make eye contact.

"The video with Joss? Different how?"

She nods to confirm, then draws in a deep breath. "There was this point after the piercing was done, when she was half-laughing and half-crying. You just looked so concerned. Like, you knew that despite her cracking up, she was in actual pain. And when a tear finally fell, you brushed it away with your thumb. It was an innocent enough gesture between friends, but... not when you look at her the way you do. It was the look. That's what made it more than *just friends.* That's what made it love."

I gaze at her a few seconds, then let my stare shift to the wood slats beneath our feet, feeling exposed. Like she's just read me.

"And... I guess I can take your silence as confirmation."

Frustration brings tension to my shoulders. "Doesn't really matter what I feel. Her mind is made up about us and I've accepted that there ain't shit I can do about it."

Shawna's thoughtful for a moment, biting her lip when I glance her way.

"While I'm more than aware that what I'm about to say will probably sound completely desperate, it seems that's a risk I'm willing to take," she says with a nervous laugh. "But if you come to the conclusion that things aren't going anywhere with her, I'm willing to let that be enough."

A solemn smile touches her lips, but I'm confused. It seems she understands that when the lighthearted expression leaves her.

"I'm... not sure I follow," I admit, which has her face tinting red.

"Shit, I don't even know how to flirt anymore," she says mostly to herself. "What I'm trying to say is, I know neither of us are emotionally available right now, but that doesn't have to mean we aren't, you know, *physically* available. To each other," she adds, gazing up through her dark lashes.

I only look into her eyes a few seconds before glancing out toward the courtyard again. For some reason, even *imagining* what she just offered feels like I'm cheating. But how fucking ridiculous is that?

Shouldering the guilt of being unfaithful, when the one girl I want refuses to admit the feeling is mutual?

Shawna takes hold of my arm, her light touch drawing me back to her stare. There's sadness in her eyes, and a bit of something else. Hope, maybe?

"Please don't think less of me for speaking my mind. I just think that since we both know how much it fucking sucks to be lonely, maybe it's okay if we're... you know... lonely together."

I have nothing to say, nothing to combat that.

"Just... think about it," she says.

With that, her grip on my arm loosens, and I watch her walk away, weaving back through the crowd until she disappears.

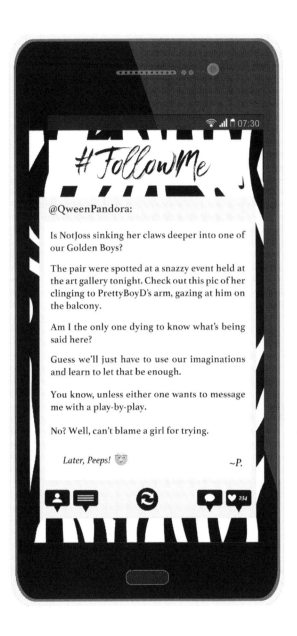

#FollowMe

@QweenPandora:

Is NotJoss sinking her claws deeper into one of our Golden Boys?

The pair were spotted at a snazzy event held at the art gallery tonight. Check out this pic of her clinging to PrettyBoyD's arm, gazing at him on the balcony.

Am I the only one dying to know what's being said here?

Guess we'll just have to use our imaginations and learn to let that be enough.

You know, unless either one wants to message me with a play-by-play.

No? Well, can't blame a girl for trying.

Later, Peeps!   ~P.

Chapter 24

Joss

"Thanks for coming."

I trudge slowly down the steps of me and Dane's building and Sterling hands me one of the two lidded coffees he holds.

"You kidding? Something had to be done. Your lame weekends are starting to make the crew look pathetic as a whole," he teases.

Laughing, my steps sync with his and we move at a slow pace down the mostly deserted sidewalk. Seeing as how it's already midnight, that makes sense.

Thinking of the time serves as a reminder that Dane hasn't come home yet. I'm pathetic enough to admit that I checked the Arland-Danton event calendar. Tonight's meet-up was scheduled to end at ten, so he's just hanging out, I guess.

With Shawna.

Which is my own damn fault.

Which makes me hate myself a little.

Why can't I just take a chance? Why can't I separate my parents' past from whatever future Dane and I could possibly have? It sounds so simple in thought, but as the one caught in the thick of it, there's nothing easy about it.

And that fucking sucks.

Sterling's random check-in call is how he found out I spent my evening working, instead of hanging out like most nineteen-year-olds do on Friday nights. But nope, not me. I was nerding out, working on Dane's website until Sterling threatened bodily harm if I didn't swear I'd meet him out here in fifteen minutes.

Clearly, he won the argument.

"So, this moping thing you're doing, does it have anything to do with that pic Pandora posted?" he asks casually, sipping his coffee afterward.

I shrug and let out a sigh. "It does and it doesn't. I was already kind of fucked up before I even saw it," I admit.

Now that Sterling's brought it up, the image is in my head again—the one of Dane looking so damn sexy in his suit, leaning on the balcony rail at the gallery with Shawna clinging to his arm.

"Talk to me. I'm great at solving other people's problems. It's my *own* shit I can't seem to manage," Sterling says with a laugh.

After excusing ourselves when cutting through a group of teens whose open-mouthed stares mean they definitely know who we are, I let out a breath. My hesitation doesn't go over Sterling's head.

"You two been fucking or something?" he asks with a smirk.

Caught off guard by his bluntness, I burst out laughing. "What? No!"

At first, I'm staring straight ahead, but then my eyes flicker to his. He's got this smug grin on his face like he knows more about the situation than even *I* do.

"Why'd you assume that? Did he tell you something?"

Just to get under my skin, ensuring that I die of anticipation, Sterling still isn't answering. All I'm getting is more of that wicked grin.

It's so weird talking to him about this. Subtle physical differences aside, it's like I'm speaking directly to Dane.

"Well, is there anything *to* tell?" he asks, prompting me to roll my eyes, unsure of why I even doubted that he knows. The Golden boys tell each other everything.

"Cut the shit, Sterling. He already told you about our arrangement, didn't he?"

His grin turns into quiet laughter. "He did, and I'll tell you like I told him. It was only a matter of time before you two went all the way.

You can only dry-hump a guy for so long before he talks you into letting him fuck you for real."

He's laughing, but it literally feels like I'm talking to my brother about this. I don't have one of those, but if I did, I'm positive I'd have this same, uncomfortable feeling in my gut.

"Now, let me guess what happened next," he continues. "Sex complicated things and you're pissed he's got this work thing with that Shawna chick. Sound about right?"

I'm shaking my head before he even finishes, thinking he's got me and Dane pegged.

"Actually, you're mostly wrong. For starters, we haven't had sex. Second, you know me, Sterling. I'm rational and I've never been much of a jealous person, but—"

"But all that shit went out the window when you started falling for him," he cuts in, plucking words from my thoughts that I never would've said aloud.

Only, he's gotten something else wrong. I fell for Dane years ago. These feelings are nothing new.

"I told him to go tonight," I admit, lowering my gaze to the sidewalk. "He wanted to stay in and hang out together, but I turned him down. Because I'm a dumb-ass," I add with a sigh.

When I finally meet Sterling's gaze, his brow quirks. "And... that was easier than just telling him you're into him?"

I see what he's trying to do, hear it in his tone. "It's not as simple as you're making it out to be."

He's quiet for a moment, then drops his arm around my shoulders with a sigh. The feel of it is comforting, reminding me of the many times he and his brothers pulled me into their circle, making me feel like I was more than just a friend, but a part of their world.

"At the risk of Dane killing me later, I'll let you in on a little secret. Whatever bad thing you see happening down the road if you open up to him, it ain't happening," he says with surety I wish I had.

"How can you know that?"

"Because you aren't just some crush for him, Joss. You're not some chick he'll get tired of and toss aside a month later," he says in that big brother tone he takes with me sometimes.

When I peer up, I know there's more he wants to say, but he's holding back.

"Shit, he really *is* gonna kill me," he says mostly to himself. "Fuck it. He's in love with you. Has been for a very, *very* long time. And if there's one thing I'd bet my life on, it's that he'd never fuck it up if you gave him a chance."

My stomach feels all fluttery hearing him say these things. Yes, I know Dane's feelings are strong like mine, but hearing it from Sterling makes it that much more real.

Breathing deeply, I share more than I planned to tonight. More than I was able to share with Dane when we talked about it.

"My parents were best friends once. Before eventually hooking up and trying to make a romantic relationship work."

"You never mentioned that," Sterling says gravely, maybe sensing that there's a bleak story ahead when I nod.

"They were tight like me and Dane, but then it turned into more. They did the break-up and make up thing for a while before finally calling the relationship *and* friendship quits. Then, they ran into each other at a party," I add with a sigh. "Both had a few drinks too many and she went home with him that night. Mom says they woke up in the morning regretting it, dressing in silence with plans to go their separate ways. Again."

"Damn."

I nod slowly, sharing Sterling's sentiment.

"They'd already seen how toxic they were together, so they weren't even considering trying to work things out this time. That is, until about a month later when Mom found out she was pregnant with me."

Sterling's gaze shifts and I feel his stare, but he doesn't speak.

"She scheduled an abortion, even showed up at the clinic, but couldn't go through with it. Eventually, she got up the nerve to tell my dad she was pregnant, and I guess they thought the right thing to do was to make it work. For *my* sake," I add.

We're both quiet and I feel sick to my stomach thinking about how they could easily be a cautionary tale for Dane and me.

"So, you were, like, a breath away from not existing. That's kinda deep."

"It's one of the reasons it's been relatively easy for me to stay a virgin," I admit with a faint laugh. "Things happen, and if I were to ever face something like that, I don't think I'd be able to choose differently than my mom did. It's not a political or moral thing. It's just that… it stays with me that her split-second choice is the only reason I'm here."

"Damn," Sterling says again, taking it all in.

"From there, shit went from one end of the spectrum to the other. They ended up at the altar," I reveal. "Because of *me.* Not love, but out of obligation. Taking things too far in their friendship ruined them in more ways than one. It's the reason my mom's a shell of who she would've been without my father, and it's the reason *he's* bitter and unhappy. And it's probably also the reason he's a fucking cheater."

I didn't mean to let that last part slip, but it just sort of rolled off my tongue. Guess it's out there now.

We continue to walk without saying a word, his arm still tight around me, holding me close. I don't even know why I've said so much, but maybe I just need to be understood. Need someone to know I'm not keeping Dane at arm's length to be a bitch. I do it because I refuse to lose him.

"I get it," Sterling says solemnly, finally speaking. "You've got good reason for being afraid."

The statement makes me feel like someone gets me, makes me feel seen. I'm not some frigid, cold-hearted monster who enjoys seeing the only guy I've ever loved suffer. I suffer, too.

"I've come to the conclusion that the only way to keep Dane close is to keep him at a distance," I say, summing up the thoughts I had earlier during the car ride.

It's the reason I set him free tonight. Because we both need to learn how to live with things being exactly the way they are, which probably also means our arrangement should end sooner rather than later.

Like, immediately.

The phone buzzes in my back pocket and my heart leaps a little. When I glance down, hoping it's the one person I shouldn't be hoping for, I'm admittedly disappointed to see Carlos' name.

"One sec," I say to Sterling with a sigh as his arm slips off my shoulder.

We step closer to the brick building we walked beside when I take the call.

"Hey, mind if I hit you back in the morning?" I answer.

"This won't take long. Just check your messages. I sent you something."

Trying not to roll my eyes, I pull the phone away from my ear and find his text. And... the image of a roundtrip plane ticket to the airport located on the outskirts of the city.

I feel the tension in my brow and I'm certain Sterling can see it when I bring the phone to my ear again.

"What is this?"

When Carlos sighs on the other end, I'm positive he hoped to draw a different reaction from me. But the only other reaction he might've gotten from me is 'What the fuck?'

"I... thought you'd be excited," he says, and it definitely sounds like I burst his bubble.

Letting my back fall against the brick, Sterling rests beside me, taking the empty coffee cup from my hand to toss it in the trash with his.

"Carlos, I think maybe we should've talked before you did this. I'm not sure if you coming here is really a good idea right now or... at all," I add, drawing Sterling's attention. "Things might be moving a bit fast."

"An entire year is too fast for you?" he asks with a quiet laugh. "Listen, I know you're skeptical about us, which is why this is only a friendly visit. You have my word."

My head is spinning. I've already got so much going on, adding this makes me want to vomit. I feel terrible for what I'm about to say, but I cannot in good conscience let him travel all this way not knowing my position.

"I still stand by what I've said before—that I don't see this heading in the direction you're hoping. I just really, really don't want you wasting time and money coming to see me, I—"

"Visiting you could never be a waste, Josslyn. As a friend or otherwise," he interjects. "So, with all that out of the way, do you feel a bit more at ease? Besides, you'll only have to put up with me for a couple nights."

There's amusement in his tone, not frustration or anger like I feared there might be.

Despite the shift in conversation toward lightheartedness, I still feel like I've been backed into a corner. Glancing toward Sterling, I no longer have his attention. It's gone to the pair of girls in short skirts who just walked past.

After inspecting the ticket closer, I see that it's for three weeks from today and non-refundable.

"Just as friends, right?"

He laughs again. "Yes, just as friends."

I've been open and honest with him, so if he's hellbent on coming, it seems I can't stop him.

"Guess I'll see you in a few weeks then," I concede, trying to ignore how my stomach twists into a knot.

If I'm lucky, by some small miracle, this won't end in disaster.

@QweenPandora:

We've definitely slipped into an alternate universe, lovelies. Not only are Pretty Boy D and NotJoss looking more and more like a couple, but it seems MrSilver's been called in as an understudy for his missing brother.

He's spotted here, on the streets of Downtown Cypress with VirginVixen. Coffee cups in hand, the pair appear to be in deep conversation.

Could it be that he's consoling her about that balcony pic?

Not sure, but something's definitely up.

Oh! And how could I nearly forget this juicy tidbit! It seems that after the fancy event, PrettyBoyD was spotted heading into a posh hotel with NotJoss still latched to his arm.

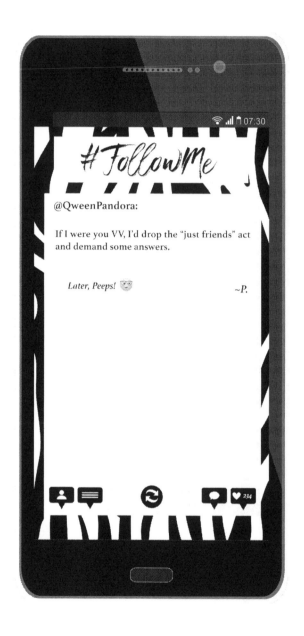

#FollowMe

@QweenPandora:

If I were you VV, I'd drop the "just friends" act and demand some answers.

Later, Peeps! 😎

~*P.*

Chapter 25

Joss

Dad: I'll be making dinner reservations before my arrival and will send the details. Once you have them, please clear your schedule for that night. I look forward to our talk.

Tucking my phone back inside my purse, I breathe deep, trying to focus only on the now. Not what will happen when my father flies into the city.

Seems I've got *two* visits to dread.

"Well, look who finally decided to show," Blue says, flashing a grin my way when she answers the door.

"Yeah, sorry I'm late. I got caught up in a new project and lost track of time. Then I had to grab the snacks like I promised."

I keep to myself that I probably would've been even later if Sterling and West hadn't shown up at the loft. They're having their guys' night there, while us girls hang here.

My hands are freed from the grocery bags when I set them down, then Blue pulls me into a hug, knowing these past couple weeks have been shitty. The night Dane attended the meet-up started a fourteen-day period of silence between us. For him, I'm guessing it was being pushed on that date with Shawna, reinforcing the false notion that I'm content with things remaining as they are. For me, it was the pics of them heading into a hotel afterward. He has to know I've seen them, has to know I'm aware of what likely went on inside the room. So, I've

181

taken it as his way of ending our arrangement, even if he hasn't come right out and said it's over.

I'm not mad. I *can't* be. This is what I wanted for him—to move on and let go of the notion of him and me. Like *I'm* trying to do. Only, I didn't expect it to sting this damn bad.

Since that night, we only speak when we have to, we don't drive to practice together even when we start at the same time, and I can't even nail down our emotional status.

Is it just frustration that's wedged its way between us?

I can't tell. All I know is it's happening—the breakdown of our friendship, and it didn't even take sex to ruin it. Kind of makes keeping my distance feel like a moot point if I was going to lose him anyway.

Trust and believe, that fact is not lost on me.

When Blue pulls away, I see sympathy in her eyes. She—like the entire city—has seen the updates about Dane and Shawna. They hang out all the time now, looking like the perfect couple. It's hard to tell if they're even still pretending at this point, or if their hookup changed things. Whatever the case, Blue hates what's happening almost as much as I do, because her rooting for Dane and me has been genuine.

"Want me to pour you a drink? You look like you need one. The bar's stocked with some pretty good shit, too. Vin may be an asshole, but the man had great taste in liquor," she says with a laugh.

"As tempting as that is, I'll pass. But thanks."

She's got that look in her eyes again when rubbing my arm. "Well, come on. The girls are all out by the pool and I want you to meet Dez."

Taking my hand, she leads the way, dragging me through her and West's ginormous house. Our steps echo across the marble tile and, through the wall of glass just beyond the living room, the girls come into view. They've formed a tight circle around the firepit, all wearing bathing suits, which means there's a swim session planned at some point.

Blue slides the door open, and we step out. I hadn't realized it through the glass, but the conversation is loud and lively—a far cry from the vibe at the loft lately, making the noise a welcomed change.

"You made it!"

Jules pops up from her seat when she spots me. She squeezes me tight and confirms it. I *did* need this—their positivity, their emotional support.

Before Blue, I didn't have many close girl friends. Yeah, there were the girls on the squad, but outside of dance, we didn't really click. Hence the reason it was always me and the triplets. But now, she's bridged the gap between me and a group of girls I might've missed out on knowing otherwise—Jules Avery and Lexi Rodriquez. This being my first time meeting Dez, it's a little early to tell, but Blue's a pretty good judge of character, so I trust that she's cool, too.

Jules eventually let's go and I drop down into the seat between her and Blue.

"Joss, this is Detective Roby's daughter, Dez. You remember me telling you she'd be here tonight, don't you?"

I smile and wave, meeting the gaze of the girl seated across the firepit from me.

"Hi, nice to meet you."

She waves, too. "Same!"

She *seems* friendly, and there's no doubt she's beautiful. Her perfect, medium-brown complexion holds a glow that rivals that of the blazing fire. Deep dimples create small sinkholes in her cheeks when she greets me, as she pushes the length of her dark hair behind her shoulder. Large, gold hoops hang in her ears, matching her metallic bikini. Having met her father once or twice during the chaos that's surrounded Vin's arrest, I expected her to be broody and rough around the edges like him, but she's anything but that.

"We were just discussing my lack of a love life," Jules offers with a laugh.

"Oooh, sounds interesting," I say, sliding the sandals off my feet before settling into the deep wicker chair, legs tucked beneath me.

"Hardly. In fact, I'm done with guys for a bit. At least, ones our age. I want someone at least twenty-three, twenty-four."

"Don't get your hopes up that'll be any better," Dez chimes in.

"Take it from me, dudes can be assholes regardless of age. Hence the reason I'm newly single."

"What's your story?" Jules asks with a gleam in her eyes.

Dez sips from the wine glass dangling lazily in her fingers.

"Well, the short version is that I'm the idiot who started dating a carbon-copy of her father without even realizing it. I mean, down to his line of work," she adds with a laugh. "He's a rookie cop and he's about as exciting as watching grass grow—straitlaced, does everything by the book, never breaks the rules. Just thinking about it has my panties dry as the Sahara."

Lexi spits her drink into the flames when she laughs.

"Damn, girl! You sure warm up quickly, don't you?" Jules says with a grin.

Dez shrugs. "My dad's profession is based solely on being able to read people. Guess some of that rubbed off on me. I knew you girls would be my new tribe the moment I stepped out onto the patio. You, too," she adds, pointing her glass at me before sipping again.

I nab a bottle of water from the cooler beside me and raise it into the air. "I'll drink to that."

"Besides," she adds with a wink, "Pandora has me and this whole city feeling like we already know you guys."

On cue, Blue, Lexi, and I roll our eyes. Jules has yet to get caught in Pandora's web, but it's just a matter of time before we're *all* entangled.

"She's not all bad, though, right?" Dez adds. "Didn't she help take down Vin? At least that's what my dad told me, during one of the few conversations we've had this year, that is."

Lexi's brow quirks when she blows a smoke ring, giving us all a bit of a contact high. "One of the few conversations?" she repeats. "You live with the guy. You two don't talk much or something?"

Dez's gaze flashes toward the pool for a second before answering. "He'd have to actually come home sometimes for us to talk. If your last name isn't Ruiz, he isn't really interested. He's been obsessed with that case for months now."

I don't miss the sadness she tries to hide. Neither does Blue, which is why she redirects the topic quickly.

"Last time we talked about school, you were thinking you'd enroll at one of the universities nearby. That still your plan?" she asks.

Dez shrugs. "Honestly? I've given college two years and I still don't know what I'm doing with my life. Breaking up with Tony helped me realize I might not be cut out for the shit most girls are looking for. I don't dream about picket fences and barbecues with the neighbors. I need some excitement. I need... something unexpected."

She zones out after that, maybe dreaming of this life of excitement she craves.

"Well, if there's one thing this city is sure to give you, it's the unexpected," Lexi teases with a smirk. "While you wait, feel free to come to my house and sunbathe by the pool. That way, my mom can yell at us *both* for being complete derelicts."

Dez snaps out of the daze that stole her attention for a moment and smiles. "Ohh... nice! I've never experienced someone *else's* parent looking down on me. I'm in!"

Shaking her head with a laugh, Blue turns to me. "What about you, Joss? How's work going?"

I appreciate her not bringing up Dane. My heart can only take talking about him so much.

"Work's fine. I'm starting to find my sea legs, I guess. I've started a new ad campaign I think will bring in a ton of followers. Dane will appreciate that, plus it'll help me build my portfolio. Two birds, one stone."

"And how's that going? Living with the guy *and* working for him?" Jules asks.

I shrug. "It's going fine."

I stretch the truth a bit because what's wrong with Dane and me has nothing to do with me working for him.

"You two have had some interesting photos floating around lately," she adds. "Which makes it super jarring when the next ten photos are of him and Shawna."

And here we go.

I draw in a breath and respond as best as I can. "Well, we're friends, so we spend a lot of time together. Plus, we live together."

We were doing a lot of other things together, but we'll leave that part out for now. Especially seeing as how those days seem to be behind us.

"At any rate, Dane's free to do whatever he wants," I add.

"Speaking of, have you gotten around to telling him about the visitor yet?" Blue bounces her brow with the discreet question.

I shake my head. "Not yet, but I will."

Although, I'm pretty sure Dane's and Carlos' paths will never cross. Especially seeing as how Dane and *I* are barely even speaking.

As if having just heard my thoughts, that sympathetic look returns to Blue's eyes, which is why I feel her hurting for me.

"And he'll be here next weekend, right?"

I don't miss the hint of nervousness in her tone. My only response is to nod when my own anxiety creeps in.

"Well, you know what I think? For tonight, we should all set our real-life shit aside and just… be free," she announces as she stands and pulls off the t-shirt that covers her bikini. Her shorts come off next, then she cannonballs into the pool.

We scream a bit when the huge splash reaches our seats. It's insane seeing this girl so carefree and happy. And watching her move through the water like a fish is nothing short of a miracle seeing as how, before West, the girl couldn't swim to save her life.

Literally.

"Come on. I could use a little of whatever she's got," Jules says, following Blue into the water.

Soon, we're all in, deciding to put our B.S. on hold for a bit. Pretty sure none of us believe this will actually fix anything, but we're going to have fun and leave the drama behind.

Well… for tonight at least.

I could sure use the break.

@QweenPandora:

Looks like while the Golden Boys are spending a chill night at PrettyBoyD's loft, the girls are having their fun at the Bellvue mansion.

Fun Fact: There seems to be another newcomer in the mix, so I'll be watching to see if she's sticking around long enough to earn a moniker. You know, if this city doesn't eat her alive before she even gets the chance.

If she survives the gambit, I'll be back with all her stats.

Later, Peeps! 🐨

~P.

Chapter 26

Joss

If I'd been a minute later coming out of my room, I would've missed him. He's dressed for the gym, with his duffle bag slung over his shoulder. He hears my footsteps and casts an emotionless look my way.

Swallowing before I speak, I pretend it doesn't bite a little seeing how things have changed between us.

"Hey, mind if I talk to you for a sec?"

His hand falls away from the doorknob and he faces me. "Sure. What's up?"

I swallow deeply, searching for courage I'm not sure I have. When I got in from Blue's last night, he was busy editing video footage to upload, so I didn't bother him, making myself scarce because it was the easy thing to do.

But it's now or never. With only one week until Carlos arrives, I can't keep putting this off.

"So, there's something I've wanted to tell you, but I went back and forth between not being sure how to bring it up, and not being sure it was even worth mentioning," I ramble, pushing a stray curl out of my face.

"What is it?" he asks flatly, letting his back fall against the door while he listens.

There's a lump in my throat the size of a golf ball. I swallow and just spit it out.

"It's not my doing, but... Carlos will be here next weekend. He'll be staying in a hotel, so you won't likely see him, but I thought you might want to know."

My tone lightens at the end, hoping to make this sound like nothing. Technically, it *is* nothing, but Dane would never believe that.

Now, he's quiet. *Too* quiet. It's even more awkward because this is the most we've talked in weeks. But he can't possibly be upset, right? After all, he and Shawna are involved.

"Okay."

That one word falls from his mouth and I'm silent. He holds my gaze and holds that expressionless look on his face.

"Just... okay?"

"What the hell else am I supposed to say, Joss?" he says with a short laugh. "You told me before that he might be visiting, so... it is what it is."

I breathe in slowly and let it out the same.

It is what it is—a vague-ass statement that's always grated my fucking nerves. Even more so with him using it now, while I'm trying to discuss something serious.

This conversation makes it feel like the gulf between us just widened by a mile. He seems so cold and indifferent. Telltale signs that a guy's emotions have detached, likely the result of whatever it is him and Shawna have been up to lately.

"Fine. Guess that's it then."

"You sure?" he asks, popping a brow like the cocky dick I've seen him be toward other people, but not with me.

Never with me.

Guess this is where we are now.

"Yeah, I'm sure." I force a smile, pretending not to notice how different he is.

He's about to turn and leave, but halts with his hand on the knob. "I'm supposed to have another thing going on with Shawna next weekend, so I was gonna suggest that we double, but why don't we just have something here? We can invite people and get a caterer. It'd be fun."

My heart's racing and I can only hope I'm hiding it well. I force another smile and nod.

"Sure, I'll shoot you a text of a few caterers I think might work."

He seems so casual about this. So… indifferent.

"Sounds like a plan. Maybe we'll talk more about it when I get back from the gym."

Dumbfounded, I nod and can't say another word as he steps out and closes the door behind him. Meanwhile, I've got one thought running through my head.

What the actual fuck just happened?

Chapter 27

Dane

I hate this shit.

Pretending not to care because *she* pretends not to care. If our conversation this morning taught me anything, it's that Joss doesn't know me as well as either of us thought she did.

Now, on top of everything else—Rose's bullshit, stressing over my *Dad's* shit—I'll have to keep it together while Carlos' ass is in town.

And what the fuck was I thinking suggesting that we throw a party here? The last thing I want to do is watch her with him all night. But since my dumb ass already brought it up, she'll know there's something up if I back out now.

No emotion, right?

That was her rule.

Shit. I'm fucked.

Flipping my pillow to the cool side, my head slams against it and I stare at the ceiling. Just like I have been for the last three hours. There's movement in Joss' room, but she hasn't been out in quite a while. Not since she grabbed a glass of water and passed a discreet glance this way, maybe trying to see if I was asleep. Even when we locked eyes, neither of us spoke. She just went back to her room and closed me out.

Which seems like how things have gone between us lately.

I'm not sure how much longer I can keep this up, pretending not to care just so she isn't uncomfortable. At what point do I just say fuck it and *make* her see what I see?

Fighting anger, I flip onto my side and focus on the window, on the rainwater pouring down it in sheets. Since sleep hasn't come naturally, I force my eyes closed and just... hope for the best.

"Dane!"

The sharp scream that hits the air has my lids wide open again and I swear I'm off the couch before her voice even fades. Hurdling the armchair in my path with one swift motion, I sprint down the hallway faster than I've ever moved down the field.

Throwing Joss's bedroom door open, my gaze shifts from one side to the other, searching for the threat.

"What the hell happened?" I ask, glancing as she squeezes herself into the corner near her bed, clutching a t-shirt over her bare tits. She's naked from the waist up, and only wearing panties from the waist down.

Shit. Focus.

"There's a fucking spider in my sheets!" she shrieks, pointing at the dark spot I hadn't noticed before. It's moving fast toward her headboard, but I'm faster.

Grabbing a sheet of paper from the notebook on her nightstand, I head it off before it knows what's coming, then move to the window. Joss stares with relief as I crank the glass open, then let the eight-legged terror out onto the fire escape.

By the time my eyes are on her again, she's panting a little less wildly, but with the threat gone I'm staring at her tits again.

"Thank you," she says breathily, snapping me out of it.

"No problem."

"I was changing for bed and sat down on the edge of the mattress to put my shirt on, then I spotted that thing out of the corner of my eye."

She's still worked up so I'm holding in a laugh now, recalling her overreaction to the bug.

"It's nothing. I wasn't asleep."

She seems surprised by this, and before she can read more into it than I'd like, I turn to leave.

"Night."

"Night," she echoes, then I close her door behind me and head back to the couch.

No fucking way I'll fall asleep now.

I fall against the cushions with a grunt, drawing in a deep breath to help me relax, but nothing works. Part of what's kept me awake is that I'm horny as fuck. And now seeing Joss half-naked has made things even harder.

Literally.

My head pops up off the pillow and I glance toward the hallway through the darkness, making sure I'm still alone. After confirming, I try to alleviate the problem the only way I can, seeing as how our friends-with-benefits arrangement seems to have expired.

My hand lowers into my boxers and I stroke my dick once, remembering the feel of Joss' soft palm working it up and down. That was unexpected, her wanting to touch me like that.

I lower my waistband a bit, until my dick's free and aiming skyward. One last peek to make sure it's just me out here, then I go at it, jerking myself off to the thought of flawless brown skin, dark curls that fall on smooth shoulders, and a body so perfect it's painful to look at.

"Shit."

The word hisses through my teeth as the fantasy in my head runs wild, as images of her touching herself dance into my thoughts. Biting my own lip, I imagine her mouth against mine, the moist heat of it driving me insane.

I'm getting close, feel my sac tightening. Any second now, I—

The sound of lightly squeaking hinges has me yanking the blanket over my waist and flipping onto my side at record speed, breathing hard like I just finished a workout.

Correction: *almost* finished a workout.

Soft feet pad down the hallway and stop somewhere near the

entrance of the great room. I don't look her way, though, for fear that she'd somehow know I was beating off while thinking about her.

"Are you still awake?" she asks quietly.

Trying my hardest to hide that I'm out of breath, I answer. "Yeah, I'm up."

She takes another few steps, then stops again. Her silence is hard to read, so I eventually force myself to peer up to where she stands. With a pillow tucked beneath her arm, a sliver of moonlight cuts diagonal across her face, showing only her full, parted lips as she watches me.

"You okay?"

She doesn't answer right away, so I prop myself on my elbow to get a better look at her. Her thighs are still exposed, with dark satin covering the triangle at their apex. The t-shirt she held over her a few minutes ago is now on, covering her tits and half her midriff.

Is it possible for an erection to get so out of control your dick explodes and kills you? Cause I think I'm about to fucking find out.

"I don't think I can sleep in there after the whole… spider thing, so I was hoping I could lay with you."

She sounds sweet, innocent even, but that's a far cry from what I'm staring at right now. With her curls wild and covering her face a little, she looks like a Playboy model. My gaze wanders down the well-defined curve of her hips, making me envision the perfect ass that's currently hidden from view. She's always hated the size of her thighs, but I sure as hell don't. They're smooth and athletically toned, making them slightly larger than her ideal, but whatever her measurements are, they're definitely *my* fucking ideal.

Shit. I was supposed to respond.

"Uh… yeah. Of course."

Scooting a few inches higher, I drop my head onto the armrest. Joss sits, then leans to the side to rest on her pillow, drawing both feet onto the couch. Smoothing the sole of one up my inner thigh, she stops just shy of my dick. Our legs are loosely tangled now, locked into some kind of figure eight.

She's completely silent when I spread my blanket over us both. My thoughts are on football, ice baths, and even my grandfather—anything that'll make this hard-on go away.

"I'm sorry."

The softly spoken words surprise me, so I lift my head a little to look at her. Dim light filters in through the window and shadows of the raindrops streaking down the glass move over her skin.

Football.

Ice baths.

Grandpa Boone.

"What do you have to be sorry about?" I finally ask.

"I haven't been myself lately and it's caused me to be really cold and distant toward you, which you don't deserve. I'm working on finding a way to work through my shit without it affecting the people I care about," she says.

"You don't need to apologize. Neither of us have exactly been warm lately."

She's silent, thinking as she blinks into the moonlight.

"At the end of the day, all I want is for you to be happy and for us to be… us."

"Same goes for me," I say. "So, how do we fix it?"

She shrugs and settles in a bit more, moving her knee across my leg while she thinks.

"I believe the first step was for us to stop pretending there wasn't anything wrong. Now, maybe we can move forward, being mindful of each other's feelings. Being mindful that, above all else, what's most important is our friendship."

I can do that. To start, I initiate a conversation we would've had before all the other shit got in the way.

"So, this Carlos guy is really making his way here, huh? Guess it's been a long time coming. The two of you have gone back and forth for a while."

"It's not really like that," she says with a sigh, hinting at frustration. "By the time he told me his plan, he'd already bought his ticket."

This shouldn't make me feel relieved, but it does, knowing she's not nearly as into this guy as he seems to be into her. I'm not naïve, though. Her mind could easily change when he gets here.

"That's kind of a bold move, isn't it?"

She nods and releases another of those tense sighs. "That's one word for it. Like I said, though, he won't be here very long. Just a couple nights."

Now *she* sounds relieved.

"So… you really don't feel anything for him?" I'm aware that the question could be perceived as invasive, needy. But I don't really give a fuck about that at the moment.

She shakes her head first. "Not as anything but a friend."

Hearing her admit that twists me in knots, because I know for a fact that she sees *me* as more. Even if her stubborn ass won't admit it.

My eyes are glued to her, and with each deep breath she draws in, her tits lift. Firm nipples poke through the fabric of her tee, making my mouth water for her more than it already was.

Damn girl's gonna be the death of me.

When she stretches one arm above her head, I can only guess she's just as restless as I am, which leaves me to wonder if she's restless for the same *reason* I am.

My mind starts to wander, questioning whether a girl comes to lay with a guy in only a shirt and panties if she truly wants to be left alone. Or… maybe she hoped something would ignite between us. Like it usually does.

As I think it, the smooth sole of her foot slides higher up my thigh, reaching my boxers. She stops there at first, but to my surprise, answering my question, she grazes lightly over my sac, then my dick. The lingering contact lasts far too long to be an accident,

"You didn't come to me because you're scared." That isn't a question. It's a fact I've just been made aware of.

"I… no," she admits, sounding like she might've considered lying first, but knew I'd see right through it anyway.

The hammering in my chest is telling of how she gets to me, draws a physical reaction from me that no other girl's been able to evoke.

My thoughts run wild, imagining all the shit I could do to her right now if she'd only let me.

"Come here."

She hesitates at first, but then moves the cover, revealing the rest of that sexy-ass body. She stands and takes my hand when I reach for her. I rest on my elbow, smoothing my fingertip across the waistband of her panties, staring up while she watches.

"Is it okay if I touch you like this?"

Distracted and maybe letting her imagination run wild, too, she nods.

My gaze lowers to where her thighs touch, to the outline of her slit through her panties, which brings an even better idea to mind.

There's only one question.

Will she let me have my way tonight?

Chapter 28

Joss

Every nerve in my body is alight with anticipation, with need. He's only stroked the elastic of my panties and, already, I'm so wet for him.

A breath hitches in my throat when his fingers loop around my waistband and he tugs, dragging the dark fabric down my thighs to my knees, until it falls to my ankles. The action is triggering, reminding me of all the reasons I should stop this, all the reasons I should tell him that touching me is off limits.

Starting with him following Shawna into that hotel.

I try to hold onto that thought, try using it to slow this down, but nothing works. I want him too badly, regardless of the pile of broken rules mounting between us.

He gestures for me to remove my t-shirt and I do so without question. The subtle roughness of his palms pushes up the backs of both thighs and I can't breathe. He has this way of stealing all the air from the room, leaving me to pant and writhe for him.

"Do you trust me?" he rasps, peering up.

The question makes my brow gather.

"Of course," I answer, but secretly wonder what he has in mind that warrants that he even needs to ask.

Slowly, he pulls me closer as he lays back again. But my heart races when I realize what he wants. It isn't until he takes me by my hips and guides me down onto him, positioning my thighs at either side of his face, that I fully grasp it. A hint of stubble brushes against my skin and the sensation arouses me even more. Then, the next second, he brings me down lower, until my pussy covers his mouth.

There's no time to breathe, no time to ask him to go slow, because his tongue's already inside me.

Deep inside me.

"…Dane."

His name leaves me with a whisper and the room fills with the echo of my heavy panting, laid over the soundtrack of rain cascading down the window. Weakening me, he draws my clit between his lips, sucking while I whimper and grind into him. It dawns on me that I didn't know pleasure before this, before *him.*

Touching myself, using my vibrator… neither compares.

The sudden movement of his shoulder beneath me has my attention divided, luring my gaze behind me, down his long, muscular body. Gray boxer-briefs cling to his thighs in the most delicious way, emphasizing the bulge that swells in front. I fixate there, on his hand when it slips inside the fabric to free his heavy cock. It springs toward the ceiling and I swear I salivate, seeing his tight grip encircle it. When his fist begins moving up and down his impressive length, my breaths become erratic to the point of feeling lightheaded.

I'm torn between focusing solely on how he's completely devouring me, and watching how he pleasures himself. The visual of it—his hand wrapped around his thick shaft, the large crown I fantasize pushing its way inside me—has me on the verge of coming. His thighs tense. He's close, too. I feel it even more when he squeezes my ass with the hand not stroking his dick. His hips writhe and he pumps his fist faster, just as a fluttering deep within me rises and euphoria floods my senses. I can't take anymore.

A cry leaves my mouth when I come to the deep vibration of him moaning into my pussy. I fight the urge to close my eyes, as wave after wave of pleasure slam into me, but I'm determined to keep my eyes trained on him. A struggle that pays off when a deep groan leaves him, and I get to witness his sudden release. A torrent of wet heat reaches my lower back when he erupts. My teeth sink into my lip, savoring the visual of him that will forever live inside my head.

Sated, his dick relaxes, and I turn to stare down my body at him, feeling heat from his breath against my inner thigh before he places a kiss there. I can't help but to wonder how he turned me into this person. This girl who craves something so badly that she's never even had. He's gifted in ways I never dreamed, with every part of his body I've experienced so far.

I can only imagine what he can do with the rest.

Slowly, and weak in the knees, I stand to my feet, eying his perfection sprawled out on the couch. His gaze is locked on mine and he doesn't bother to cover himself, not an ounce of discretion or self-consciousness in his body. He knows he's a fucking fantasy in the flesh.

My fantasy.

He stands and lowers his boxers, kicking them off, but he grabs his t-shirt from the floor before straightening. Using the soft fabric, he wipes my back clean as he towers over me. I will myself not to glance down at the girth hanging between his legs, but I swear he feels the struggle. Hence the reason those green eyes never leave me when he speaks.

"I'll get the shower going so you can clean up," he rasps, lust still heavy in his eyes.

He doesn't wait for a response, just drags his palm across my stomach as he passes. My eyes chase after him, gawking at the thick muscles in his back and that perfect ass when he walks away.

Even when he's gone, I stare in the direction of where he's just disappeared, completely aware of how each encounter draws us in deeper, bonds us more than we already were. And while I also know leaning into what I'm feeling crosses our boundaries… I'm not sure I can stop this.

Not sure I can stop myself from falling deeper, from wanting to be with him.

This girl who was once drowning in rules might finally be learning what it means to live.

And it only took Dane showing me how.

Chapter 29

Joss

And guys say girls are teases.

I beg to differ.

My eyes flash to the mirror while brushing my teeth, meeting Dane's gaze in the reflection as he slides past on his way to the shower. There's a smirk on his lips as his dick brushes across my ass, with only my towel and his between us. Then, he drops his, and I see *everything* before he steps beneath the stream of steaming water.

The 'couch incident' was a full week ago and we haven't touched since then. There's been a lot of flirting, a lot of me dreaming about how far things could've gone, but no actual contact. I'm trying to resist, knowing he's broken his end of the deal with Shawna, but I've thought about giving in every day.

Every. Single. Day.

"Excited for tonight?"

I spit toothpaste into the sink before answering. "Should be fun."

That's kind of a lie. In truth, I'm nervous. Not only will I be seeing Carlos in person for the first time in over a year, I'm worried I'll somehow hurt his feelings once we're face-to-face. He'll see there's no chemistry on my part, and I can't guarantee things won't go bad with him and Dane meeting.

"Shawna coming?" I ask, trying to sound as neutral as possible when her name leaves my mouth. Trying not to sound like the idea of her turns my stomach.

"She can't really miss it," he says with a laugh. "For us, this is work. She texted a few minutes ago to say she'd be late, but she'll be here."

I pop my toothbrush into the cup and face the shower. A glimpse of Dane's silhouette catches my eye as I lean against the edge of the counter.

"Cool."

He chuckles to himself, but doesn't speak.

"Will I like her?" I ask next.

"She's pretty chill, so maybe?"

He doesn't sound so sure about that and I have more questions—about her, about *them*—but I keep them to myself for the sake of not sounding insecure.

Even if there is a bit of truth to that.

"Well, I'm sure it'll be fine," I say with a sigh.

"Just fine?" There's a laugh in his tone when asking.

I shrug like he can see me and push off the edge of the counter. "It'll just be an interesting night."

The conversation ends there because I leave to change. I slide into the outfit I grabbed from the mall this afternoon—a denim, overall minidress, a white, off-the-shoulder crop top underneath. Styling my hair, eyeing myself in the mirror, I'm aware of having chosen an outfit I thought would get Dane's attention. Carlos wasn't even a thought when I decided.

Placing hoop earrings in my ears, I try to settle my nerves, praying tonight doesn't end in total disaster.

Dane

West and Blue showed up first, coming through with the drinks they promised. Next, Sterling arrives with bags of ice, and within fifteen minutes of him crossing the threshold, our place is packed with at least fifty people. That number includes members of our new team as well as the old. And the extension of our regular crew—Lexi and Jules—plus Dez, some new girl Blue's been hanging with. Add in the caterers and we're almost at max capacity.

Almost.

Still no Shawna or Carlos.

Conversation about two sisters one of the guys fucked last week goes in one ear and out the other. Not only because I'm completely uninterested in hearing about how both were "squirters", but also because a pair of smooth brown legs just walked past, distracting me like she's done the past seven years.

I trail up the firmness of her thighs with my eyes, tilting my head slowly as I wish I had x-ray vision to see under that short-ass skirt she's wearing. Beneath it, her curvy hips and round ass are physically painful to look at. But that doesn't stop me. As if she feels my eyes on her, she glances back, meeting my gaze from over her shoulder. She fights a smile, facing forward to keep from giving in to it.

My thoughts slip back to a week ago, to the softness of those same thighs tightening against my jaw when I ate her until she came. I'd be lying if I said that was enough for me. I want it all, but for now I'll settle for us at least being civil again.

I'm on my way to the door when someone knocks, and I have Joss' attention again. She hasn't said it, but she's dreading the arrival of her guest and mine. She isn't alone, though. Twice this week, I considered calling this whole thing off, opting to go back to me and Shawna's original plan this weekend—an invite to hang in a nearby club's VIP room. It's always about the photo ops and connections. The biggest part for us right now is keeping up appearances, continuing to see our numbers grow and the opportunities rolling in like they have been.

My hand lingers on the door knob before telling myself to man-the-fuck-up and just open the damn thing. When I do, Shawna greets me with a huge grin that tells of her *own* nervousness.

"I come bearing gifts," she announces, holding up a bottle of wine.

I take it and she leans in for a hug while we linger in the doorway for a bit.

"Thanks. You didn't have to do this, though," I say, eyeing the bottle.

"It's no bother. I actually enjoy buying this shit now that I'm legal."

I glance up and she's still smiling, but scanning the room over my shoulder.

"Come on in. I'll introduce you to everyone. Well, the people you haven't already met."

Her lips widen and as soon as I close the door behind her, she latches on to my hand, lacing her fingers with mine. The feel of it makes my gut twist and my anxiety spike. On cue, I glance toward Joss. Her eyes flicker down to my hand locked in Shawna's, then she meets my gaze for half a second maybe, before she falls back into conversation with Blue and the other girls. Of *course*, she misses the part where I let go, pretending to need both hands to set the bottle on the counter as we pass.

Shit.

"Is that her?"

Shawna points and I'm not even surprised she's aiming right at Joss.

I nod. "Yep."

I don't miss how she scans Joss with only her eyes, never moving her head as she gives her a sweeping look.

"Do you... want to meet her first?"

She sucks in air and I'm reminded of the many, many chicks I've come across who Joss manages to intimidate before they even exchange a word. Guess that's the cost of being a fucking knockout.

"Sure," Shawna sighs, pushing her shoulders back when she smooths her hair.

We walk that way, me with my heart in my damn throat. It's Blue who slides a look our way this time, and I don't miss it when she mouths the words *'They're coming this way,'* to Joss, which means they were definitely talking about us. Joss doesn't move, appearing to be the picture of confidence as she sips from the glass she holds.

"Ladies, mind if I interrupt?"

Four sets of eyes land on me when I ask—all except for Joss'—then those probing looks shift to Shawna, judging everything from her hair, to her outfit, to her shoes. All with one collective glance.

They scatter slowly without a word, leaving Shawna and me to face Joss alone. She turns with this freakishly natural smile on her lips.

"Shawna, Joss. Joss, Shawna."

I hold my breath once the introduction is out of the way, having no fucking idea how this shit's about to go.

"Hey!" Joss says sweetly.

"Nice to finally meet you," is Shawna's enthusiastic reply. She's someone who likes to be liked, so I know Joss' warm welcome resonates with her.

"I'm glad you made it. Dane's told me a lot about you," Joss continues, still giving nothing away with her expression.

"Same. I feel like I know you already. By the way, I cried with you when you got that foot tatt. You've got bigger balls than me," Shawna adds with a laugh.

"Oh gosh, you saw that?" Joss says with a grin. "I tried to get Dane to shut the camera off."

"No, I loved it! It was real! You don't get a lot of that with social media these days. People are up for posting their latest clothing hauls and vacations and shit, but no one posts the real, day-to-day shit. Whenever you and Dane hang out, you two give tons of footage like that."

When she finishes speaking, she does that thing again, where she slides her hand into mine, and there's no smooth way out of it this time. And, like before, Joss doesn't miss it.

Her smile is still there, but it's not quite as light and easy as it was a moment ago.

"Well, I'm going to let you two hang out," she announces, only now letting her true emotions seep through. "I'll be around."

With that, she's gone and back talking to her girls where they've gathered near the fire escape. Her back's to me, but the sympathetic looks on *their* faces tells me all I need to know.

This party—having Shawna here—was a bad fucking idea.

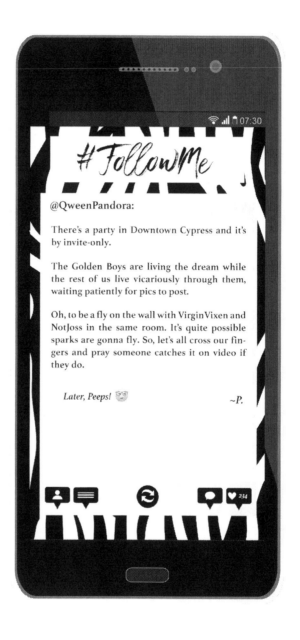

#FollowMe

@QweenPandora:

There's a party in Downtown Cypress and it's by invite-only.

The Golden Boys are living the dream while the rest of us live vicariously through them, waiting patiently for pics to post.

Oh, to be a fly on the wall with VirginVixen and NotJoss in the same room. It's quite possible sparks are gonna fly. So, let's all cross our fingers and pray someone catches it on video if they do.

Later, Peeps!

~P.

Chapter 30

Joss

Bass thumps low from the speakers Dane purchased online this week, just for tonight. They got here quickly, which is more than we can say for his special-order bed. I pointed this out and he didn't find it all that funny.

I focus on those speakers and the music pumping through them, because they help keep me from looking at the two smiling and laughing in the kitchen.

I was nice, but it took a lot out of me, draining my social battery like you wouldn't believe. The first indicator that this was going to be a shitty night was her grabbing his hand within seconds of her ass walking through the door.

She's familiar with him.

Really fucking familiar.

"You okay?"

I tear my eyes away from Dane and meet Blue's gaze when she asks. "Peachy," I say, sounding like the bitch I feel raising her ugly little head in my soul.

Seeing him with her in pics was one thing, but having her in our loft, breathing the same air as her, is another. Knowing she either touched, sucked, or fucked him in that hotel room.

"Easy killer," Lexi says in that calm way she has, easing an arm around my shoulders as she takes the glass from my hand.

It isn't until she touches me that I realize I'm shaking, completely enraged.

"She's got a pretty nice ride from what I've seen in pics. It'd be easy to spot it in the parking garage. Say the word and I'll grab a bat from my trunk and fuck her shit up," Lexi offers, drawing a laugh out of me despite my mood.

"You know, Blue made a similar offer, but I'll pass. This time," I add.

My gaze is set on Dane again, remembering that the whole reason he started giving Shawna the time of day in the first place is because of me. It's this thought that keeps my emotions in check, keeps me from throwing a bitch-fit I'm not entitled to throw.

A knock hits the door and I breathe deep.

"I should grab that."

I push off from the brick beside the fire escape, headed toward the door. Passing Dane and Shawna, I can't help but glance over. She's running her mouth about something, but instead of giving *her* his attention, Dane's eyes are glued to *me*. He's watching with this mean-ass look on his face as I snatch the door open and, the next second, my eyes lock with Carlos'.

Letting my gaze settle on him, I breathe in and release it slowly. Time apart had distorted my memory, so his staggering height catches me by surprise. With the breadth of his shoulders, he carries almost the same presence about him as Dane.

Almost.

A wickedly intense smile touches his mouth when I invite him in and re-lock the door.

"You're even more beautiful in person," he says in a low voice. It's deep and mellow just like over the phone, but more so now that we're face-to-face. He doesn't bother with discretion when his eyes sweep over me with a look.

Before I have a chance to even register what's happening, I'm drawn into a slow, gentle hug that ends with Carlos' hand settling at the small of my back.

"I'm... glad you made it. How was your flight?"

"Long," he answers with a laugh. "I had time to drop my bags at the hotel and catch a nap before heading over."

"I'm so sorry I couldn't pick you up from the airport. I had a ton of last-minute shit to do to get ready for tonight."

"Please, don't apologize. I'll take what I can get."

He locks me into his gaze, wetting his lips.

"We, uh… would you like to meet everyone? Or are you hungry? We have food and—"

"Relax," he croons, cutting me off when I start rambling. "You seem nervous."

I fight the urge to glance toward Dane again, because I shouldn't care if he's watching.

"Sorry. Just a little tightly wound with everything that's going on."

"What'd I say about apologizing?"

"Right."

He hits me with that half-smile again, and I'm certain it's melted the panties off a few dozen women. Hell, maybe more.

"My girls are anxious to meet you," I say, tearing my eyes away from him.

"Lead the way."

I breathe deep as we walk back to where Blue and the others are waiting. When I walk up towing Carlos behind me, all four seem to forget what they were saying, staring up at his killer smile and dark features. He laughs quietly, maybe used to getting this response from women.

"Evening, ladies," he says, his smooth accent wooing the crew even more.

"Well, damn!" is Dez's less-than-subtle greeting.

"Damn is right," Jules says under her breath, but not so quiet that Carlos doesn't hear it.

He takes each of their hands and places a kiss on the back, near their wrists. The only one who has any kind of chill is Blue, and I'm willing to bet that's only because she's completely whipped and only has eyes for West.

But these other three?

Sloppy, swooning messes.

I hold in a laugh and get on with the introduction.

"Carlos, I'd like for you to meet Blue, Jules, Dez, and Lexi. My friends."

"Pleasure meeting you all," he greets them.

"No, the pleasure is *all* ours," Lexi adds, shamelessly eye-banging the shit out of him right now.

"Gonna be here long?" Blue asks, only making small talk. She already knows all the details of his visit, including what hotel he's staying in.

"Not nearly long enough. If it weren't for work, I would've arranged to have more time," he answers, casting a look my way that's fleeting, but I didn't miss it. I'm guessing my girls didn't either.

"What do you do for a living?"

He smiles at Blue before answering. "Well, by trade, I'm a personal trainer, but my passion is art."

"The watercolor on my bedroom wall is one of his," I interject.

"It's not my best work, but Josslyn inspires me," Carlos adds with a smile.

Jules' brow quirks. "Well, lucky Joss," she teases.

"On that note, you sure I can't get you a drink?" I look up at him to ask, needing a break.

"Actually, I think I'll take you up on that. Water, please."

I nod, then leave him with the wolves. Heading toward the kitchen, I remember why I should've avoided it. Dane and Shawna are still chatting near the fruit tray. That glare is still set in his eyes and I roll mine at him.

"Excuse me," I say as nicely as I possibly can when I need to step past them to get to the fridge. I grab out a bottle of water with plans to just leave them to it, but Dane's voice halts me when he cuts Shawna off mid-sentence. Like she hadn't even been speaking.

"You planning to let me meet your friend?" Dane asks, eyeing me with that same evil-ass look he gave when I went to let Carlos in.

Taking a breath, I face him. "You're more than welcome to come speak if you'd like to."

I flash a friendly smile and don't miss how uncomfortable this exchange is making Shawna.

He sets down the cup in his hand and doesn't hesitate to trudge toward Carlos, leaving me and Shawna to trail behind him. His shoulders are squared and there's an angriness to his slow, cocky stride. He walks up on Carlos and the two are eye-to-eye.

I get there just in time to do the talking myself, so Dane *doesn't* come across like the rude asshole I know he can be when left to his own devices.

"Carlos, there's someone else I'd like you to meet," I say, stepping between them. "This is Dane and his friend Shawna. Dane, Shawna, I'd like you both to meet Carlos."

You could cut the tension between us all with a knife. The silence coming from Lexi, Blue, and the other girls isn't helping.

"Nice to finally put a face with the name," Dane speaks up, offering Carlos his hand, but nothing more. Not a smile. Not an ounce of friendliness.

"Same," Carlos says, echoing an identically flat, unfeeling tone.

I'm stuck, unsure what to say to lighten the mood.

"Your accent, are you from Cuba?" Shawna chimes in, rescuing the conversation from the brink of death.

"I am. Have you ever been?" Carlos asks, only *now* losing whatever that vibe was between him and Dane.

"Once, but it was a quick trip for a photoshoot," she answers. "I keep saying I'll get back there one day, but you know how that goes. *'One day'* never seems to come."

Carlos nods. "I know exactly what you mean. I've said the same about New Zealand. I've been twice and keep planning to get back there eventually."

"Well, you made it *here,* so maybe all you need is a beautiful girl like Joss here to make the trip worthwhile."

Shawna's comment has me snapping a look her way, not missing her subtle attempt at playing wingman. She wouldn't be the first of Dane's girls to try pawning me off on another guy to put distance between him and me. Usually, though, it's one of her ugly brothers or cousins I get stuck with.

"I suppose you're right," Carlos replies, hitting me with a warm look that has Dane's eyes narrowing with frustration.

"Well, I'm gonna go grab a plate," Shawna announces. "You coming with?"

Her eyes land on Dane and he takes a moment to meet her gaze. All because he's so focused on me, on Carlos when his hand settles on my back again.

The centers of Dane's eyes gleam with darkness, with anger, when his stare meets mine again.

"Sure. Let's go," he finally answers.

Shawna does that thing again, where she reaches for his hand like he belongs to her. Only, this time, he seems to reciprocate her interest, clinging to her like she's clinging to him.

I've gone back and forth wondering what tonight would bring, what it would *prove,* and as I watch the pair walk off hand-in-hand, I think I've figured it out.

It was meant to help me realize just how wrong we are for each other.

So very, very wrong.

@QweenPandora:

It's official. The newbie by the name of Dez Roby has popped up on the scene again, so do you lovelies know what that means?

We're one step closer to bringing this mysterious beauty into the fold.

I've got a bit more research to do before branding her with a moniker, but just know it's in the works.

But while on the subject of beautiful mysteries, someone from inside the party shared a very interesting pic.

It's this image of VirginVixen with her arms wrapped around the neck of a tall heartbreaker we've never seen before...

@QweenPandora:

Shame on you, GoldenCrew! Have you been keeping secrets?

Later, Peeps! 🙈

~*P.*

Chapter 31

Joss

We've cleaned nearly the entire loft and haven't spoken one word to each other. As far as shitty nights go, this has been one for the books.

By the end of the party, I was so pissed off that it made things super weird and tense between Carlos and me, which he didn't deserve. My anger was only for the asshole currently straightening the coffee table. He doesn't see it when I roll my eyes at him, but I sure as hell hope he feels it.

I put the last clean dish back in the cabinet, head toward the hallway and flip the light switch, bathing the great room in darkness.

"You don't see me working in here?" Dane barks at me.

I stop halfway down the hall before deciding not to be *completely* petty. When I double back and flip the switch again, he's already glaring in my direction. Turning, I take one step toward my room before his voice halts me.

"Are we gonna talk this shit out? Or should I plan for another two weeks of the silent treatment?"

His words feed my anger, making goosebumps prickle my arms as rage flares inside me.

"The way I'm feeling right now, trust me, you don't want that. I'm going to bed."

I take another step, but he's not done yet.

"Then *I'll* do the talking, and you can fucking listen," he says, sounding frustrated and on the brink of losing his shit. Hence the reason I said we should wait to talk.

"I hated tonight," he begins. "I hated seeing you with bitch-ass Carlos, hated seeing his damn hands on you, hated that you *let* that asshole fucking touch you. Hated him in general."

He's filled with rage, and now I'm the one glaring. "You barely said two words to him. How the hell would you even know what he's like?"

Dane's shaking his head before I even finish speaking. "Do I look like I fucking care what he's like? You could be dating a saint who rescues children from burning buildings for a living, and I'd *still* hate his ass," he seethes, panting with fury I don't fully understand.

"You've got some *serious* nerve," I hiss, charging toward him. "You're pissed because Carlos *touched* me? At least I didn't fuck him and pretend that shit didn't happen."

Whatever words he'd been about to speak died on his lips as his frown deepens. "What the hell are you talking about?"

I stare into his eyes and there's genuine confusion in them. I didn't mean to say so much, didn't mean to let on that I *care* so much.

"That bitch was all over you tonight, but I'm supposed to feel guilty Carlos was being friendly? No, fuck that and fuck you."

I attempt to storm off, but he grabs my wrist and I stumble back in his direction, slamming into his chest. My gaze lands on him and his stare darkens.

"You know everything that goes down with Shawna is work shit," he says, his face only inches from mine, anger still smoldering in his eyes.

I was fully prepared to drop it, but since he wants to keep going, I may as well lay it all bare.

"Was taking her to a hotel a few weeks ago work shit, too, Dane?"

You could hear a pin drop. His eyes narrow on me and I'm breathless.

"I saw Pandora's pics of you two after the meet-up at the gallery," I admit.

His eyes stay trained on me and I feel his heart thundering just as wildly as my own.

"You saw that post and your first thought was that I fucked her? Your first thought was that I'd break our agreement over a piece of random ass?"

His tone is scolding, like I'm some wayward child he needs to put in her place. Feeling so small where he still has me drawn to his body, my lashes flutter with his gaze locked on me.

"I saw the pictures. Then you came home well past two in the morning. What the hell else could you—"

"It was an after party," he snaps. "I haven't laid a finger on that girl. Tonight, her hanging on me, that's the most physical contact there's ever been between us. We've never kissed. Hell, we've never even hugged," he confesses and, despite having created numerous scenarios about that night, and despite the mounting rage I've stored up when I think about it... I believe him.

Shit.

"I just... I thought—"

"You thought I settled for *her* because I can't have you."

The statement makes me cower a bit, knowing I really fucked up this time. He releases my arm and I wish I could read his mind. His energy has shifted from anger to something else, but it's still powerful, still overwhelming.

I take several steps back, until my shoulder blades touch the brick wall. My thoughts are a tangled mess of what I *thought* I knew and what I *should have* known. I can't even look at him now, realizing the only one who messed up is me.

Even when I hear his steps coming closer, I don't lift my eyes. Not until his palms press flat against the brick at either side of my face. So close, I'm trapped, *forced* to meet his gaze. I'm caged in, inhaling traces of expensive cologne permeating from his skin, trying to hold my ground.

"I gave you my word, Joss. Didn't I?"

I breathe him in deep, causing my chest to press into his.

"You did, but I—"

"And have I ever lied to you?" he rasps.

I rack my brain for an answer, but don't really need to. "Never."

He draws in air and his eyes lower to the base of my throat, where I imagine he's noticed my racing pulse.

"So, tell me, when the hell are you gonna accept it?"

I blink, swallowing deeply. "Accept what?"

"That the only girl I want to touch, the only one I want to *fuck*... is you?"

He flashes a look to my eyes again and I feel frozen, stunned that he's dared to say so much. I should've known there was an explanation, but my emotions got the best of me, made me crazy, made me jealous, and—

He kisses me rough, parting my lips with his tongue as I moan into his mouth. All I can think about is getting closer. Closer than we are, closer than we've ever been. Both hands slip down his toned torso, moving over the soft fabric of his t-shirt before I lift it to touch his skin. He's raw tonight, still toggling between anger and lust, carrying so much tension in his back when my palms slip around to pull him closer. Heat from his mouth moves to my jaw, then my ear.

"Will you ever stop thinking so damn much and just... take what you want?"

Those words ring inside my head, forcing me to answer the question *"What do I want?"*

He pulls away and I stare up, dazed by the deep green of his eyes.

"All I want is *you*."

He doesn't move after I speak, just keeps me caged there while he gnaws the side of his lips, thinking. "I'm gonna need you to be a bit more specific than that."

My heartrate's nearing critical, but I'm not unclear where this is going. So, despite my nervousness, I slowly push my hand down his stomach, then grip his dick, forming my fingers over the thickness of it.

"I want you. *All...* of you," I add, trying not to lose my breath, aware of what I've just said, aware of the invitation I've just given.

A dark look sweeps over me as Dane scans me from head to toe, like he's seeing me for the first time. He backs off slowly, wetting his lips.

"Your room. Five minutes."

Is it normal to be this scared?

Is it normal to shake so hard my entire bed is trembling and he isn't even here yet?

Deep breath. You'll be fine. It's Dane.

I take the pep talk to heart and breathe deep, but my nerves are still shot. I lit a candle, then blew it out, then lit it again, figuring that it's best if I'm able to see at least a little. That way, I'll know exactly what's happening.

Well, sort of.

I undress, then slipped beneath the covers, hoping that's right. Maybe he would've liked to take my clothes off for me, though.

Don't overthink it. Just go with the flow.

The sound of footsteps down the hall have me sinking deeper beneath the blanket, eyeing the doorway when he steps into the room still clothed, which has me thinking I should've waited to take mine off.

Shit. It's too late.

My gaze follows when he approaches the bed, keeping my eyes trained on him when he slips off his shirt, then unbuttons and unzips his jeans. He pauses to remove a condom from his pocket and places it on the nightstand before removing his pants completely.

I've come to love the sight of him in boxer-briefs, how they squeeze and showcase his best below-the-belt features. I only get to gawk for a second, though, because he removes those next.

I draw in air and wet my lips, realizing that taking all of him in won't be easy as far as first times go, but I trust he'll be gentle.

Candlelight flickers against his skin as he slips beneath the sheet beside me. He's so warm and I love the feel of his nakedness.

He scans me with a look that honestly takes my breath away. All because it says so much without a single word having left his mouth.

"You're so fucking beautiful, you know that?"

My neck and face warm with the compliment. "Thank you."

Like always, he leaves me swooning, hanging on every syllable he speaks.

His lips find my shoulder, kissing down to my breasts where he draws my nipple into his mouth, teasing it with the tip of his tongue. It's a distraction from his hand leaving my stomach, wandering between my thighs. I open for him, letting him explore. The tip of one finger strokes my clit until I moan into the darkness, inspiring him to sink two inside me.

His mouth leaves my nipple to harden in the slight chill of the air and he brings his lips to my ear, still pushing and stirring his fingers.

"You're sure you're ready for this?" he rasps, sounding like he'll die of depravation if I change my mind.

I'm barely coherent when the question registers, but even still, I'm not confused about what I want.

I nod and he exhales against my cheek, gradually sliding his hand from between my thighs. When he reaches for my finger, my eyes are glued to him, focused as the ring I've worn for many years is removed. The gentle clang of the metal dropping to my nightstand when he places it there makes me want this more. Hence the reason my eyes stay trained on him when he positions himself between my legs, and then lowers his mouth to my slit.

I press my head into the mattress, and it all comes rushing back to me, how good this felt last time, how good I imagine it'll feel *every* time. I gladly endure the pleasurable assault from his tongue and lips —flicking, sucking, licking. Dane patiently feasts until I'm drenched, dripping wet and ready to take him in. Only then does he lift to his knees and grabs the condom, rolling it into place. He hovers over me with one hand pressing into the mattress just above my shoulder, the other gripping the base of his dick, slowly caressing my slit with its tip. My entire body buzzes with nervous energy, anticipation as I open my knees further, inviting him in.

Then, finally, we quench a thirst we've suffered through for seven… long… years.

The smooth, blunt head of his dick opens my pussy and I gasp, feeling him sink into me slowly.

"Fuck," he hisses with a long breath. His eyes flutter closed, and I sense him struggling with patience.

My channel barely gives, gripping him tight as he pushes deeper, cautiously giving me more. There's a sudden heaviness in my eyelids, making them want to close as the contrast of intense pleasure and pain takes me over. I swear I feel everything, the thickness of his shaft filling me when he finally pushes to the hilt.

A deep groan rumbles in his chest, but he wrangles it in, quickly refocusing his attention on me.

"Was that okay?"

I nod against the pillow, feeling a tear streak from the corner of my eye and into my hair. He pauses, leaning in to kiss me there, then his lips find mine. There's a feeling radiating from him, and it says more than he's dared to say aloud, but I feel it. Feel *him*.

"I'll take it slow," he promises, whispering against my mouth.

His hips lift and then slowly lower again. He slides his cock in and out, deep like before but at a gentle pace I can manage. We fall into a steady rhythm as the pain subsides. He takes everything away, then gives it all back. Over and over and over again. It isn't long until I'm hooked on the delicious friction mounting between us, addicted to the way his dick fills me, hits every single pleasure point. He's so, so deep, changing his pace as his hips thrust in shallow, grinding pulses between my thighs, rocking into my core. My head pushes into the pillow and that once-controlled look in Dane's eyes is long gone, and a new feeling emerges within me, one that's deeper than any time he's made me come before this.

My nails bite into the skin of his back, but he doesn't even seem fazed. A breathy cry leaves my lips and I'm devoured by the ecstasy of an orgasm so powerful it's not only physical, it's emotional.

The sensation lingers with me, and I savor it, seeing how tension floods Dane's expression next. He pushes into me, and my arms sweep beneath his to hold his back again, feeling his muscles flex and release against my palms. Then, he lets out a pleasure-infused groan that has me biting my own lips, mere seconds before I feel him throbbing inside me as he comes.

Our heavy breaths are synced, showing how our bodies are completely in tune with each other. He presses a kiss to my mouth and I peer up at him, aware of never having felt closer to another human being in my entire life.

"You okay?" he asks quietly, panting a breath away from my lips.

I nod. "Better than okay."

That draws a smile from him, and he pulls out of me slowly before going to the edge of the bed to remove the used latex. He disappears in the bathroom for a second then comes back—still naked, still unshakably beautiful from every possible angle.

At first, I'm focused on his dick, feeling possessive as hell of that shit, possessive of *him*. It's my incessant staring that accounts for why I'm only now aware of the sound of running water.

When I finally tear my eyes away from his package and meet his gaze, Dane's smiling a bit, noticing my curiosity.

"The bath is so you're not sore in the morning. Well, not as sore as you would be without it," he clarifies.

Already, my thighs ache somewhere deep I didn't even realize they could hurt.

There's a lingering look in his eyes that has *me* smiling now. "What?"

His stare flits to my breasts for a second, then he refocuses.

"Just thought I might join you in the tub." His tone is so gentle, so sweet I have to steady my thundering heart as I nod.

"I wouldn't say no," I say coyly, liking this idea of his.

He takes my hand and helps me to my feet, and it hits me that I feel less self-conscious. Even being completely naked in front of him. If tonight has taught me anything at all, it's that, more than anyone, I can trust him.

As far as firsts go, Dane leaves nothing to be desired. Moving forward, let's just say I'm starting to believe we could make this work.

But even if there's no guarantee... I think I'm ready to at least try.

Chapter 32

Joss

The flames of ten candles flicker around the edge of the tub, our only source of light. Water rushes down both arms when Dane's hands grip them, and my head falls back, landing on his shoulder. When my eyes close, there's one thought cycling on repeat.

I think I love him.

Not as a friend. Not simply because he just blew my mind. But because I can't think of anyone I'd rather have hold me like this on the entire planet.

"Did I hurt you?"

With the question, my eyes reopen slowly. "No more than I expected."

His chest swells and lifts my head a bit when he breathes. "I tried to take it easy, but… you felt so damn good," he admits with a small laugh, bringing a smile to my lips. "And in my defense, I've been dreaming about this day since we were twelve, so I was bound to get pretty fucking excited."

"You've legit wanted to fuck me since we were in sixth grade?"

I cast a look over my shoulder when asking, and the expression he wears says it all, setting off a laugh inside me.

"Perv."

"Would you prefer it if I lie? Fuck *yeah* I've wanted you that long."

His arms encircle my ribs, brushing underneath my breasts when he embraces me from behind. His cock presses into the small of my back, but he isn't hard. Bathing together tonight isn't about sex. It's about intimacy.

I settle into him again, feeling weak. If he hadn't made a good point about being sore in the morning, I'd be fast asleep right now. Hopefully, with his warmth beside me.

"I uh… I've been thinking."

The sound of his voice has me alert again. "About what?"

"I want you to know I heard what you said about your parents, and how they remind you of us, and I also want you to know I respect that."

"But?" I ask with a laugh, feeling that coming from a mile away.

"But… I also know what I want. And what I want is you, Joss. Bad."

He's motionless after admitting this, and so am I.

"I think we should be together, and I think you should consider it. Consider *me*," he adds, making my heart skip ten beats.

I hadn't shared what my thoughts were when we finished a while ago. Hadn't told him that my resolve was weakening, so these are simply his true feelings, aligning so perfectly with mine.

My lips part to speak, but before I can even get the words out, a pang of fear strikes, stealing the smidge of courage I'd just gathered. This pang rests heavy on me. It screams that, if we do this, something at some point will go wrong and we'll both regret this decision. Even if it takes months, years. We'll regret it.

My eyes slam shut, then I exhale sharply, trying to rid my thoughts of the negativity. I manage to at least quiet it, although a trace lingers behind.

"I agree with you. We should give it a try."

His hand smooths across my stomach and it's almost scary how natural this feels, how quickly we found our way to this place.

"Just say when," he whispers against my ear.

I smile and breathe him in. "When."

He chuckles quietly against my skin, and the feel of it arouses goosebumps to the surface.

"Then, I guess that's that. It's just you and me."

"Guess it is."

I tilt my head to catch his lips and we share our first kiss as an actual, legitimate couple. It's unrushed, sensual, deep. When we finally pull apart, I feel the tide shifting between us. By owning what was in our hearts, by finally taking what we wanted, we changed our course in a big way, and we've changed it forever.

"I'm calling Rose as soon as I think she's awake to let her know I'm done with the whole Shawna thing."

His statement, while sweet, makes me feel like a complete dick.

"You don't have to do that, Dane. I was being stupid last night and... those weeks I closed you out. I should've known there was more to the story. Or in the very least, I should've come to you and asked. Shawna is work. I get it."

"But you know where we live. Pictures will keep surfacing and—"

"That's been our whole lives," I cut in. "Pictures will surface and people will talk, but we can choose not to let that shit affect us, choose not to let it tear us down."

When I lift his hand away from my torso and kiss it before placing it over my heart, I hope he knows I'm being sincere. The jealousy and rage I felt was due in part to holding in what I felt for him for so damn long. But now that he knows, now that we've moved forward, it won't happen again.

"Joss, I—"

"You don't have to worry about me," I assure him. "Trust me, Rose might be batshit crazy, and Shawna wanting you might tap dance on my last nerve, but... it's working. Your followers have skyrocketed and offers are coming in left and right."

"Maybe, but none of that shit's more important to me than you."

I'm certain that, with his palm splayed flat against my chest, he feels my heart beat wildly when he admits that.

"I know. And I trust you, which is why I'm not asking you to give anything up for me," I explain.

His eyes follow when I shift in his arms until I'm facing him, lifting my thighs to straddle his waist. On instinct, his hands push down my hips until he's gripping my ass. I have his eyes focused right on me, which is good. He needs to hear this.

"I don't just trust you; I *know* you. And despite the rage-fueled, crazy person you saw me turn into tonight, you know that's not me either," I remind him. "I'll be fine. Promise."

He searches my eyes and I let him, wanting him to know I've only spoken the truth to him here. Eventually, he nods, and I believe he sees I'm sincere.

"If anything ever makes you uncomfortable, or if you ever want me to let all the work shit go… just say the word. I'd do that for you."

He makes my stomach flutter with so few words.

"I know and I appreciate that."

A kiss lands on my collar bone and it draws a sigh from me. His arms lift, encircling my back in an embrace.

"Josslyn Grace Francois, you have my word that I'll make you happy. Every damn day," he promises, squeezing me tight, and I swear I hope we stay like this forever.

"There's only one thing wrong with that statement," I say, feeling water pool in my eyes. "You can't make me happy, Dane. Because I already am."

Chapter 33

Joss

You're not breaking his heart. You're simply confirming the point you tried getting across before he came all this way. You can't blame yourself for feeling nothing for him. No more than you can blame yourself that you've fallen for Dane.

One deep breath later and my fist taps the door of Carlos' hotel room. He's expecting me and likely has no idea why I suggested coming to *him* instead of him meeting me at the loft.

The door swings open and I'm terrified to have this conversation, but with his flight leaving early tomorrow morning, it's now or never.

A smile parts his lips when our eyes lock.

"Come in."

I step aside and slip through when he gestures for me to enter, then he closes the door behind me.

As far as awkward conversations go, this one will take the cake, I'm sure. Especially seeing how happy he is that I stopped by.

"You look beautiful." His dark eyes slink down my frame slowly, and back up again.

"Thanks."

"Please, have a seat," he says gesturing toward two armchairs situated near the balcony. Per his request, I lower into one.

He joins me and there's a bit of an awkward vibe that reverberates between us.

"I know you mentioned not wanting to go out, but I thought you might be interested in room service. How does that sound?"

Nervous, I wet my lips and inch toward the edge of my seat.

"Actually, I won't be staying long."

His smile fades and there's this deflated look on his face that makes me sick to my stomach.

"I see."

"I'm only here because I think it's time we talk things over face-to-face."

There have been a lot of open-ended conversations between us, and my hope is that he leaves here with clarity and... closure.

He pushes a hand behind his neck and his face reddens with what I guess to be embarrassment.

"I suppose I misread your call earlier. I didn't realize this would be our last time speaking."

"It's not like that," I rush to say, seeing the hurt I caused despite my best efforts to spare him.

"Then, what's it like?" There isn't an ounce of anger in his tone. Only hurt, confusion.

"We're friends, like we've always been."

I lose his eyes when they focus on the floor now. "There was something more than that between us once. Unless I completely imagined last summer."

"You didn't imagine it," I say. "I've just come to see things differently than I saw them back then."

He nods slowly, seemingly deep in thought.

"So, this is it?"

When his gaze flashes back toward me, that hurt in his expression multiplies. Now, *I'm* the one whose head lowers.

"It is. I tried telling you that before you wasted your time and—"

"I haven't changed my mind, Josslyn. Visiting you could never be a waste of time. Even if I've lost you to someone else."

I peer up again and there's a soft smile on his lips.

"It's him, isn't it."

My stomach twists into a knot, realizing that was a statement and not so much a question. It'd be so easy to lie even if for the sake of letting him down gently, but that doesn't feel right. So, when I nod, I'm at peace with what I'm about to say.

"It's always been him."

Carlos' lips purse together, making it clear that this revelation has wounded him, but I also know this was needed in order for him to let go.

"You're a good, honest woman. May he never forget what a gem he's won."

With that, Carlos stands and offers me his hand. Once I'm on my feet, he draws me into an embrace that can only be described using one word—comforting. He ends it with a kiss to the top of my hair, then releases me.

"I hope to hear from you again one day."

I nod, reassuring him. "You'll hear from me, and I wish you all the best."

As I exit and the door to his room closes again, it isn't lost on me that our parting is bitter-sweet. The bitter—I know severing any semblance of romantic ties with Carlos has cut him deep. The sweet— I believe we'll get through this. I've been honest with him since day one and the payoff is that I believe I've gained a friend for life.

My phone sounds off and, automatically, a smile curves my lips. I assume it's Dane, but when my eyes land on the screen, all traces of that smile fade into nothing. All because of the name that's just caused my heart to sink to my stomach.

Dad: Here are the details for dinner. See you next weekend. We have much to discuss.

Well, shit.

Just when I thought things were finally starting to turn around...

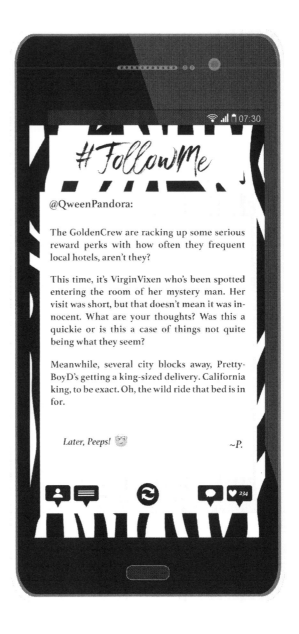

@QweenPandora:

The GoldenCrew are racking up some serious reward perks with how often they frequent local hotels, aren't they?

This time, it's VirginVixen who's been spotted entering the room of her mystery man. Her visit was short, but that doesn't mean it was innocent. What are your thoughts? Was this a quickie or is this a case of things not quite being what they seem?

Meanwhile, several city blocks away, PrettyBoyD's getting a king-sized delivery. California king, to be exact. Oh, the wild ride that bed is in for.

Later, Peeps!   ~*P.*

Chapter 34

Joss

It only seemed right that we christen Dane's new bed tonight, not even five hours after it was delivered. There was no actual sex. Mostly because the mere thought of it reminds me that it feels like someone's set off a box of fireworks between my legs, despite how gentle he was last night. So, we opted to do... other things to quiet our urges. Now, I can barely keep my eyes open.

"You up?" Dane asks in a low voice.

I nod against the pillow. "Not for long."

"Sorry, but I was thinking. What if we get away for a while?"

My brow lifts, wondering if he's really thought that through. "I can lie my way out of cheer practice, but Coach Wells would have your ass if you missed. You know that, right?"

"We'll cross that bridge when we get there. For now, I only care about having *your* ass," he teases, drawing a laugh out of me.

I turn toward his voice, opening my eyes as the tip of his finger traces a line between my breasts. One that started at my throat and eventually ends at my navel.

"Where would we go? We've already got Puerto Rico on the calendar for Spring Break."

He shrugs, resting his palm flat against my stomach. "Just... somewhere no one can find us."

When he smiles, I give his idea some thought, imagining how

incredible it would be to come and go as we please without Pandora spamming the internet with pics of us. Especially seeing as how, against Dane's wishes, I've promised to keep our relationship secret for a bit, for the sake of not interfering with his career. This means we'll have to do a lot of sneaking around, continuing the "just friends" routine no one ever really bought anyway. At least for the next few months.

Honestly, though? I don't exactly hate the sneaking around part. Could be kind of fun.

I turn completely now, kissing him once we're facing each other. "I have a better idea."

He kisses me back, then drags his teeth across my lip. His sex-drunk gaze lands on me and I'm not sure I remember what I was going to say.

"I'm listening," he says, the depth of his low voice making my nipples harden against his chest.

"What if we go back to Louisiana? The whole crew? It'd be nice to see Grandpa Boone again, Aunt Sheryl, maybe even your cousins," I add with a laugh, remembering how wild those five were.

"Seriously?" he asks, smirking a little.

"Seriously. Oh! And what if we wait and go for Christmas again?"

"So, no secret hideaway?"

I shrug. "I'm not saying no, just that if I have to choose one thing, it'd be Christmas in Louisiana. Besides, we could maybe talk your mom into going. With your dad's trial starting soon, she'll probably appreciate the time away by then."

Dane stares—searching my face for something.

"So... I suggest that we plan a romantic getaway, but you rather road-trip it with the *whole* gang, down to Saint Delphine's Parish, where we'll be surrounded by even *more* of my family. Hm."

I'm not sure where he's going with this, so I shrug. "It just sounds fun."

A smile touches his lips before they press to my forehead. "Thank you."

"For what?" I ask, feeling my brow tense with confusion.

"For surprising me with how amazing you are. As a friend. As my girl."

I don't get to respond because my mouth is suddenly busy, welcoming his tongue inside it. Heat from his palm smooths across my ribs to my back, pulling me closer. He's hard again, pressing into my thigh. Not even when his phone rings does he pull away.

"Don't you need to get that?"

His breath moves over my throat when he speaks one word against my skin. "Nope."

I let it go, but then the ringing starts again. "You sure? Might be important."

"*This* is important. Whoever that is, they can fucking wait," he says, lowering to where he's cupped my breast, drawing my nipple into his mouth.

My head shifts against the pillow, feeling myself become so easily aroused. His hand pushes between my thighs and his touch has me reconsidering.

"Ok, so maybe I spoke too soon. A weekend away sounds good," I say breathily, trying to focus long enough to get the words out.

His soft laugh awakens my skin. "I'll set it up first thing in the morning. We'll leave next weekend."

"Good."

My knees part for him and his fingers slip in, but he's careful not to hurt me.

"Right there?" he asks when a pleasure-filled sigh leaves me.

Nodding slowly, I let him know I want him to keep going. I'm starting to think I'll simply never get enough of him.

Like, ever.

"I'm not stopping until I make you come," he exhales against the rim of my ear. "All over my fingers. I fucking love that shit."

And so do I.

Wanting him to know this, I turn to face him, capturing his lips while he plays.

The phone sounds off again on the other side of the mattress, but he ignores it, keeping his promise to finger me until I reach orgasm.

He swallows every single moan that leaves my mouth, only stopping when I'm satisfied. But his lips are still moving with mine, their softness proving to be my undoing.

"If I ever let you leave this bed, it'll be a damn miracle," he says in a low, confident voice.

To some other girl, that threat might seem menacing. But to me, coming from him, I just know he better keep his fucking promise.

As if to only test his patience, the phone sounds off again, but this time it's just a text. Dane's eyes slam shut while he gathers himself, then he reaches across my body to finally answer someone's obviously desperate plea.

He unlocks the screen and doesn't hold it out of view, so I see the message clearly.

Rose: You received an invitation to attend a charity event next weekend and it's not one you'll want to miss. The guestlist is not only the Who's Who of this city, but of the state, the country even. That means plenty of networking opportunities and a chance for you to really show them what they'd be missing out on if they pass on a chance to work with you. I didn't get an answer, so I accepted the offer on my own. I'll send details once I have more information.

Dane: This isn't next weekend, is it?

I know why he asks that particular question. We hadn't made plans to get away more than ten minutes ago. Now, here Rose is trampling all over them with a simple text.

Rose: Yes, and if you think you have something better to do, you don't. This could make or break your career, Dane. Don't screw this up for yourself. Shawna will be there to keep you company and you were also given a handful of additional tickets. I think it'd be a nice touch to bring your brothers along. People love seeing you three together. They can bring dates. Just, please, no stragglers.

Stragglers.

We both know she's talking about me. Hence the reason there's a thick vein throbbing in the center of Dane's forehead right now.

When his fingers move across the screen the next second, my hand lands on his, stopping him from ruining his career. Based on the message he's typing starting out with the words, *"Listen, bitch..."* I'm positive that's exactly what will happen if he continues.

"Hold on," I say quietly, trying to soothe the beast Rose has awakened in him. "You should do this. She said there will be people there that you need to get better acquainted with, so just focus on that part. Not Rose's bullshit. Besides, it just dawned on me that next weekend is bad timing for me to leave the city anyway. My dad's coming, remember? We can postpone for a month and still be in the clear to make it back before school starts."

Dane studies my face and I know what he's likely searching for—a sign that I'm only saying what he wants to hear. But he won't find that. I really do want what's best for him, even if it takes a little bit of sacrifice on my part.

"I fucking hate this shit."

"I know you do. But it'll all be over soon."

His eyes continue to linger on me, then I see the moment the rage starts to slip away. It's enough that he lets me take his phone and respond to Rose for him.

Dane: I'll be there. Thanks.

Chapter 35

Joss

No one should dread a visit from their father, but that's practically all I've done this week—cycling through every worst-case scenario to decide how I should cope when one of them happens.

When, not if.

Now that the night's finally arrived, I'm still unprepared and scared shitless about seeing him for the first time since he and Mom took off.

I tried on at least a dozen dresses, searching for the perfect one. I finally settled on a sleeveless A-line piece that I paired with nude heels. Only, I couldn't quite get my hair right. I fussed over it for nearly an hour before snatching it down from bun after bun, eventually getting so frustrated I let my coils spring free. My dad prefers it *'neat'* and *'tamed',* which is why the plan was to conform, giving us one less thing to argue about, but I couldn't get it to cooperate.

I'd just plugged in my flatiron, deciding to go the route of straightening it a few seconds before Dane came into my room. He approached from behind and joined me at the mirror, showered but not yet dressed for the charity event he committed to. He had no clue about the hell I'd just put myself through, or how insecurity was starting to slip in, but I swear he must've felt it. He touched my hair gently, twirling his finger around a single ringlet while his other hand moved down my torso. I watched in the reflection as four words rolled off his tongue.

"You look fucking amazing."

He sealed the compliment with a slow kiss to the side of my neck and with so few words, convinced me to leave it. Now, as I walk toward the restaurant, I cling to that memory and hold my head high.

Ambient chatter floods my senses when I enter the sheik lounge and instantly begin scanning for my father. Our reservations were for five minutes ago and that man is never late for anything. A hand shoots up across the room and I point him out to the host, who then escorts me to the table. I thank him but keep my eyes on my father as he stands to greet me. To my surprise, I'm brought into a warm hug that matches the kind smile on his face.

"It's wonderful seeing you," he says, still holding me tight.

"You, too. I'm glad you had a safe flight."

He finally releases me and pulls out my chair before returning to his own. He scans me with a look that sends heat rushing up my neck to my face, wondering what scathing thing will leave his mouth as he evaluates my appearance, but his eyes simply lower to his menu.

"We should decide what we'll order first, then we'll talk."

His eyes flash up at me again, and then they're gone, leaving me to wonder why I've been asked here today. The unknown admittedly has me terrified.

"I'll just have whatever you're having."

"Very well then. We'll both have the tomato basil linguine." He lifts his finger into the air to signal a waiter to order, then after he finishes, it's just us again.

"How's Mom? I'm surprised she didn't travel with you."

"When I got called back to the city, she decided to stay behind to oversee the contractors in my absence. She sends her love, though."

I nod, keeping to myself how I'm aware that he's likely the reason she hasn't called. I also keep to myself that she should've gone against his wishes and reached out anyway.

"Well, we could chitchat all day, but you know I've never been one to mince words. I've got something on my heart, and I must say it."

I blink into his stare, breathing deep to calm myself.

"I should begin with an apology," he says, shocking me half to death because my father does not apologize. Like, ever. "I dealt with you harshly the night we spoke in my study and I should have had more compassion. What your mother and I proposed wasn't something we should've expected you'd take lightly."

Still in disbelief, I nod slowly. "And... I accept your apology. Thank you."

He nods once. "I've also regretted interfering with your internship. You worked hard to earn it and I had no right to cost you such a great opportunity."

I don't speak this time. Partly because that has been such a bitter pill to swallow, but also because there's clearly more he'd like to say.

"It's been so strange. Your mother and I have tried hard to settle in, make ourselves at home although our current residence is not permanent, but nothing works. No matter what we do, we still feel a void. And what's missing is you, Josslyn."

My heart nearly shutters to a stop when he admits that. All because he doesn't let his feelings show like this.

"I've missed you both, too, Dad, but I haven't changed my mind about leaving."

And what I don't say is that I'm even *stronger* in my decision to stay in the city now that Dane and I have finally found our way to one another.

My father's gaze lowers, and I can actually sense that his remorse is genuine.

"I've made quite a mess of things. Even before our last argument," he admits.

He doesn't say as much out loud, but I can't help but to wonder if he's referring to his affair. Or should I say *affairs...* plural.

"And while I certainly accept the blame for the current state of our family, I also think it's the reason we should all be together right now. It's the only way we'll heal."

He's being less abrasive about it this time, but his narrative is still the same. He wants me to drop everything and *everyone* to run off to Haiti with them. Only, my narrative hasn't changed either.

"I really appreciate you bringing me here, but more than that, I appreciate that you were able to acknowledge my feelings," I say. "But my mind is still made up, Dad. Cypress Pointe is my home, and I can't just walk away from it."

A long, solemn stare stays trained on me and I know he hates not having the same control over me that he used to, but his anger doesn't flare like it would have in the past. Instead, he releases a breath and I follow his hand when it drops into his pocket, then lands on the table with an envelope between his fingers.

"I was going to wait until after dinner to give you this, but now seems like as good a time as any. Open it," he instructs.

With my pulse racing, my hand meets his at the center of our table, but he doesn't release the envelope as easily as I expect. When I follow his gaze, I understand why. He's fixated on my hand or, rather, my empty finger.

An image flashes in my head, of Dane sliding the ring off before I gave him everything that night. No, my father can't say for sure I'm not wearing it because I'm no longer a virgin, but that look on his face says otherwise.

He seems to realize that I've noticed his observation and he relaxes his grip. I breathe through the spike of anxiety and finally reveal what I've just been given.

"It's a plane voucher. Good for a one-way ticket to your mother and I. Whenever you're ready," he adds. "Although, my hope is that you will join us sooner rather than later."

I'm certain it's killing him not to try ruling me with an iron fist, but I'm pleased I'm being treated like an adult for once.

"I appreciate this, but I won't be using it."

When I try to hand it back, he doesn't accept it.

"It's still yours. In case you change your mind. I'll be in town a few more days and it's my hope that I won't be leaving the city alone. I need you. Your mother needs you," he adds.

We hold one another's gaze for a moment, then I decide to just slip it inside my purse to maintain the civility between us.

"I've only ever meant to do right by you, Josslyn. I hope you know that."

His words have me thinking back to what it must've been like when he got the call from Mom, letting him know their last night together resulted in my conception. They chose to be together, so I'd have both parents in the home, which was what they believed to be the best thing at the time. So, while my father's methods are sometimes heavy-handed and harsh, I do know that I'm loved. And I do know he's made sacrifices with my best interest at heart.

When I nod, acknowledging this, he seems satisfied.

The waiter returns with our meals and the conversation comes to an end. Neither of us truly got what we wanted, but I think we both got more than we expected. While my father hasn't changed his mind about me continuing to live here, he at least seems to realize I'm old enough to make decisions for myself, which is something.

For the first time in a long time, the air between us is clear.

So, if that's true, why the hell do I still feel so shitty?

@QweenPandora:

Look what the cat dragged in. The dog of all dogs has flown back into the city to dine with his lovely daughter, so why does it look like she'd rather be anywhere else but seated at that table?

Perhaps she's still not over all Daddy's dirty little affairs. Or maybe she's just miserable because she'd rather be on the arm of her bestie as he's been spotted leaving their loft wearing a dapper French-blue suit, climbing into a limo that later made it's rounds to gather the other Golden boys, too.

Don't worry VV, I'm pretty sure Daddy's gonna be back on that plane headed God-knows-where soon. Then, you can go back to playing house with PrettyBoyD, uninterrupted.

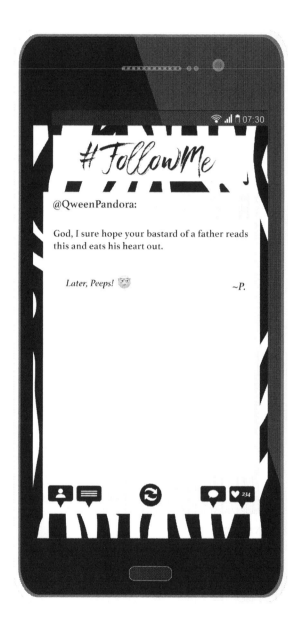

Chapter 36

Joss

Dinner left me emotionally raw, driving home in a daze.

Kicking my shoes off at the door, I head to my room on autopilot, sorting through the menagerie of feelings bogging me down. The onset of a headache signals me that I need to hit reset on this day. I just want to lay in bed and start over in the morning.

I barely get a breath out when the door to the loft opens and shuts. I hear Dane's steps as he moves through the great room, then the knob turns again. Only, he doesn't leave.

"Joss?"

A quick glance in the mirror reveals that my eyes are as red as expected from tearing up. There's no way Dane won't notice, and definitely no chance he'll let it slide.

What the hell is he doing here anyway?

Pandora's last post showed him heading out to the event, but something's brought him back.

"In here," I call out, knowing there's no point in trying to hide.

His steps carry him in the direction of my room, and he doesn't stop until he gets here. Right away, his expression tells me the switch has flipped and he's gone into protective mode. That's ended badly for more than one person over the years. Even dressed to the nines, he looks like he'd commit murder on my behalf.

"What are you doing here?"

He seems only half-focused on my question as he evaluates what he's just walked in on—my teary, red-rimmed eyes I'd just seen in the mirror.

"I forgot the tickets," he answers, but his stare darkens. "Now, tell me what the fuck your dad did *this* time? Then, tell me where I can find him." His voice is low and menacing when he asks.

My hand lands on his chest and I feel his racing heart against my palm. "He didn't do anything. It's not that."

My words relax him a bit, but he's still far from settled.

"What happened?"

Breathing deeply, I take the flight voucher from my purse and hand it to him. Now, since he asked, I'll do my best to explain feelings I haven't even sorted out myself.

"Things went well, but he's still pressuring me to go with them."

Dane's quiet when he glances up from the slip I gave him, and I don't miss that look in his eyes. It's almost as if he feels physical pain, maybe at the thought of me leaving.

"And... are you considering it?"

Hearing his question, tension spreads across my brow. "Do you even need to ask? Of course not!"

When I reach for his hands, he squeezes mine.

"This doesn't change anything, the wounds are still just a little fresh, you know?"

"I get it," he says, and I know he does. "If it helps, I booked our trip. I'm taking you away from all the bullshit in just a few weeks."

I do feel relieved knowing there's something to look forward to, but I'm still a bit bummed. Dane does that thing where he studies my face, reading me, then he presses a kiss to the center of my forehead.

"Know what? Change of plans," he says. "Put your heels back on. You're coming out with me tonight."

A laugh leaves me. "You're kidding, right? Weren't you expressly warned about bringing stragglers?" I tease, pushing a tear from my cheek.

"Fuck Rose and anyone else who doesn't like it. I'm not leaving my girl home alone, feeling like shit."

There's a wild look in his eyes and it's just enough to tempt me.

"Dane, I don't want to ruin anything. I—"

"The only thing that can ruin tonight is you making me go to this bullshit event without you."

He casts this wickedly sexy look down on me and I swear he's got magic behind those green eyes.

When I roll mine with a sigh, he likely already knows what I'll say.

"Okay. I'll go."

One corner of his mouth curves up with a smile and he leads me toward the door. With him holding my hand for balance, I step back into my shoes.

"Ready."

He smiles at my lack of enthusiasm, then holds out his arm for me to take. "It'll be fun."

Famous last words.

"What kind of event is this anyway?"

Dane shrugs, hearing my question. "It's a charity auction, I think, but… who gives a fuck? We're doing our own thing tonight."

He grins and I have no idea what that means, or what trouble he'll face when Rose finds out he's bailing, but there's something to be said about Dane. Once his mind is made up, there's no changing it.

Chapter 37

Joss

Seeing my dad messed with my head a bit, even though the visit was more civil than expected. But Dane knew exactly what I needed, knew that being with friends would burn away the sadness. He brought me to the one public space where we always feel safe and welcome—Dusty's Diner.

Dusty puts up with how loud we are and lets us in on nights like this, long after he's closed simply because he knows we need a haven. His restaurant is the only public place we can draw the blinds and not worry about the things we do and say making it into Pandora's posts.

And to top it all off, we're allowed to have our fill of whatever dessert we want at no charge. Although, the boys always sneak a sizable tip near the back grill, more than covering our tab.

I scan our crew—the Golden boys in expensive, tailored suits, Blue and me in dresses and heels, stuffing our faces with apple pie and ice cream. We're tightly packed into a booth, me wedged between Dane and Sterling with West and Blue across the table. It's only us in here, so we're loud and free and, before long, I feel like nothing even happened tonight. That's the power of friendship, I guess.

I'm grateful we ended up here instead of some stuffy auction, surrounded by snobs and pretentious businessmen. For Dane, I would've endured it, but this is *so* much better. The loud laugh he belts out at the end of the batshit crazy story Sterling just told tells me that he agrees.

A knock hits the glass door and it's entirely possible some of Pandora's minions spotted us as we headed in, finally working up the nerve to get a closer look.

Blue hops up from her seat with West's eyes glued to her ass, of course. "That's Jules, Lexi, and Dez. I told them to meet us here."

She bounds toward the entrance while the rest of us hang back, finishing up dessert.

"So, Dane and I were thinking. What if we do Christmas in Louisiana again?" I dip the spoon back in my ice cream dish after asking.

"What's that about Louisiana?" Blue chimes in when she returns with the other three girls trailing right behind her.

"They want to head back to the Bayou." The faint smile on West's face when he explains tells me he's already in.

"Am I invited? I was so bummed I didn't get to go last time," Jules says before pulling up a chair from a nearby table.

Dane laughs as he nods. "*Anyone* who wants to go is free to do so. Grandpa Boone loves having guests to entertain. The interesting part will be keeping our cousins from humping your legs like dogs in heat once they find out we're bringing girls. Just ask Blue and Joss."

"He isn't lying, but the one who can *truly* attest to that is my sister."

None of us miss the tension in Blues expression after she speaks. Her sister, Scarlett, was like fresh meat to the boys when we last visited. Well, to one of them in particular—Linden.

"Would you bring her this time?" There's a smirk on West's lips when he asks.

"Possibly. Maybe," Blue wavers with a shrug. "All I know is I'm getting her fitted for a chastity belt first if I do."

"Nah, no need. All it'd take is one of us scaring the shit out of Linden one good time and I guarantee he wouldn't be a problem," Sterling offers, drawing a laugh out of everyone.

"As much as I'd love to see that, I'm pretty sure that'd just make Scar even *more* interested," Blue reasons.

She probably isn't wrong.

"So, who's down?" All eyes are on me and I'm not surprised when all hands shoot up into the air, making our plan official. Come December, we'll be back in the Bayou and away from Pandora and all the other bullshit that happens in this city.

Speaking of, all our phones sound off at the exact same time. No question what the notification will be.

"Bitch doesn't waste any time, does she?" I don't think any of us miss the air of frustration in Sterling's voice when he asks.

Pandora's just given away our crew's location, with a well-timed pic of Dane and I heading into the building last, with his hand dangerously close to my ass as we entered.

Lexi chuckles a bit. "Well, damn. If half the city didn't already think you two were a thing, they sure as shit will now!"

Her teasing has the rest of the gang laughing, too, but I feel my face turning redder by the second. I suppose I should've just laughed it off, because now Blue and Jules are giving me *the look*.

"Something you two aren't telling us?" she asks. I guess Dane's lack of denial in response to Lexi's accusation didn't help much either.

"Well?" Jules' eyes are alight with hope, intrigue.

My eyes flit to Dane and he clearly doesn't care who knows, so it's on me to decide whether I'm ready to let the cat out of the bag among friends.

"It's a new development," I confess, and before I can even elaborate, the girls are squealing and asking all kinds of invasive questions.

How'd it happen?

Since when?

Does this mean Pandora can't call you Virgin Vixen anymore?

Are you going to give us the details?

Dane's smile grows when he glances down on me, probably loving how uncomfortable I am right now.

"It happened after the party last weekend," I reveal.

"You've been holding out on me for an entire week?" Blue tries to glare at me when asking, but she's way too excited for it to seem threatening.

"We decided it'd be best to keep it on the hush. You know, because of Dane's work with Rose."

"*You* decided it'd be best," he adds with a smirk.

"Well, yeah... It's just that he's worked so hard, I didn't want *us* to get in the way of that."

"Hell, I'd keep that shit secret under *any* circumstances," Dez chimes in with a laugh. "Pandora doesn't seem to believe anything involving you five is sacred."

"Fucking tell me about it," Sterling grumbles.

"Well, I'm over the moon for you two. This is awesome news, and my lips are sealed," Jules says with a huge grin.

"Same."

"Won't breathe a word about it to anyone."

Lexi and Dez make their promises in unison. As two of the newest additions to our group, they're loyalty still has yet to be proven, but they've kind of been grandfathered in due to our trust in Blue.

"So?"

My eyes flit toward Sterling when he says that one word. "So... what?"

He shoots me a *cut-the-bullshit* look. "You're gonna just leave us all hanging?"

I'm still not sure what he means, but when he leans in to whisper, I know it's about to be something I probably don't want to answer.

"Aren't you gonna tell us if you fucked him yet?"

"Sterling!" I shove him away with a laugh. Thank God he was at least discreet enough not to ask out loud in front of everyone.

"I'll take that as a yes." He nods at Dane after that, in such a way that the gesture conveys congratulations.

Sick freak.

"Anyway, we—"

I fall silent when Dane's phone goes off with a text. "Shit. It's Rose."

"Ignore her ass," West says with a laugh.

"That'd be easier if she weren't out in the parking lot right now."

No sooner than those words leave Dane's mouth is there another knock at the door, and *this* time, I'm positive the person on the other side is no friend.

So much for this being a safe space.

"She saw Pandora's post and wants to talk," he says in a clipped tone, motioning for Sterling to shove out of our side of the booth. I follow right behind him, giving Dane room to stand.

"Is everything okay?" I sound nervous because, shit, I *am* nervous. Something told me there'd be drama when he didn't show to the event, but I didn't realize it'd catch up to us so soon.

The kiss Dane presses to my forehead is meant to calm me down, but it doesn't work. If the knot in my gut is any indication, our night is about to take one hell of a turn.

Dane

The door closes behind me and I lay eyes on Rose—pacing in a parking space, glaring once she finally meets my gaze. I swear there's steam rolling off the top of her head, fire in her eyes. I've seen her mad before, but never *this* pissed. Now, lucky me gets to feel her wrath.

Great.

Can't fucking wait.

"Oh, well how nice of you to join me after I've spent the entire night wondering where the hell you've been." She stops with the pacing and perches both fists on her hips.

"Something came up," I explain with a sigh. "Didn't bother calling because I knew you wouldn't understand."

I'm aware that my response will only make matters worse, but it's the only answer she's owed.

"You're damn *right* I don't understand!" she snaps. "Do you have any idea the hell I went through to get you an invitation to that auction? Or any idea how unprofessional it made me look after making arrangements for you to meet some very important people in attendance? And not to mention Shawna! She was dateless and spent most of the night making excuses for your absence, only for pictures to surface of you with your hand on some other girl's ass."

"I—"

"No, you don't get to speak yet," she hisses, maybe a couple feet away now. "I put my neck out on the line for you, Dane. But not just tonight. I've done this on *many* occasions, and I'm convinced you think this is all one big joke—your life, your career, your *future*."

Her steps carry her away from me when she starts pacing again, only to come right back to get in my face a second time.

"And what are you gaining from any of this? A chance to fool around with a girl you'll forget about the second a pair of nice tits in heels walks past?"

I shove both hands inside my pockets and don't speak right away. I'd prefer to weigh my words, evaluate the situation, preserve my anger. When I let it run rampant, I see red, and then shit gets ugly.

Fast.

"If you keep screwing this shit up, you're gonna wake up one day and realize she was never fucking worth it. And what's worse is, you'll realize she was never even on your damn level," she adds.

She moves in closer, keeping her eyes trained on me. Meanwhile, I'm trying to figure out who the fuck this bitch thinks she is.

"You've got a bright, *bright* future ahead of you, but I get scared for you, Dane. Because sometimes, I think you're gonna piss it all away for what feels right *today*." The stern look in her eyes softens a bit as she exhales. "You wouldn't be the first to regret putting temporary emotion before a promising career. I've seen it before and I hope it doesn't come to this, but... I can't shake the feeling that it'll take one hell of a wakeup call to help you get your shit together."

She steps away and her eyes never leave me. Since day one, she thought she had me pegged, thought my main objective in life was to amass some unholy fortune, but she missed that that's not really me. Yeah, I'm driven and have goals, but not to the point of risking it all to climb the ladder. My father was that guy and his greed tore our family to shreds. Which is why I vowed a long time ago to be deeper than that, to have more integrity than that.

"Rose, I agreed to bring you on board to oversee my career. Not to run my entire fucking life," I snap, losing my cool despite trying to reel it in.

"The two are one in the same," she insists, "and the fact that you don't realize that means you still have so, *so* much to learn."

"Or maybe it means that, until now, you've only worked with a bunch of assholes whose grand plan is to work their lives away, only to end up rich and alone when all is said and done."

My words seem to shock her into silence for the first damn time ever. I'll take the win, *and* the opportunity to get a few things off my chest.

"I'd like to be the type of guy who doesn't measure his worth by what's in his bank account. And I'm aware that this means I'll miss an opportunity here and there in order to be around for my family, but I'm willing to accept that."

"Like hell you will," she scoffs. "How soon you forget all I've done for you, Dane. How soon you forget that you wouldn't have *half* the success you've found if it wasn't for me. You fucking owe me! Do you really think I'll just let you mess this all up for me? For Shawna? No. *Hell* no."

Lowering my head, I fight the urge to blow up again, feeling the rush of blood behind my ears, feeling both hands tremble as I suppress my rage. All that keeps me from acting on it is knowing Joss and the others are waiting inside. Rose won't change my mind tonight, or ever for that matter. So, I decide to make this quick.

"Thanks for making this shit so much easier," I say. "Consider our work together done."

An incredulous laugh leaves her, and she stares, completely thrown off by what I just said. For so long, she's had me by the balls, unable to move left or right without her say so, but those days are gone. I'm determined to live my life the way I want to live it, and a huge part of my life includes Joss.

"Mark my words—you will regret this decision," she yells as I walk away. "Your father's trial starts soon. You'll need me more than ever then. Everything will fall apart without me."

I don't have any words for her, and I feel her desperation growing with the space between us.

"Don't walk away from me! We're not done here!"

Her quick footsteps approach from behind, but I don't turn.

"Because I know how incredibly pigheaded you can be, I'll give you until noon tomorrow to rethink this. After that, you have my word that I'll rain down hell on your entire fucking world, Dane Golden. I have power you can't imagine, power to make or break you, you little shit. Cross me and you'll see just how cold it is out there alone."

I slip back into the diner with Rose still shouting at my back, and when I lock the door behind me, I feel nothing but relief. I've finally closed this wicked cunt out of my life.

Literally.

Figuratively.

Good riddance, bitch.

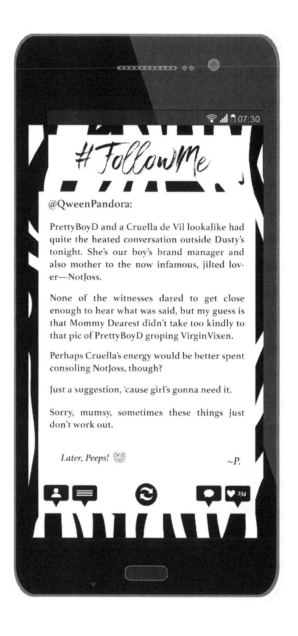

@QweenPandora:

PrettyBoyD and a Cruella de Vil lookalike had quite the heated conversation outside Dusty's tonight. She's our boy's brand manager and also mother to the now infamous, jilted lover—NotJoss.

None of the witnesses dared to get close enough to hear what was said, but my guess is that Mommy Dearest didn't take too kindly to that pic of PrettyBoyD groping VirginVixen.

Perhaps Cruella's energy would be better spent consoling NotJoss, though?

Just a suggestion, 'cause girl's gonna need it.

Sorry, mumsy, sometimes these things just don't work out.

Later, Peeps!   ~P.

Chapter 38

Joss

A smile curves my mouth having read Pandora's post at least 4 times now. Knew I called Rose's Cruella vibe right.

Dane's keys jingle when he unlocks the door to the loft, and I follow him inside. He's been quiet since his chat with Rose, leaving me to wonder how the conversation went. He hasn't said much, which I'm guessing means *she* said a lot.

He waits and offers his hand while I lower out of my heels. Then, we walk through the darkness instead of turning on lights. With our fingers laced, our steps echo in the hallway and I expect him to stop outside my door. Only, he doesn't. Instead, I'm led toward *his* room and he doesn't release me until I'm standing near the bed, watching his silhouette as he slips out of his suit jacket, then loosens his tie.

"Do you want to talk about what happened?"

He thinks for a moment, then shakes his head, filling *mine* with curiosity.

Leaning close, heat from his mouth warms my neck when he answers. "No. The only thing I want… is to fuck you." The rawness of his voice tells of his anger.

What the hell did Rose say to him?

He slides the straps of my dress down both shoulders. The motion is rough, jerking my body toward his as he shoves the fabric from my torso to my hips. It falls to my calves and I step out of it. His hands grip my ribs and I know I'm right about him being in rare form tonight. He's raw, emotionally undone and... I don't hate what it's bringing out in him.

His fingers slip inside my underwear, then inside *me,* awakening my clit with his touch. He strokes it in deliciously soft swirls, the gentleness contrasting the tension in his shoulders as I clutch them.

My nipples harden against the lace of my bra where they're pressed against his chest. His mouth finally makes its way to mine and devours me with a deep kiss steeped in passion, frustration, need. I feel his dick against my thigh, getting harder by the second, straining against the fabric of his pants.

He's wound so tightly, and I want to help with that, want to *ease* that.

I feel his stare on me through the darkness when I pull away, dropping my hands to his zipper. His eyes stay locked on me as I push the waistband down his rock-hard thighs, and then lower to the floor with them, taking his boxers with me.

At the feel of the smooth head of his cock pushing between my lips, he draws in a sharp breath. Thick, ridged veins caress my tongue when I take in more. He's so fucking big, which is why I'm careful not to gag, but the sounds leaving his mouth make it more than clear I'm doing this right.

"Fuck, Joss."

His fingers twist loosely into my hair with those words, prompting mine to grip the firmness of his thighs. I suck faster and take him in just a little deeper. Seeing how much this turns him on has me so, so wet for him. Phantom traces of pleasure from the last time we fucked makes my walls clench the emptiness where his dick should be. I'm torn between wanting him to come like *this* and wanting him to fuck me again.

But when it comes down to it, there's really no competition.

I'm off my knees and slipping my panties down both hips after deciding. He quickly undoes my bra and tosses it across the room while I climb onto the bed. One perfectly toned arm stretches toward the nightstand drawer and I stare as he removes a condom from the wrapper. Once he rolls it into place, my knees part for him.

He enters with less caution than before—a little rough, impatient —and I feel the burn, the maddening friction I didn't know I missed so badly until now. He cranes his neck down until his mouth meets mine and I suck his tongue, gripping the rolling hills of his back with both hands.

"You're fucking *mine*."

He growls those words against my lips, power-driving his hips between my legs, going so deep I swear he's a part of me. When I whimper, letting my lips graze his shoulder, I couldn't agree with him more.

"I mean that shit," he rasps. "Not just now. You've always been mine. And you always will be."

His promise moves over me like it has life coursing through each and every syllable.

"I need to hear you agree. Tell me you understand," he demands. "Tell me you'll never give this pussy to anyone but me." His voice is strained, showing signs that he's nearing his own release.

With the sweet tension of an orgasm building in my core, it takes a second to find words.

"I swear," I finally answer, feeling my eyes roll back as my walls clench around his dick.

"You swear *what?*" The deep tone of his voice when asking sounds so menacing, making me even wetter.

"I swear you'll be the only one. Always."

My chest moves with rapid breaths, feeling the weight of what's just been promised. Mostly, because Dane's just made it clear that I'm all he wants.

"Good," he says, staring down on me in the darkness, "because I'm in love with you."

Heat moves through my limbs and warms my face as I let that sink in. I felt it before now, but never imagined he was ready to admit it.

I'm unable to get actual words out, but choose to show him

instead, letting him feel that the emotion between us is one-hundred-percent mutual.

My fingers move to the back of his neck and I lift my head from the pillow to kiss him. Our tongues move together slowly and the tension I managed to stave off before now catches up with me and I moan into our kiss. When his hips pump harder, slamming into me as a throaty grunt rumbles inside his chest, I feel the sudden rush of heat as his cum fills the condom.

We both go still but cling to one another, his entire body shuddering from the powerful release. I'm still in a daze, hearing his words echo on repeat in my thoughts.

He's in love with me.

We're in love with each other.

Slowly, he pulls out and slips to my side, but the connection between us is still so strong, like nothing I've ever felt. He moves to the edge of the mattress and lets his feet touch the floor while I stare at the ceiling, trying to steady my breath *and* my heart. It's so liberating to no longer be in denial about my feelings for him.

"I've been so afraid to love you," I admit, placing my hand on his back as he draws in a deep surge of air. "It's one of those things I've always known, always *felt*, but the idea of really letting myself own it... I guess I let myself believe it'd come with some sort of tragedy attached. Some disaster that would tear us apart."

He's quiet, letting me get my thoughts out.

"We're not my parents. You said that and you were right. We're not tragic or doomed. We're just us—Dane and Joss," I say with a smile.

My eyes flash toward him when he doesn't respond, doesn't even move.

"Um, you listening?" I ask, sitting up on my elbows to see him better. There's still no answer, just silence. "Dane..."

He turns, but he moves slowly, finally meeting my gaze after several seconds. Immediately, I know something isn't right. Before he even says a word.

"What is it? What's wrong?"

"I—" His voice trails off and he draws in a breath to start over.

Then, with so few words, he sends me into a spiral. "...The condom broke."

Wrecked.

That short, simple sentence completely wrecks me. In fact, I break into a full sweat and sit up straighter in his bed.

"What? How? I don't—"

I'm panicking and can't even wrap my head around what he's just told me.

"It's okay," he says, trying to calm me down. "I can run to the drug store. They have a pill that—"

His words cut off when I stand and dash toward the bathroom. The second the door closes behind me, everything I'd just confessed comes rushing back, taunting me for being so fucking naïve, so careless.

We're not tragic. We're not my parents. We're not doomed.

But right now, in this moment, with my heart pounding inside my chest and Dane pounding on the other side of the door... it feels like we might be all those things.

Chapter 39

Dane

"She text you back?"

I snap out of a daze and glance toward West when he emerges from the fieldhouse, hiking his practice bag higher on his shoulder. To my surprise, both my brothers are taking the shitshow from last night seriously. There hasn't been a single joke.

Not yet anyway.

I shake my head. "Nope. Nothing. I heard her moving around inside her room this morning, on my way here for practice, but I didn't bother her. If she wanted to talk, she would've opened the door last night."

Thinking about it, everything, I feel sick to my stomach.

"Did she say anything when she left the bathroom and went to bed?"

I shake my head again. "I didn't wait around to see. After a few hours of not getting any response, I walked to the drugstore, got that pill, then set the bag on her bed."

West's brow quirks. "And... you're sure no one shared that shit with Pandora?"

"Honestly, I was so fucked up at the time, I didn't even think about it. Guess the only thing to do at this point is pray she has mercy if someone did. Like before," I add, remembering how not so long ago,

Pandora withheld a few details to cover our crew while our father was still on the streets, raising hell.

"Yeah, maybe," he concludes.

Sterling finally joins us, and we head toward the parking lot slowly. My damn head's still in the clouds, trying to process everything.

"Any clue how it happened?"

I glance toward Sterling after he asks. "How what happened?"

"How the condom broke. It's never happened to me."

Taking a breath, I shrug. "Beats the hell out of me. Just one of those things, I guess."

"What'd you do, run out of Magnums and tried to use a regular one?" There's a laugh in West's voice that has me shaking my head.

"No, dipshit. I'm not an idiot."

"Well, at least you *tried* to prevent this. My dumb ass thought I was invincible and raw-dogged it, which landed me knee-deep in the Casey situation," West adds.

The situation he speaks of happened years ago and isn't one we talk about often. But with all the shit swirling around inside my head, I'd forgotten all about it.

"So, do you think Joss took the pill?" Sterling asks.

"Probably," I answer, but then backpedal. "Fuck if I know."

He thinks for a moment, then hits me with another question. "If she didn't and... you know... what's your next move?"

I try to imagine it, going through that scenario with Joss.

"You mean aside from being scared shitless?" I ask with a short laugh. "I guess once the shock wore off, I'd man up and get shit done, step up for her. *With* her," I add. "For some reason, because it's Joss... it doesn't feel like it'd be the end of the world. Because it's her, I know we'd find a way to be okay."

We all fall silent when a group passes by, knowing how info flows through this city like water if we're not careful.

"Oh, Rose is gonna *love* this," West says, the statement dripping with sarcasm, but she hadn't even come to mind.

"Doesn't matter what she thinks. I fired her ass last night. I swear she hexed me, though. Damn witch."

My brothers run out of things to say, because there isn't much *to* say. Not to them, anyway. The one I need to be having this conversation with won't even talk to me, but that has to change tonight.

"You're taking off?"

I nod, doubling back toward my car, instead of toward West's truck like we planned. "Yeah, just need to figure shit out. I'll catch up with you guys later."

Hanging with them for a bit would help keep my mind off things, but that's the opposite of what I need right now. I need to focus, figure out what to say to Joss once I do finally convince her to talk.

Because whether she likes it or not, I won't let her shut me out again.

I drove around all day, making myself scarce. Hopefully, it gave her time to think and calm down.

I let out a breath as I unlock the door to the loft, a little surprised to find it's completely dark inside. There isn't even a light coming from Joss' bedroom, which is unexpected. I thought she'd be hiding out in there, hunkering down until she's ready to face me.

I drop my practice bag, lock up, then walk that way, to where I hoped to find her. But when I flip the light switch, it's like hitting a brick wall. Her bed's made and everything's in place as usual, but... something feels off. For some reason, my first thought is to check the dresser and what I find there has my heart racing.

Or rather, what I *don't* find there has it racing.

She's gone. The plane ticket's gone.

I'm in a full panic now, dropping down to the edge of her bed to scroll Pandora's posts. If anyone knows where she's gone, it'd be her. I sift through image after image and nothing.

"Fuck!"

The one time I need this bitch to have information, she fails.

I'm on my feet again and storming toward the door with absolutely no plan. If Joss *did* leave, there's no telling how long she's been gone, but if she got on that plane...

Don't think like that. You can't possibly know she left.

But... I also know what it looks like.

I feel myself coming undone, losing my shit. I have to find her, and the odds are better if I have help. The thought of us falling apart over this, over something that was completely out of my control, has my head spinning with disbelief.

As hard as I try *not* to think about it, all that's cycling in my head is how she believed we were doomed from the start, destined for disaster. My biggest fear in this relationship is proving her right, and, despite what I keep telling myself, I'm not convinced this isn't that.

One big fucking disaster.

Chapter 40

Dane

"She's gone," I growl. "She left and took the fucking plane ticket with her."

I'm aware of how insane I look, how unhinged I sound, but trust me—the hurricane raging on the inside definitely matches the outward chaos.

Blue steps aside and I storm into the foyer. "Slow down. Who's gone? Joss? And what plane ticket?"

I can't even answer, feeling like I'll drown in the thoughts that fly at me if I open my mouth to speak.

"Did you two get into a fight?"

"She'd have to be speaking to me for that to happen," I seethe. "You haven't heard from her? She hasn't tried to call or text?"

Blue shakes her head. "No, the last time we spoke was at the diner last night."

Just fucking great.

"Hang on," she says. "Just… wait here. I'll go grab West."

I pace across the marble tile while she races out to the patio, and all I can think about are the many ways I could've handled this differently. *Should* have handled this differently. All of which would result in Joss still being here, instead of on a plane flying halfway across the world tonight.

Shit. I can't believe she left.

"What happened?"

I turn to the sound of West's voice as he dries his hair with a towel. His damp swim trunks and the scent of chlorine make it clear why I didn't get an answer when I tried calling on my way over.

"I drove around most of the day, trying to get my thoughts together. Then, when I went home to see if she was ready to talk, she'd taken off. Took the ticket her dad bought her, too."

I feel that swell of rage on the inside again, but exhale to quench it.

"Ok, calm down. We'll find her," West says, but I'm not buying it. He didn't see the flash of panic on Joss's face last night.

She was already so afraid to give us a try, so afraid we'd turn out like her parents, then... that fucking condom broke. The Joss I know retreats when she's scared, and that's what this feels like—her retreating, running from me because it's easier than facing me. Easier than facing what happened last night.

My phone rings and I scramble to pull it from my pocket. Seeing it's only Sterling returning my call, my heart sinks a little.

"Everything cool? Looks like I missed about ten calls from—"

"Have you seen or heard from Joss?" I cut in, skipping a greeting altogether.

"No. Why? Should I have?"

"Shit."

"What the fuck happened?"

"Just come to Bellvue," I answer, hanging up right after.

"He hasn't heard anything either?" Blue asks, unable to hide the traces of panic in her tone.

"No. I'm guessing she wanted to make a clean break, get out of here before any of us could talk her out of it."

I go back to pacing because it's the only thing I can do to keep from going off the deep end.

Of all the ways for this to have gone, this definitely wasn't how I imagined it. Last night was a first for me. I'd never told *any* girl I love her, and the moment I let my guard down, shit blows up in my face.

"I'll get dressed while we wait for Sterling, then we can hit up some of the places she could've gone," is West's suggestion.

I don't respond, already thinking the worst.

"You don't know that she left, man. We could still find her," he adds.

I hear him but that doesn't set my mind at ease. Problem is, we don't know that she *didn't* leave.

He heads upstairs and I force myself to lean against the wall, force myself to breathe.

"I'll call around and see if I can find what hotel her dad's staying in. Maybe she went to see him," Blue says, turning to go toward the kitchen, already scrolling through her phone.

I hear Sterling's engine outside and exhale, trying to think positively. *Failing* to think positively. My nerves are fried, so within a few seconds, I'm back to pacing, worrying. I envision us racing through the city's streets half the night and still coming up empty. I know one thing, though, that won't stop me from trying. I'd move heaven and Earth for that girl. And if she *did* get on a plane tonight, I've already made up my mind that tracking her down is my next move. Hence the reason I reach for my phone and get started looking up flights to Haiti.

No matter how far she goes, no matter how pissed or scared she is, I meant what I said—she's mine.

That means through the good and the bad, whether she's right or wrong, I'll never let her go.

Sterling knocks and I rush to the door, pulling it open, ready to repeat the same information I'd just given West and Blue, but...

The wind is knocked out of me when my eyes land on a face that isn't my brother's. Before I can even form words, I grab Joss tight, squeezing as the fear I felt over losing her begins to fade.

"I thought you fucking left." I breathe into her hair as she clings to me, pressing her palms to my back.

"What? Why would I leave?" she asks with an emotion-laden laugh.

"You wouldn't talk last night, then when I got back to the loft you were gone, the ticket was gone, I just... it doesn't fucking matter."

My arms tighten around her when I give up trying to explain.

"I'm sorry about last night," she says against my ear. "I freaked out and just needed to process and… I'm sorry," she repeats.

"You don't have to apologize. I'm just glad you're here."

She nods and my eyes fall closed.

"Oh, thank God. You're okay," Blue says with a sigh of relief when she returns to the foyer.

I finally release Joss from my arms, but she clings to my hand. "I didn't mean to scare anyone. There was just something I needed to take care of."

"Listen, as long as you're fine, you don't need to explain," Blue adds, rubbing Joss' shoulder.

"Pandora said Dane was spotted racing to Bellvue, then that Sterling was seen doing the same, so I came straight over."

Our gazes lock when she says that, because I know for a fact that Pandora hasn't posted in over an hour. I know because I've been obsessively checking and refreshing, hoping to find some clue as to where Joss had gone.

"Mind if we talk?" she asks.

I nod and Blue points us toward the patio, so Joss and I head there. She drops down onto a lounger while I close the door behind us, and then join her near the pool.

Her dark stare pans the surface of the water while she thinks, and I feel her sadness without her having said a word yet.

"We've got so many memories out here—midnight swims that turned into sleepovers, parties, afterparties," she adds with a quiet laugh. "We've been at this friendship thing a long time."

I nod, agreeing. "We have, and I think I even knew back then that you're the best thing that's ever happened to me."

She swipes a tear from her cheek, and it takes everything in me not to hold her again, crowd her.

"I went to see my dad. That's why the ticket was gone," she reveals. "I gave it back and let him know I won't be using it. Now or ever."

Hearing those words is all my heart needed to settle down completely. Her eyes meet mine and I don't miss the unshed tears there.

"You're okay?"

Sniffling, she nods. "I am now," she says. "Got a message this evening. From Pandora, of all people. She sent *several* messages, actually. The last of which is how I knew to find you here."

She swipes at the tears but seems more self-assured than sad. Like she's found new strength through whatever happened tonight while we were apart.

"So… what did the messages say?"

Joss breathes deep, her skin glowing with the turquoise light that shines up from the pool.

"It wasn't so much what she said, but what she showed me."

I wait while she takes her phone from her pocket, then scrolls, turning the screen toward me when she finds what she searched for. I'm not entirely sure what I'm looking at.

"It's you, right? An old pic?"

She laughs, but it never quite reaches her eyes. "Look again."

I take the phone this time, examining it more closely. It's a girl with skin the same shade of warm brown as Joss, the same dark ringlets, the same dark eyes, but… there are slight differences. The point of her chin, the shape of her brow, a tiny mole above her lip.

My gaze narrows as I continue to study the pic, trying to make sense of what I'm seeing.

"Her name's Peyton, she's almost fifteen, and… she's my half-sister."

I lower the phone to stare at Joss.

"That's the exact look I had on my face when Pandora first reached out," she says. "This was sent to her a little after noon, then she sent it to *me.* Not sure if she was on the fence about making it public, but I guess she decided against that."

"Shit, I—I'm not even sure what to say. Did your dad know before tonight?"

She sighs when I ask.

"He did and, while that fact is super fucked up all on its own, it's not the worst part. He got a threat last month, from someone who knew he and Mom had left the country and that I stayed behind. They said they'd expose his secret if he didn't convince me to leave the city, too. Apparently, he had until summer's end to get the job done. So, there was no business he needed to handle here. Only this, getting me to leave to protect himself."

I don't miss that the solemn undertone of her voice intensifies with this realization. She's hurt, and rightly so.

"I suppose it makes sense that he was so different, so much kinder than usual. He thought he could manipulate me into following him. But the jokes on him, I guess. Whoever's blackmailing him clearly decided to pull the trigger early. He likely pissed them off somehow."

Or... I pissed them off somehow.

My head spins as pieces begin to fall into place. I hate that I'm thinking what I'm thinking, but... there's someone who fits the bill. Someone with motive, someone who's made threats, someone who would've been inspired to pull the proverbial trigger today.

Around noon...

I hold on to that thought, keeping it to myself for now. I'll confirm my suspicion soon enough. But right now, Joss is here and she needs me, so I focus on that.

"You're really okay, though?"

Her shoulders lift with a shrug and she breathes deep. "Mostly. I just told him I need space for a while, because I didn't have the energy to argue since I didn't exactly sleep well last night."

My gaze follows hers out to the water and I don't have to wonder why she tossed and turned. Mostly, because I did the same until the sun came up.

"I fucking suck," she says with a small laugh. "We should've talked shit out last night, but I ran. I ran and—"

"You were scared."

"Yeah, but I'm sure you were, too. We should've been scared together," she says, turning to face me again. "I wasn't mad at you and I didn't blame you, so I hope you didn't think that. My mind just went right to my parents and that this is almost exactly how their story played out and... I don't know. I just freaked."

Her palm is warm in mine when I take it.

"I understand but you're here and that's all I fucking care about."

She searches my eyes, only finding sincerity there. A faint smile touches her lips, then she leans on my shoulder.

"There's something I need to tell you and I'm scared shitless to say it, because I'm not sure what you'll think or say, but I—"

"Joss, it's me. You can tell me anything. You know that. Nothing's changed."

She doesn't lift her head from my shoulder, but even without seeing her eyes, I know it's all coming back to her, memories of all the shit we've faced together, secrets only the two of us know. She has nothing to be afraid of with me, in our friendship, in this relationship. I have her no matter what.

"I... didn't take the pill," she admits. "I don't really have an excuse, other than my personal convictions based on my mom's decision to have me, but... I didn't take it," she repeats.

I breathe deep and being honest, I wasn't expecting that. When it takes me a bit to respond, she peers up with worry in her eyes. Twice as much as before.

"You're pissed."

"No, not at all," I answer. "I didn't buy it to force you or anything. I got it so you'd have the option, and so you wouldn't have to risk Pandora getting wind of you buying it yourself."

When that last part leaves my mouth—considering the picture she shared with Joss in private—I'm not completely sure she doesn't already know about this situation, too. She definitely does her share of shit-stirring, but when it comes down to it, she's had our backs on the big things.

"Whatever happens, we're in this together. You and me."

There's no way Joss can question whether or not I mean those words. What I feel for this girl is so powerful, she has to feel it, too.

"I love you," I say, leaning to kiss her once. "So fucking much."

"I love you, too. Always have," she admits, warming the sides of my face with her hands.

Our future could look drastically different than either of us expected, but… at the end of the day, we've got one hell of a solid foundation. One built on friendship and fortified with love.

Come what may, we're in this together.

"I need a favor. I need you to promise me you won't leave while I make a quick run."

Joss seems suspicious when I release her and stand.

"Ok, but where are you going?"

"There's just something I need to take care of. Tell you all about it when I get back."

She nods and, with that, I rush toward my car.

The one who did this, tried to hurt Joss with that post, they're about to feel my fucking wrath.

Chapter 41

Dane

Dane: I'm sorry for ditching last night. I should've at least called you, even if I didn't reach out to your mom.

Shawna: All good. Congrats on finally making that love connection. Wishing you and your girl the best!

I smile to myself, knowing her words are only genuine. Even if things didn't quite work out like she might've hoped.

Dane: Thanks.

Dane: I'm looking for your mother. Any idea where I can find her?

Shawna: Funny you should ask, she's here visiting, tossing out everything with flavor from my cabinets and fridge. Need me to have her call?

Dane: No, don't. She's not answering for me. Mind shooting me your address? I'll just stop by.

Shawna: That depends. Are you pissed at her for something?

I hesitate, hoping she doesn't alert Rose that I'm coming for her.

Dane: Let's just say she did some shit she needs to answer for.

Shawna: Well, what kind of daughter would I be to set up my own mother?

Shawna: Just kidding. One sec.

The next message to come through is her address and I speed toward her building.

Shawna: Here you go, but hurry. I think she's leaving soon.

I lower the phone and go over the plan again. First, I need to hear

Rose say it. I need to hear her admit that she threw a fucking tantrum because she couldn't control me, resulting in her thwarted attempt to send Joss into a tailspin. No fucking way that message to Pandora about Peyton came from anyone else. I'm not sure *how* she knew, but I know she had a hand in this. Once she confirms, once I know for sure she's guilty, I've got something for her shady ass.

Whipping into the lot outside Shawna's building, I spot Rose's car and block her in before hopping out to lean against my hood. If it weren't for the *'she's on her way out'* text, I would've stormed toward the entrance, but this is better. I'll let her come to me.

Patience pays off when I spot her leaving out the front and then descending the steps. She's glued to her phone as usual, not paying attention to her surroundings as she comes my way, no clue I've got eyes locked on her.

That is, until she hears my voice.

"I bet you're real fucking proud of yourself."

Startled, she nearly drops her phone.

"Dane," she says with shock and a hint of frustration. "What are you doing here?"

I don't miss how quickly she adjusts her expression, pretending to still have the upper hand.

"You couldn't control *me*, so you thought you'd enlist Pandora's help to fuck Joss over instead."

Her brow arches and that innocent act she tried to pull fades away. "I do believe I warned you not to cross me, didn't I? You always like to think you've got everything figured out, so it seemed like the perfect time to teach you a little lesson in respect. It also proved to be an opportunity to show that you're not as invincible as you'd like to think."

A laugh slips when I realize how out of touch she is. "Invincible? Apparently, you've missed how screwed up my life has been these last few months. If there's one thing we Goldens realize we aren't, it's invincible."

She crosses both arms over her chest and scoffs. "I asked one simple thing of you in return for rebuilding your reputation, and that was loyalty. There was a plan in place that would've taken your career to the moon, Dane."

"You mean a plan that would've taken *Shawna's* career to the moon," I correct her. "You never had my best interests at heart. It was always about you securing the bag for *yourself,* to the point that you even used your own daughter, made her life fucking miserable chasing perfection."

"Who the fuck cares if her star would've risen in tandem with yours? And boo-hoo! Yes, I push you both to be the best you can be. Since when is that a sin?"

"You're physically incapable of admitting that you screwed this shit up, aren't you?"

"Screwed up? Dane, I could've made you very, very rich. The only thing I screwed up was not realizing from the beginning that you were too blinded by the hearts in your damn eyes to see the vision! So, yes, I've pushed hard, and I've played the part of the coldhearted bitch to help you reach greatness, but I'm starting to think you're a lost cause. The day you make something of your life, hell will freeze over."

"How'd you do it? How'd you dig that shit up about Joss' family?" I ask, ignoring her rant.

"You think I'd reveal my source? All you need to know is that this city is loyal to those who are loyal in return. I know low people in high places and those people *always* come through for the right price. And let's just say I was more than willing to pay whatever the cost to ensure Shawna will never want for anything. It's about foresight. Something you know nothing about."

"In case you've missed it, your daughter isn't the materialistic airhead you make her out to be. I haven't known her long enough to pretend I have her all figured out, but something tells me she'd turn down a paycheck for your acceptance any day of the week."

Rose falls silent then, looking stoic as she pretends my words didn't register.

"Shawna knows I love her. She's not some fragile bird who needs the cooing and coddling other girls are looking for. I raised her to be tough because that's what she'll need to be to survive. Tough."

This speech sounds oddly familiar, but the one whose given it in the past is currently behind bars. Thank God. Knowing there's no arguing with this level of narcissism, I decide it's time to cut my losses and move on.

When I lower my gaze and a smirk breaks free, Rose is up in arms again.

"What the hell is funny? The prospect of your shitty future?"

When I glance at her again, the smirk turns into quiet laughter. "Well, *someone's* future will certainly be shitty, but it definitely isn't mine."

She watches as I lift my phone and upload the audio I just recorded of us. Audio that will show the world what a fucking shark she really is.

"What is that? What'd you just do?"

I shrug and tuck the phone away. "Just posted an update, but you don't have anything to worry about. I'm nobody, remember? I'm sure no one will see it."

Her finger slides over her phone screen until she gets to my profile, I guess. The suspicion is confirmed when I hear my own voice playing through the speaker.

"Have a good night, Rose. And a great fucking life."

I climb into the front seat of my car while she watches in horror, witnessing the moment her career crashes and burns. The influencers who follow me will be interested to see what it's really like being one of Rose's clients. And if I know the network, the first-hand account I've just uploaded will be viral by morning.

As of tonight, her agenda for me, for Joss, just got canceled right along with her career.

She thought she was ruining me, but payback's an even bigger bitch than she is.

Epilogue

Joss

Warm sand between my toes, sunny sky above, the rush of the ocean beside me. To top it all off, Dane and I have this entire beach to ourselves. And to think, this vacation was nothing more than an idea a few weeks ago.

Here, my head and heart are both so much clearer.

Blue: Well?

I smile at my phone when she texts, knowing everyone back home is anxiously awaiting the results. Much like Dane and I are.

Joss: Nothing to report yet, but it should be noted that we only have a two-minute wait and you've already texted five times.

Blue: Cut me some slack! I just keep picturing this fat-faced cutie calling me Aunt Blue!

A laugh slips out that helps dispel some of the nervousness. No, we're not hoping it's positive, but we've accepted that it's a possibility.

Joss: Promise you'll be the first person I text either way. That is, if Dane doesn't get to West first and spill the beans.

She knows as well as I do that our boys tell each other everything.

Blue: Ok, good luck!

I smile at the phone and shove it back into the pocket of my jean shorts, seconds before my gaze is drawn toward our villa when the sliding door opens.

"It's time," Dane says with a quick nod.

Those two words have me sprinting up the stone steps, then across the patio. I'd come outside for fresh air, hoping to calm my nerves, but it didn't help much. A million thoughts have been racing through my head—*what will it say? Has the course of our lives just been changed forever?*

However, the one thing I *don't* question is whether Dane and I are strong enough for this. Whatever comes next, that small stick we left on the sink holds all the answers.

"You good?"

I glance toward Dane when he speaks, trailing me to the bathroom.

"Fine," I say, which is *mostly* true. But then, his palm warms my shoulder, halting my anxious steps.

"Whichever way this goes, we're good. You know that, right?"

He takes my face in both hands, drawing my eyes to his. The contact settles me a bit, all because I believe him. One hundred percent. Whatever the outcome of the test, we'll make it.

I nod, and he seems to realize I'm being honest. When his hands leave my cheeks, he leads the way this time. We cross the threshold, and our attention fixates on the sink. Or rather, on that tiny stick resting on it. As we approach, I imagine Dane's heart is racing just as fast and as hard as mine.

Which is pretty fucking hard.

"Wait," he says, stepping in front of me, blocking my view before I can finally put an end to my curiosity.

My eyes widen at him, finding it hard to believe he'd postpone such a pivotal moment.

"What is it?"

"Just sayin'. This is our last chance to vlog this moment. If we let it pass, the opportunity's gone forever. Well, at least until I potentially knock you up again."

He earns himself another of my hard glares with the statement. For *several* reasons.

"You know, way, *way* in the future," he clarifies with a wink that has me smiling up at him.

"As tempting as it is to let the whole world know the condom broke and this is our life right now, I'm gonna have to pass. Besides, that kind of defeats the point of us escaping Pandora."

He, legit, looks disappointed and I know it's not about clout or views for him. He just genuinely loves the idea of us and wants to share all our moments with our followers.

Our followers.

Shifting the focus of his brand to be about *us* and not just him was completely his idea. With Rose out of his life, and with me in it, he wanted to take things in a completely new direction. So, we vlog and post as a couple now—cooking videos, decorating the loft as a team, date nights, every minute of this vacation.

Well, every moment except this one.

I was pretty sure he'd see a dip in engagement after making the change, but it's been the complete opposite. We've gotten several sponsorship offers we're still trying to sort through, and his solo offers have skyrocketed, too. My uncle's even been impressed, offering us both an internship after graduation, should we decide to accept.

Apparently, Dane's fans love seeing the reformed playboy turned devoted boyfriend, finally settled and happy. They root for us almost as hard as *we* root for us, which they proved when Dane's recording of Rose went viral beyond our wildest dreams.

The end result?

The online community completely canceled her—influencers began avoiding her like the plague, which made brands view partnering with her as a liability, the kiss of death. Already, after only a few weeks, she's been dropped by several clients, and I suspect we'll see the trend continue.

Guess this goes to show you don't fuck with Dane Golden. Just ask Alex from back in the day.

Something unexpected that's come of all this vlogging stuff is that

I even find *myself* opening up, venturing to talk about my father, the insecurities that resulted from the toxicity in my childhood home. Hearing both Dane and I be transparent about real-life shit has helped a lot of people.

Dane's opened up about things with his dad, too, including how mentally preparing for the trial has affected him, and I've talked about finding out about my sister in a very unconventional way. Of course, I took a delicate approach—concealing Peyton's identity—but it's my hope that, one day, she and I can meet. When she's ready. When we're *both* ready.

It isn't lost on me that if Pandora hadn't been discreet about this, hadn't let me have this one thing, my sister might've been hurt. While I don't yet know her, I still feel the inclination to protect her. Even if the feeling in the pit of my stomach tells me she's got a hard road ahead—being my father's daughter, living anywhere *near* Cypress Pointe.

This thought leaves me, and I accept that we've procrastinated long enough. Taking a step closer to the sink, I crane my neck a bit.

"Ok, moment of truth," I say, finally getting a clear view of the test, of the tiny window in the center of it. A sharp gasp leaves my mouth and my gaze flits toward Dane. As he studies the stick, his expression reflects his mood—anxious, nervous, confused.

"No clue what that means," he admits with one eyebrow raised. "Why the hell can't they just say *yes* or no? Did we throw away the directions?"

"We don't need them," I say, locking both arms around his neck as I whisper two words against his ear. "It's negative."

His grip on me tightens slowly, not like he's overcome with relief, but I get the sense that he's just happy to know one way or another. Happy to finally have an answer.

I breathe the first sigh of relief I've breathed in weeks, all because I now know that we have time.

Time to enjoy each other with it just being us.

Time to achieve all that we're capable of achieving.

Time to plan how we want to build our future, our family.

My kiss cuts off his words just as he begins to speak, but he gets into it quickly despite being caught off guard.

"We have to tell everyone," I step back to say. However, I'm pulled close again, laughing when his lips tickle the side of my neck.

"You can't just fucking kiss me like that, then think I'll let you walk away," he says with a groan.

"Can and will," I tease. "We have calls to make. Blue's been waiting on pins and needles and I'm sure your brothers have been, too."

After a few seconds of serious deliberation, Dane finally lets go, but not without groping my ass as I exit.

Joss: Negative!

I've barely made it to the hall when I send that text.

Blue: Congrats! Although, I was kind of digging the idea of our crew having a new addition.

Joss: Believe me. There is still plenty of time for that. Just... you know... not now. Thank God.

Blue: Now that you got a redo, we should totally plan to get knocked up at the same time. That way, our kiddos can grow up together.

Joss: Can you imagine how this conversation would terrify the guys if they read it?

Blue: Nah, not with us. I think they know they're stuck with us forever.

Joss: True. But back to this totally unrealistic, obligatory friendship/ baby pact.

Blue: Seriously, though! I mean, are two girls really even friends if they don't get knocked up in the same month?

Despite her being a few thousand miles away, and completely full of shit, I laugh and swear I hear her laughing, too. Which makes me miss her and our crew even more.

Joss: You're insane, but I love you.

Blue: Love you back! Enjoy your vacation and call as soon as you two make it home. We'll have another girls' night.

Joss: Sounds perfect. Talk soon.

With that, I head back into the living room where Dane's got both his brothers on speaker phone. There's talk of Dane *'double-wrapping'* it next time and other ridiculousness. Meanwhile, I've already got a script for birth control waiting on me as soon as we're back in Cypress Pointe.

This is an experience we'll never *ever* forget.

Distracted when I begin kissing the back of his neck, Dane wraps up his conversation quickly, and then tosses his phone to the couch. Half a second later, he turns to lift me off my feet. On instinct, my legs encircle his waist and we're on the move.

"Where are you taking me?" I ask, not really caring. He could literally take me anywhere and I wouldn't complain.

"Eventually we're going out to swim," he answers, confusing me.

"Eventually?"

"Eventually," he repeats with a nod, squeezing my ass tight as he carries me. "The first thing we're doing is celebrating, and what better way to celebrate not getting you knocked up than to have a couple practice rounds?"

I smack his shoulder playfully, but don't protest.

"Ok, but you have to do one thing first."

His steps slow and he peers up. "Name it."

A smile touches my lips and I grip his hair in my fingers. "Tell me you love me."

His smirk tells me I just gave him the simplest task in the world to complete, so the words just roll off his tongue. Easy. Free.

"I love you, Josslyn Grace Francois. More than any-fucking-thing."

With that, he takes me to the suite, and I never imagined I'd ever know this kind of happiness. And to think, it only took me giving in to the one guy I should've always known was *'the one'.*

My best friend.

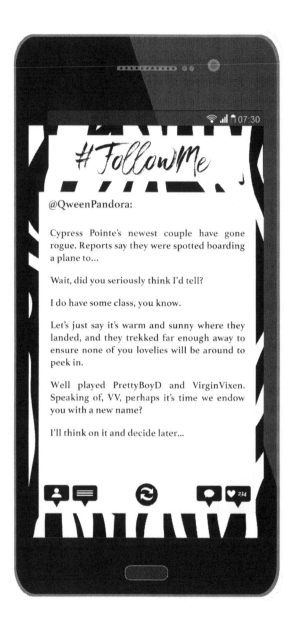

#FollowMe

@QweenPandora:

Cypress Pointe's newest couple have gone rogue. Reports say they were spotted boarding a plane to...

Wait, did you seriously think I'd tell?

I do have some class, you know.

Let's just say it's warm and sunny where they landed, and they trekked far enough away to ensure none of you lovelies will be around to peek in.

Well played PrettyBoyD and VirginVixen. Speaking of, VV, perhaps it's time we endow you with a new name?

I'll think on it and decide later...

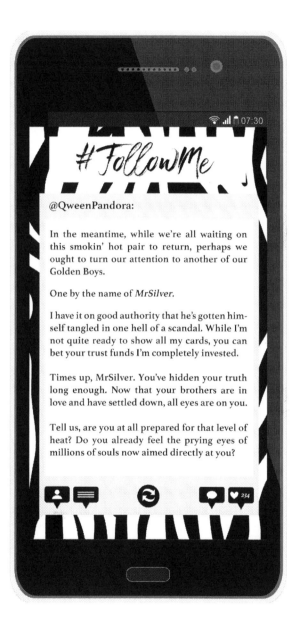

#FollowMe

@QweenPandora:

In the meantime, while we're all waiting on this smokin' hot pair to return, perhaps we ought to turn our attention to another of our Golden Boys.

One by the name of *MrSilver.*

I have it on good authority that he's gotten himself tangled in one hell of a scandal. While I'm not quite ready to show all my cards, you can bet your trust funds I'm completely invested.

Times up, MrSilver. You've hidden your truth long enough. Now that your brothers are in love and have settled down, all eyes are on you.

Tell us, are you at all prepared for that level of heat? Do you already feel the prying eyes of millions of souls now aimed directly at you?

234

#FollowMe

@QweenPandora:

It's time for your story to be told and I, personally, look forward to finding out what you have to hide.

I think I speak for us all when I say...

Bring. On. The chaos.

Until next time, Peeps! 🐱

~*P.*

1-click your copy of Mr. Silver today!
https://amzn.to/2TLs4gj

BONUS CONTENT & MORE FROM THE GOLDEN CREW

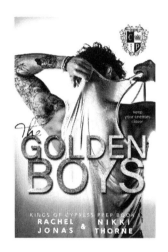

Want more Dane & Joss?
Then don't forget to grab the completed
KINGS OF CYPRESS PREP trilogy
(enemies-to-lovers/bully romance) that started it all!
https://amzn.to/3gFShWx
Book one is only $0.99 for a limited time, and the entire series is
available for FREE with Kindle Unlimited.

I'd also love for you to pop into the *KINGS OF CYPRESS Spoiler Room.*

There, you'll find tons of bonus content and access to early chapters from upcoming books, including Mr. Silver once available.

You won't find these goodies anywhere else!
Check out the group's pinned announcement post for all the extras.
See you there!

Love ARCs, random giveaways, and fun bookish conversation? Come hang out in my Facebook group for readers, THE SHIFTER LOUNGE!
Can't wait to chat with you :)
For all feedback and inquiries, email me at author.
racheljonas@gmail.com

A NOTE FROM THE AUTHOR

Thank you so much for reading **Pretty Boy D**, *A Kings of Cypress Pointe Standalone.*

If you have enjoyed entering the world of Cypress Pointe, show other readers by leaving a review!
Just visit: Pretty Boy D. https://amzn.to/3gHVdle

Join my readers' group for more news The Shifter Lounge
https://www.facebook.com/groups/141633853243521
and my Newsletter today!
https://us14.list-manage.com/subscribe?u=
73f44054c9dda516cc713aea7&id=ad3ee37cf1

SOUNDTRACK
(Listed in no particular order)

Music is a very integral part of my writing process and I carefully choose songs that fuel each scene. The lyrics may not always be spot on, but sometimes it's more about the emotion evoked. While writing *PRETTY BOY D*, I selected music that brought out the intense emotions Dane & Joss felt during various scenes throughout their journey. I hope this list enhances the reading experience for you, like it did for me while writing.

Note: Piracy is unlawful and using sites where music can be downloaded for free is equivalent to stealing from the musician. Buying the song or album directly from the artist will always be the best way to show support and appreciation for the artist's work.

"I DON'T TRUST MYSELF" by John Mayer
"HUGGIN AND KISSIN" by Big Black Delta
"STAR SHOPPING" by Lil Peep
"LIKE YOU DO" by Joji
"BETTER" by Khalid
"DREW BARRYMORE" by Bryce Vine

"LIKE I WANT YOU" by Giveon
"STUNNIN" by Curtis Waters
"MINE" by Bazzi
"CRUSH" by Yuna
"TEARING ME UP" by Bob Moses
"POWER TRIP" by J. Cole
"LEARN YA" by 6lack
"LOVEEEEEEE SONG" by Future ft. Rihanna
"HEAT WAVES" by Glass Animals
"KISS ME MORE" by Doja Cat
"SLOW MOTION" Trey Songz
"KISS IT BETTER" by Rihanna
"WATER UNDER THE BRIDGE" by Adele
"WATERMELON SUGAR" by Harry Styles
"EGO" by Beyonce
"MAGIC" by Coldplay

About
The Author

~Rachel Jonas also writes as Nikki Thorne.~

Hey, I'm Rachel! Consider this your formal invitation to hang out in my private Facebook group, THE SHIFTER LOUNGE. You'll get fun book convo, exclusive giveaways, and other random acts of nerdiness!

   Don't usually talk to strangers? No worries! Allow me to introduce myself. I'm a Michigan native, wife, and mother of three who made a career of indulging the voices inside my head :) With several completed series, and stories in both the paranormal and contemporary YA/NA romance categories, there's something for everyone!

   Happy Reading!

Twitter: @author_R_Jonas
IG: @author.racheljonas
Rachel's Facebook: https://www.facebook.com/authorracheljonas/
Reader Group:
https://www.facebook.com/groups/141633853243521/
Amazon: amzn.to/2BHiLlS
Goodreads:
https://www.goodreads.com/author/show/16788419.Rachel_Jonas
BookBub: https://www.bookbub.com/profile/rachel-jonas
Nikki's Facebook: https://www.facebook.com/nikkithorneauthor/

Printed in Great Britain
by Amazon